W9-BZD-944

THE HARDY BOYS®

UNDERCOVER BROTHERS™

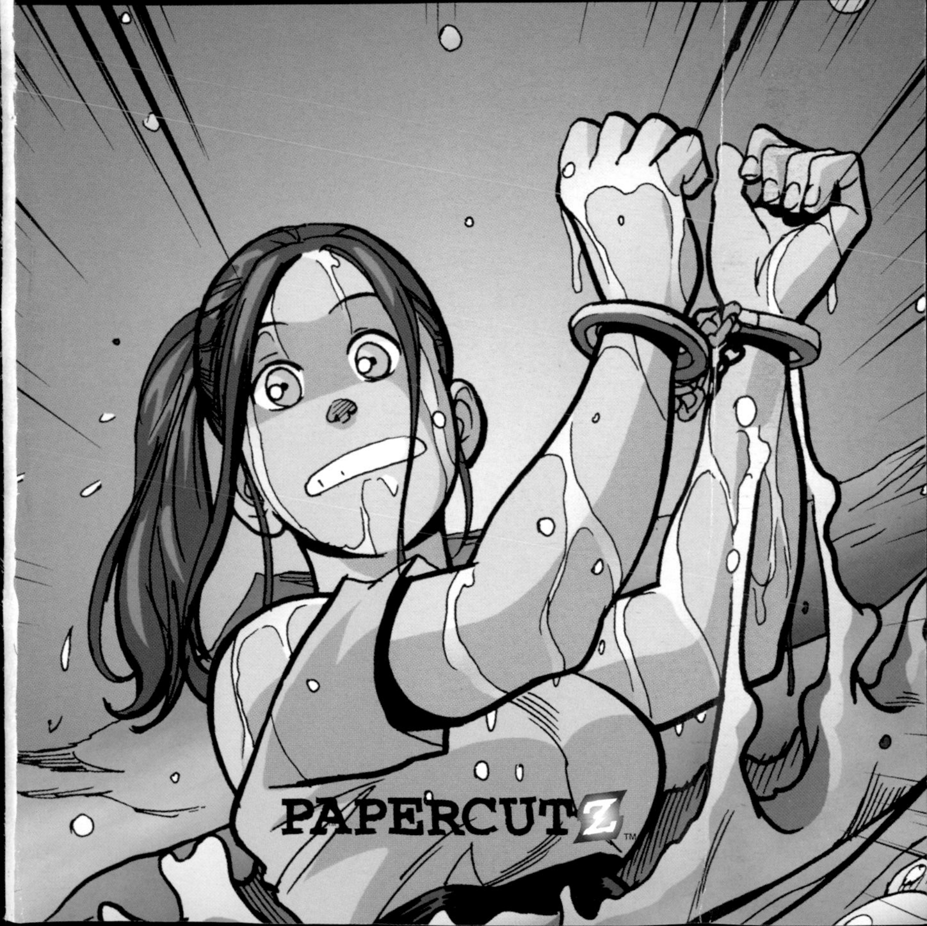
PAPERCUTZ™

THE HARDY BOYS GRAPHIC NOVELS AVAILABLE FROM PAPERCUTZ

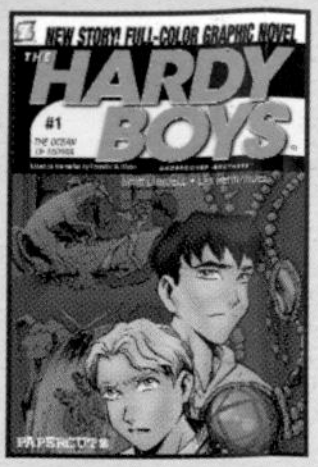
NEW STORY! FULL-COLOR GRAPHIC NOVEL
THE HARDY BOYS
#1
PAPERCUTZ

#1 "The Ocean of Osyria"

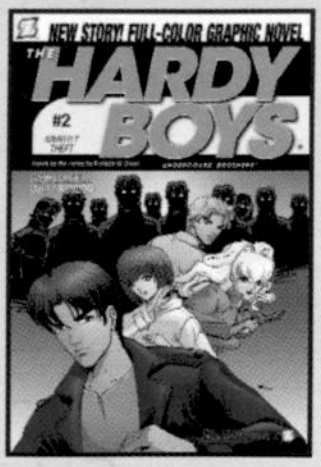
NEW STORY! FULL-COLOR GRAPHIC NOVEL
THE HARDY BOYS
#2

#2 "Identity Theft"

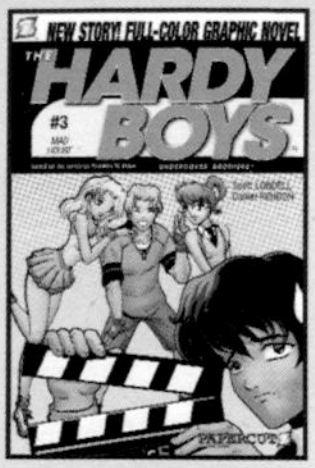
NEW STORY! FULL-COLOR GRAPHIC NOVEL
THE HARDY BOYS
#3
PAPERCUTZ

#3 "Mad House"

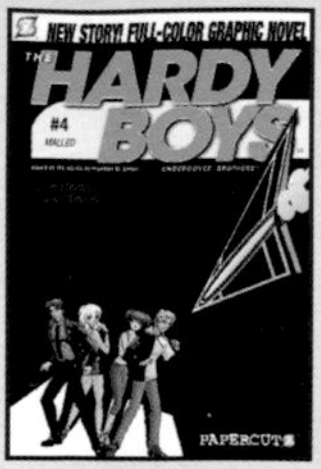
NEW STORY! FULL-COLOR GRAPHIC NOVEL
THE HARDY BOYS
#4
PAPERCUTZ

#4 "Malled"

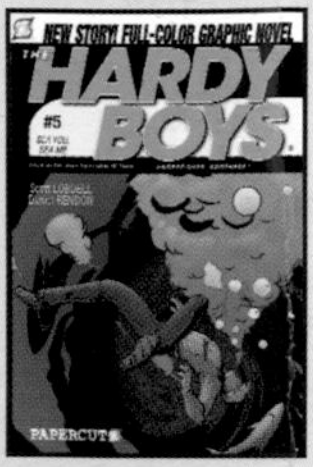
NEW STORY! FULL-COLOR GRAPHIC NOVEL
THE HARDY BOYS
#5
PAPERCUTZ

#5 "Sea You, Sea Me!"

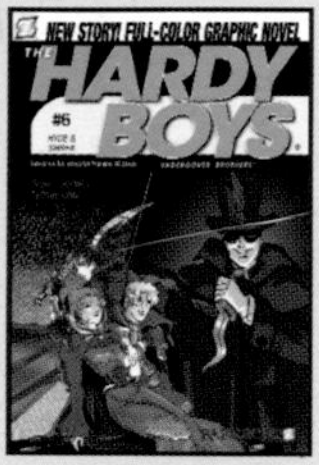
NEW STORY! FULL-COLOR GRAPHIC NOVEL
THE HARDY BOYS
#6

#6 "Hyde & Shriek"

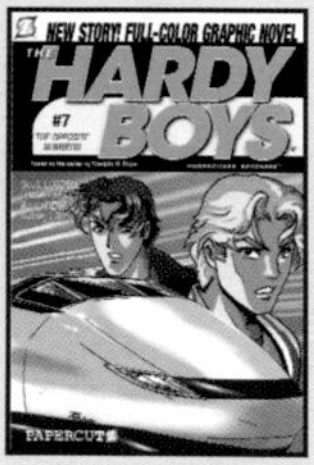
NEW STORY! FULL-COLOR GRAPHIC NOVEL
THE HARDY BOYS
#7
PAPERCUTZ

#7 "The Opposite Numbers..."

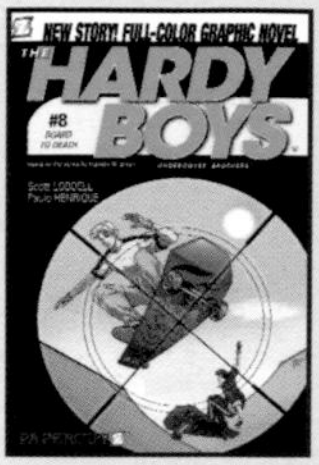
NEW STORY! FULL-COLOR GRAPHIC NOVEL
THE HARDY BOYS
#8
Scott LOBDELL
Paulo HENRIQUE

#8 "Board To Death"

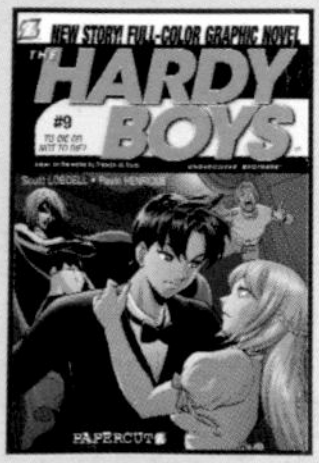
NEW STORY! FULL-COLOR GRAPHIC NOVEL
THE HARDY BOYS
#9
Scott LOBDELL • Paulo HENRIQUE
PAPERCUTZ

#9 "To Die Or Not To Die?"

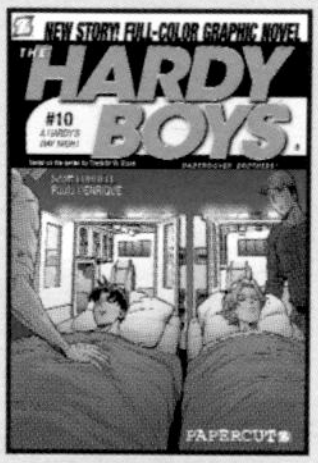
NEW STORY! FULL-COLOR GRAPHIC NOVEL
THE HARDY BOYS
#10
PAPERCUTZ

#10 "A Hardy Day's Night"

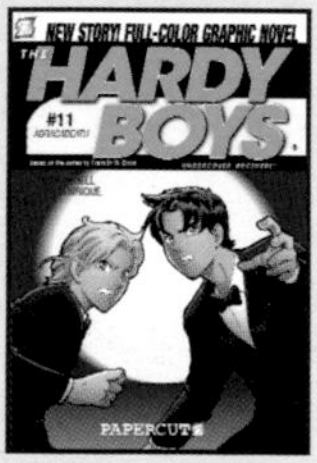
NEW STORY! FULL-COLOR GRAPHIC NOVEL
THE HARDY BOYS
#11
PAPERCUTZ

#11 "Abracadeath"

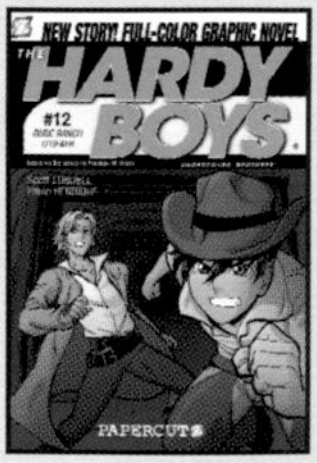
NEW STORY! FULL-COLOR GRAPHIC NOVEL
THE HARDY BOYS
#12
PAPERCUTZ

#12 "Dude Ranch O' Death"

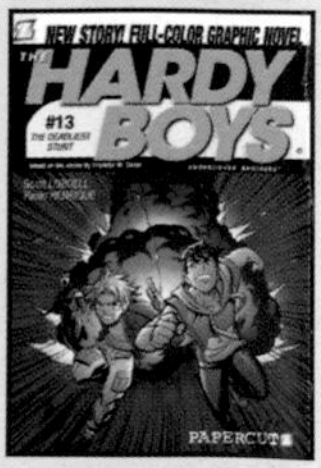
NEW STORY! FULL-COLOR GRAPHIC NOVEL
THE HARDY BOYS
#13
PAPERCUTZ

#13 "The Deadliest Stunt"

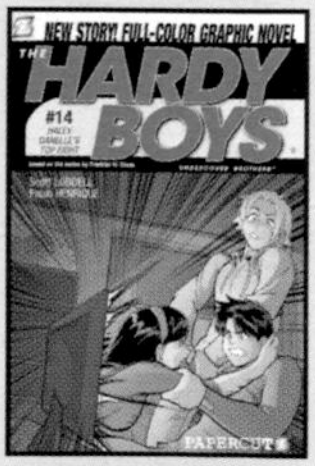
NEW STORY! FULL-COLOR GRAPHIC NOVEL
THE HARDY BOYS
#14
PAPERCUTZ

Coming Soon! #14 "Haley Danelle's Best Eight"

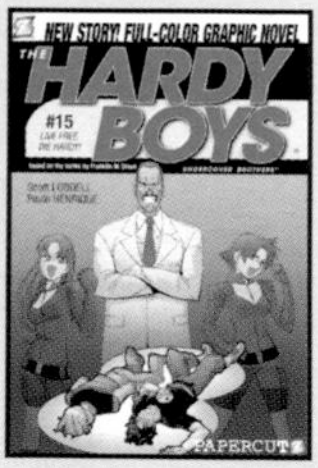
NEW STORY! FULL-COLOR GRAPHIC NOVEL
THE HARDY BOYS
#15
PAPERCUTZ

Coming Soon! #15 "Live Free or Die Hardy"

$7.95 each in paperback, $12.95 each in hardcover.

Please add $3.00 for postage and handling for the first book, add $1.00 for each additional book. Please make check payable to NBM Publishing. Send to:

Papercutz, 40 Exchange Place, Suite 1308 New York, NY 10005 • www.papercutz.com

THE HARDY BOYS

#13

UNDERCOVER BROTHERS™

The Deadliest Stunt

SCOTT LOBDELL • Writer
PAULO HENRIQUE MARCONDES • Artist

Based on the series by
FRANKLIN W. DIXON

PAPERCUTZ
New York

The Deadliest Stunt
SCOTT LOBDELL – Writer
PAULO HENRIQUE MARCONDES — Artist
MARK LERER – Letterer
LAURIE E. SMITH — Colorist
JOHN McCARTHY— Production
JIM SALICRUP — Editor-in-Chief

ISBN 10: 1-59707-102-1 paperback edition
ISBN 13: 978-1-59707-102-4 paperback edition
ISBN 10: 1-59707-103-X hardcover edition
ISBN 13: 978-1-59707-103-1 hardcover edition

Published by arrangement with Aladdin Paperbacks,
an imprint of Simon & Schuster Children's Publishing Division.

Distributed by Macmillan.

Printed in China.

10 9 8 7 6 5 4 3 2 1

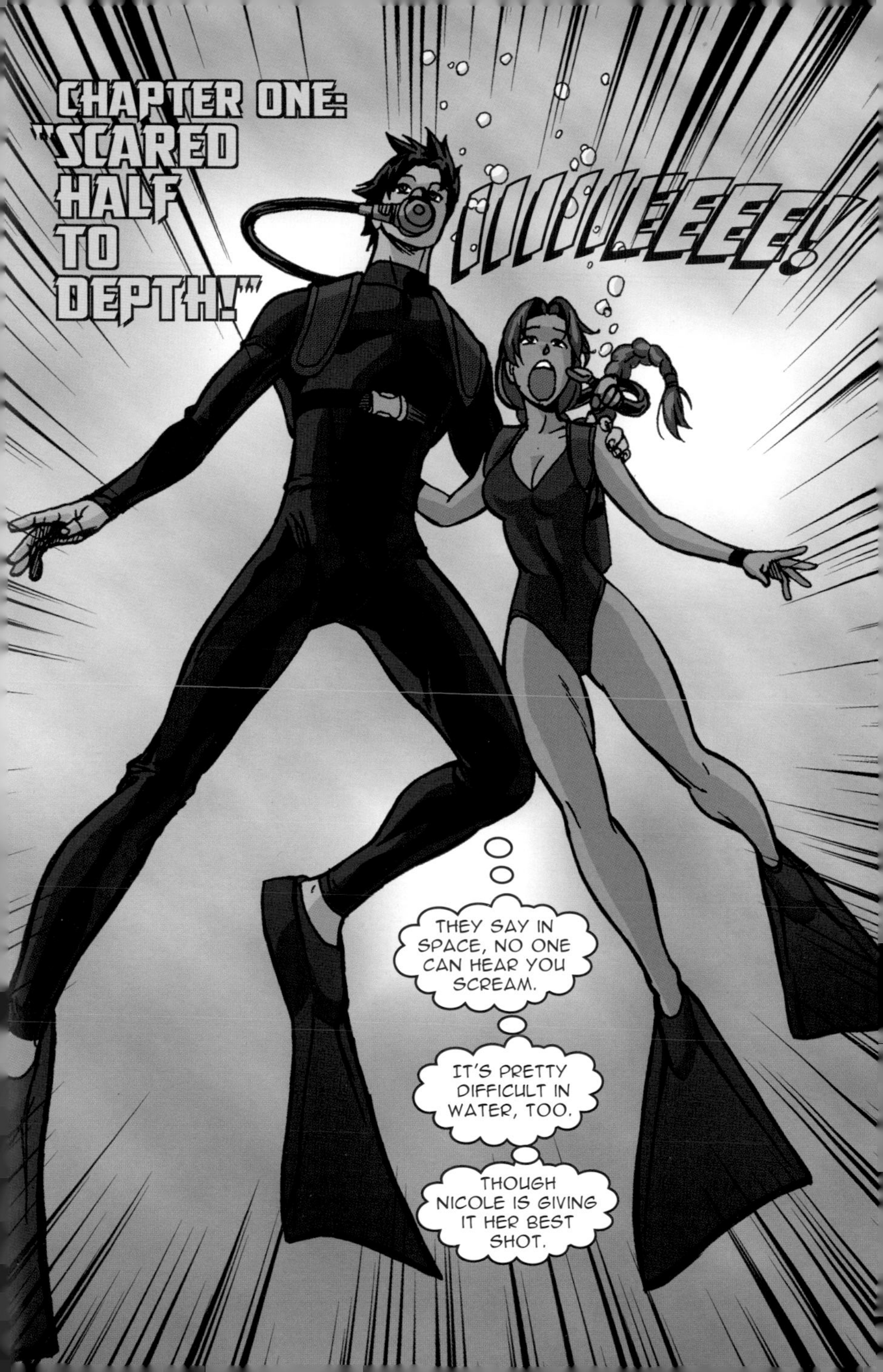
CHAPTER ONE: "SCARED HALF TO DEPTH!"
IIIIIILEEEE!
THEY SAY IN SPACE, NO ONE CAN HEAR YOU SCREAM.
IT'S PRETTY DIFFICULT IN WATER, TOO.
THOUGH NICOLE IS GIVING IT HER BEST SHOT.

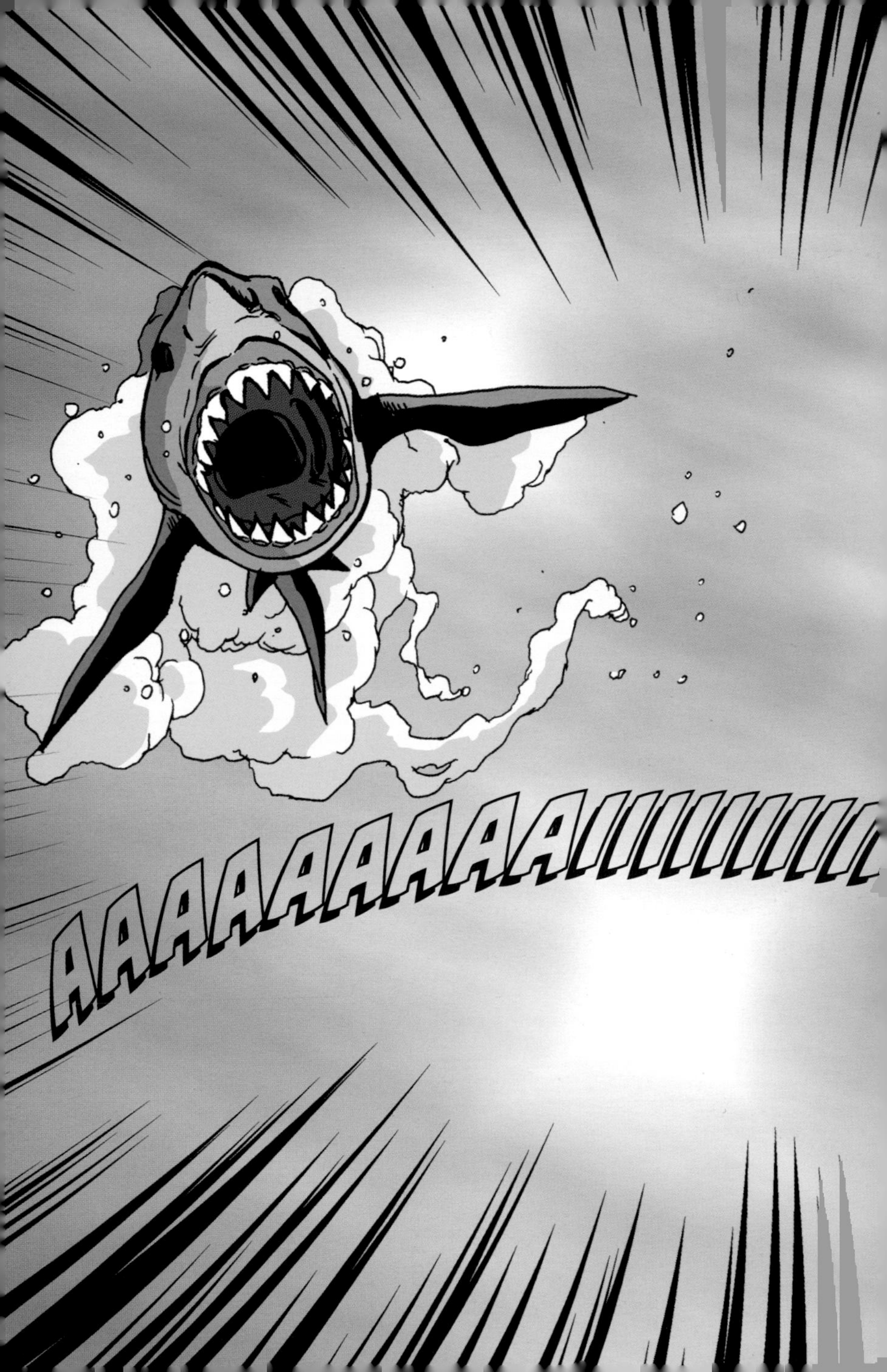
AAAAAAAAAIIIIIIIIII

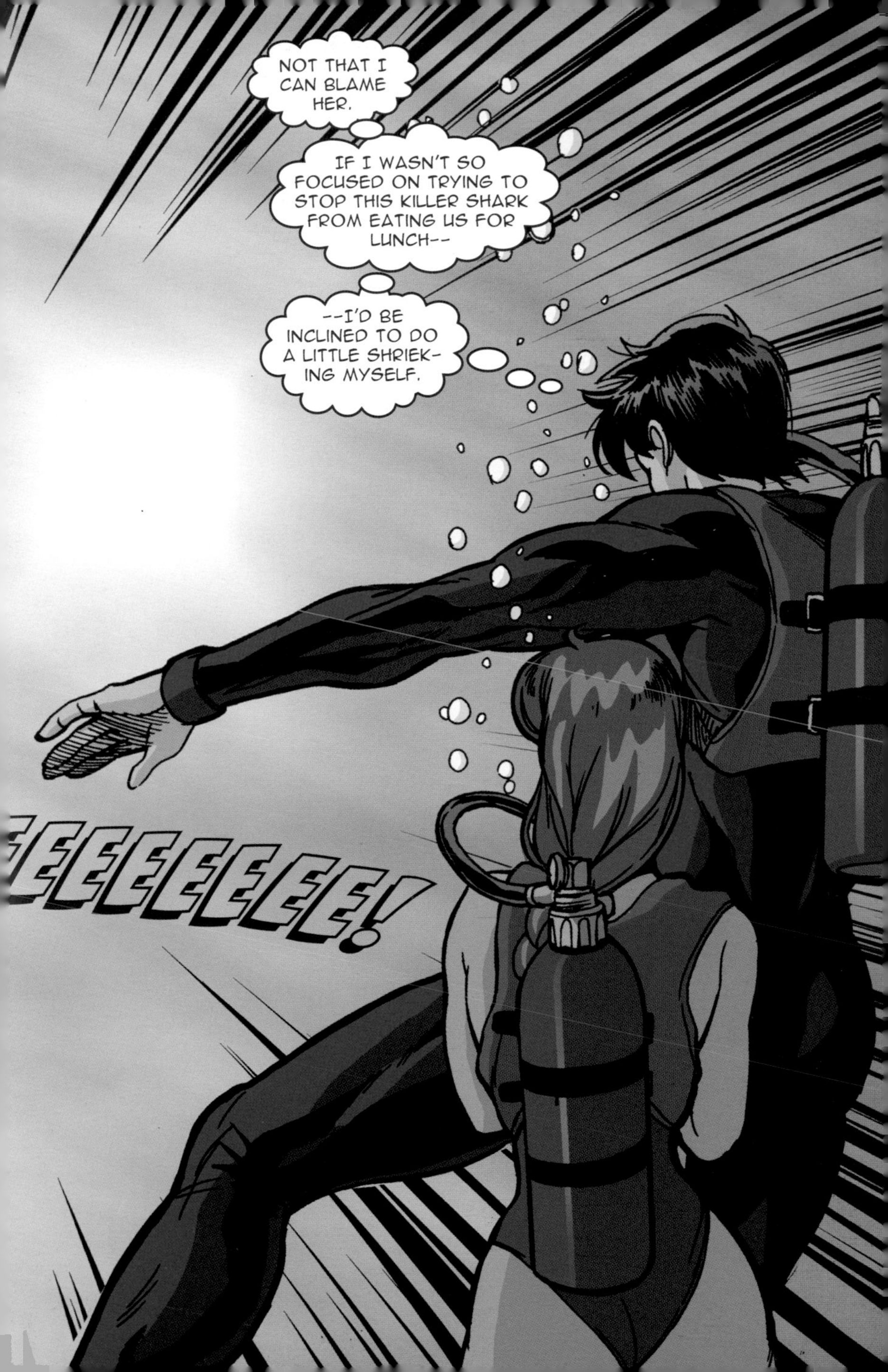
NOT THAT I CAN BLAME HER.
IF I WASN'T SO FOCUSED ON TRYING TO STOP THIS KILLER SHARK FROM EATING US FOR LUNCH--
--I'D BE INCLINED TO DO A LITTLE SHRIEK-ING MYSELF.
EEEEEEEEE!

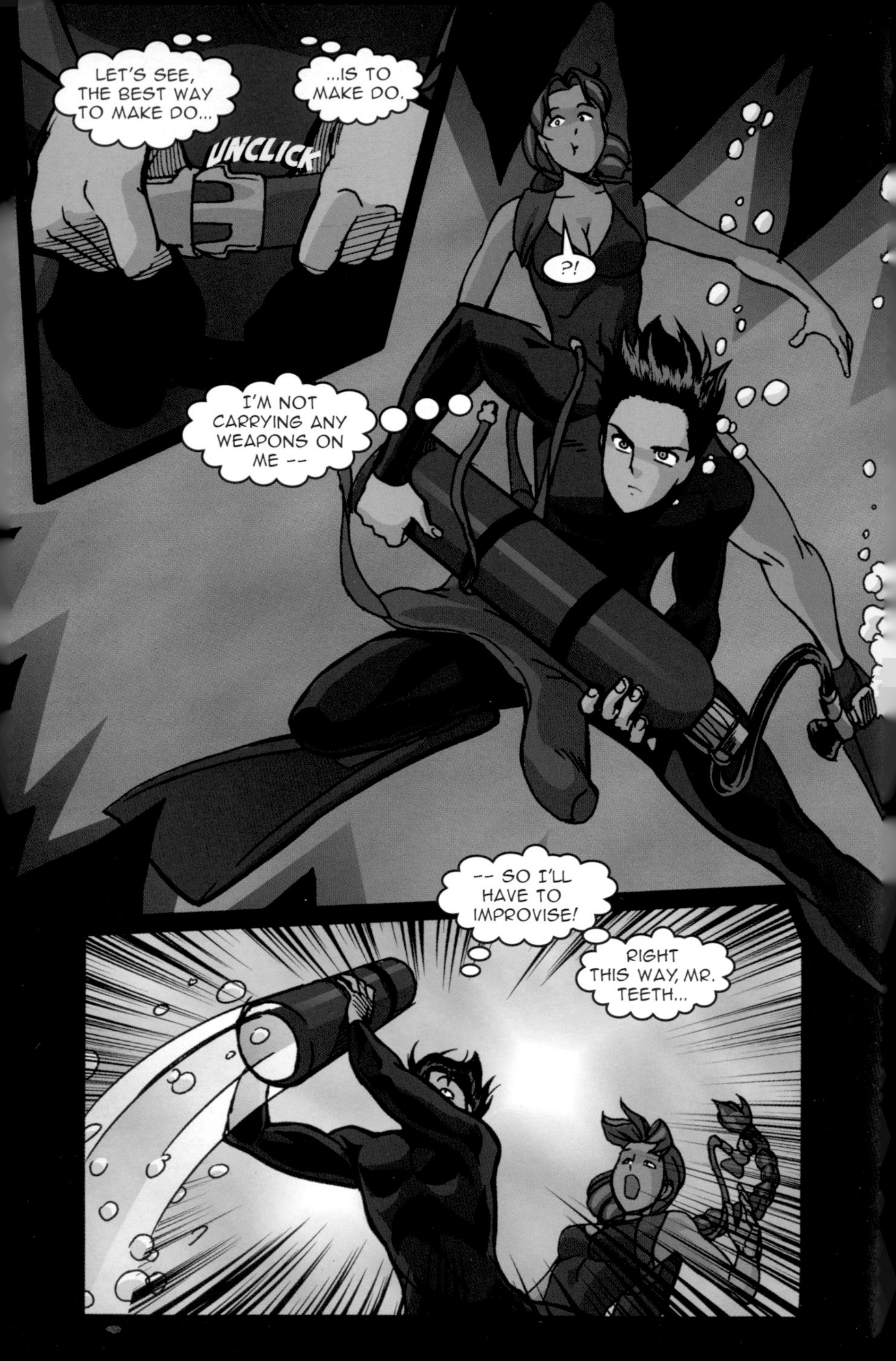
LET'S SEE, THE BEST WAY TO MAKE DO...
...IS TO MAKE DO.
UNCLICK
?!
I'M NOT CARRYING ANY WEAPONS ON ME --
-- SO I'LL HAVE TO IMPROVISE!
RIGHT THIS WAY, MR. TEETH...

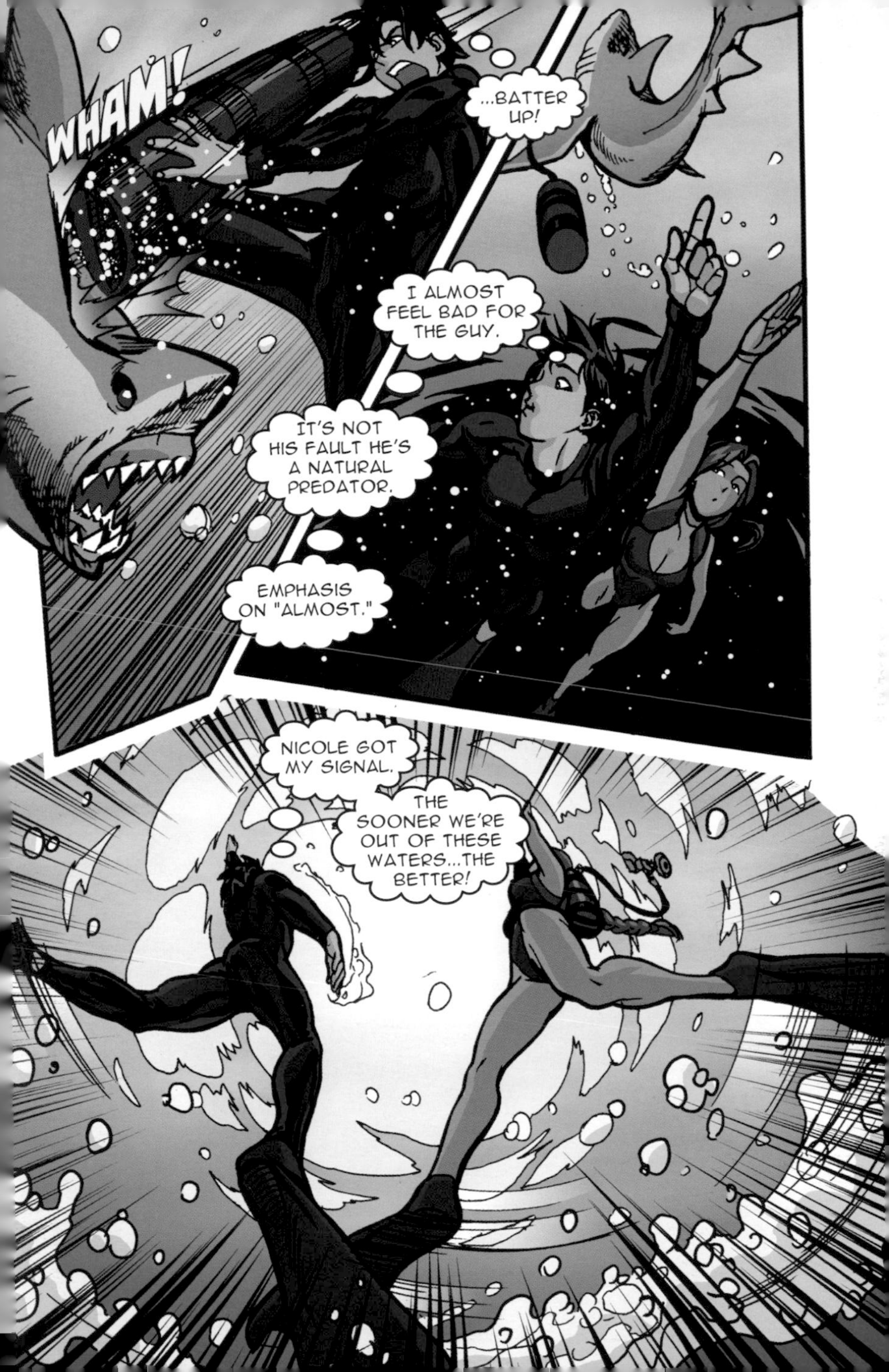
WHAM!
...BATTER UP!
I ALMOST FEEL BAD FOR THE GUY.
IT'S NOT HIS FAULT HE'S A NATURAL PREDATOR.
EMPHASIS ON "ALMOST."
NICOLE GOT MY SIGNAL.
THE SOONER WE'RE OUT OF THESE WATERS...THE BETTER!

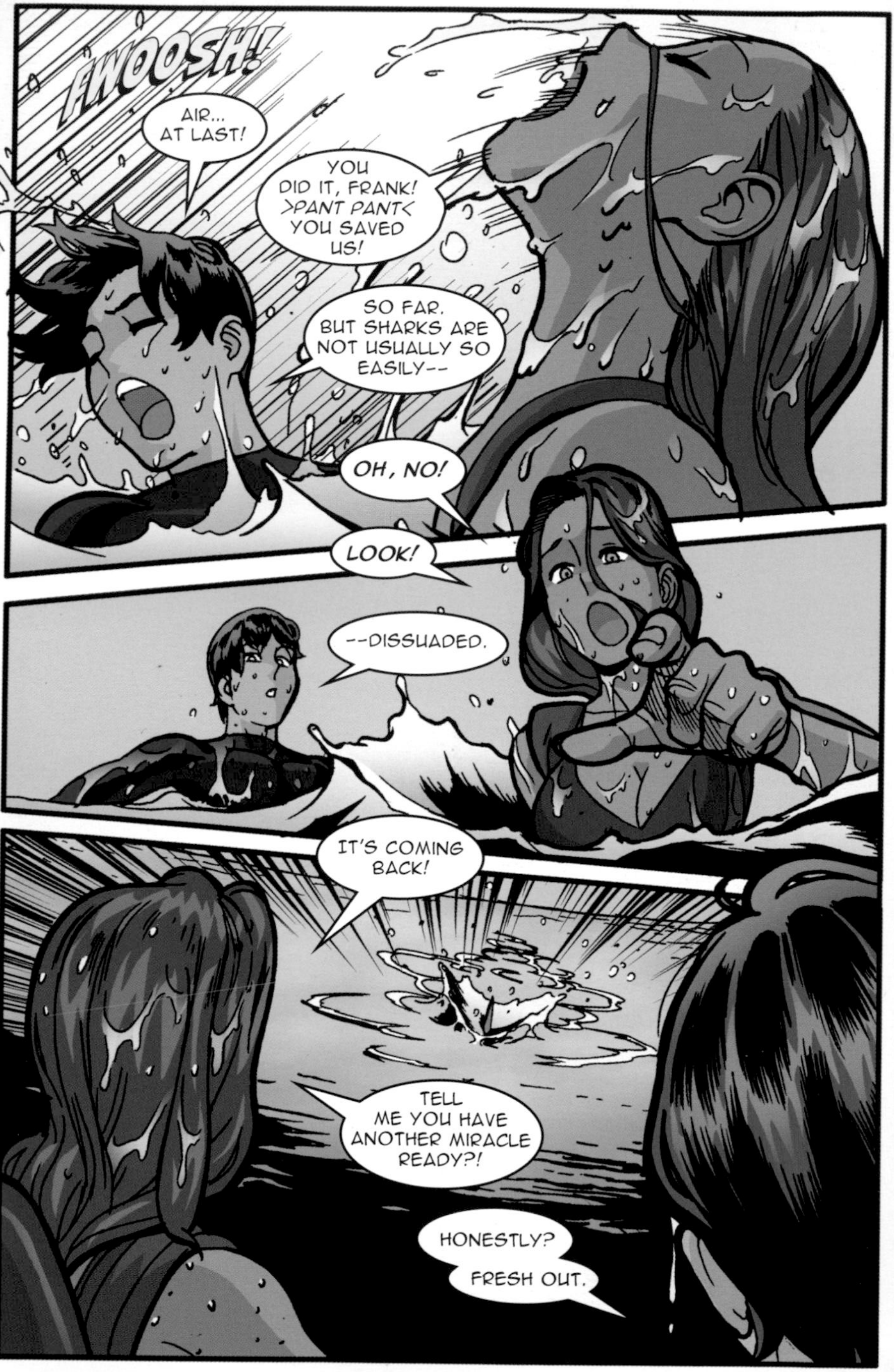
FWOOSH!
AIR... AT LAST!
YOU DID IT, FRANK! >PANT PANT< YOU SAVED US!
SO FAR. BUT SHARKS ARE NOT USUALLY SO EASILY--
OH, NO!
LOOK!
--DISSUADED.
IT'S COMING BACK!
TELL ME YOU HAVE ANOTHER MIRACLE READY?!
HONESTLY?
FRESH OUT.

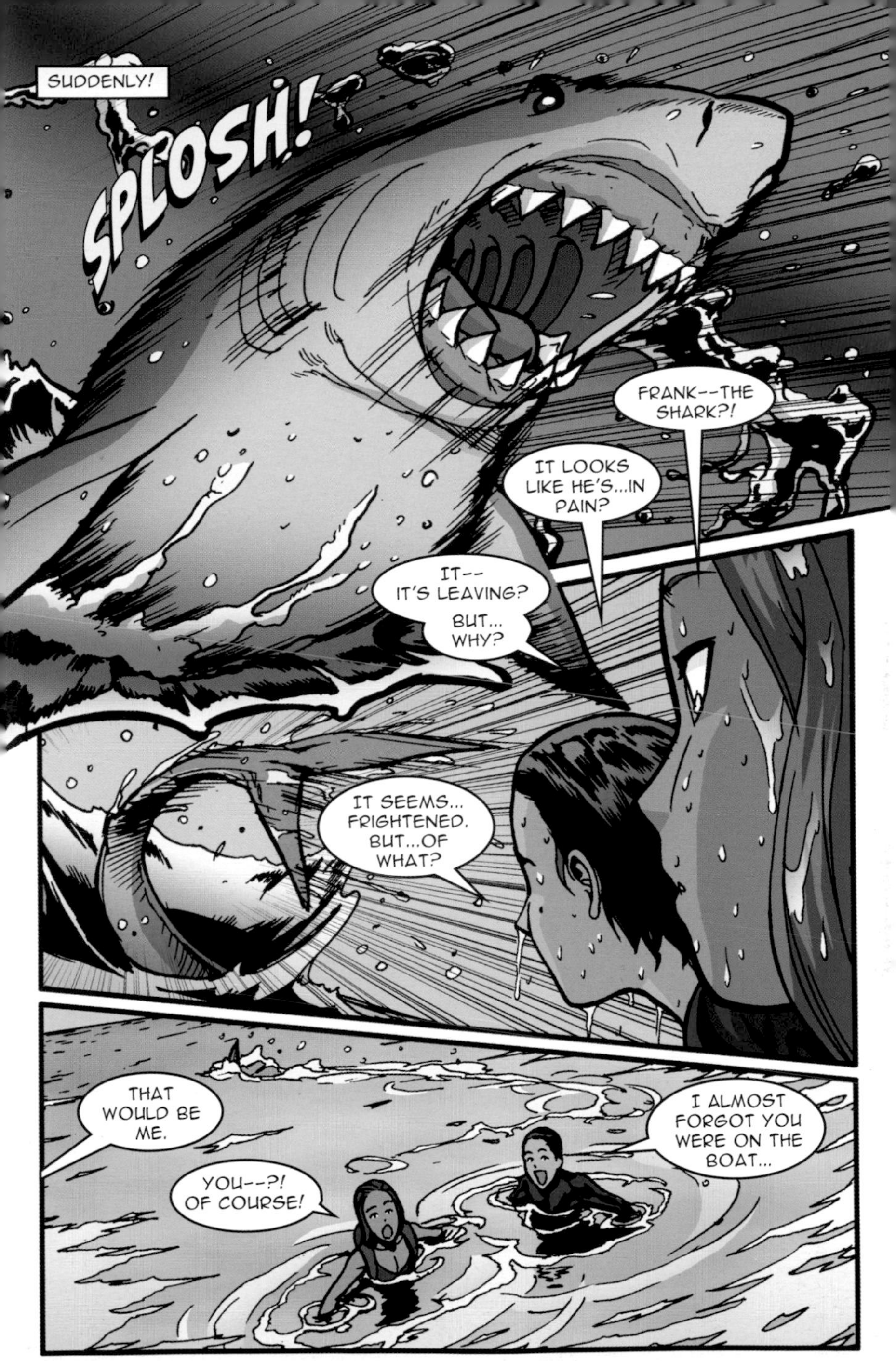
SUDDENLY!
SPLOSH!
FRANK--THE SHARK?!
IT LOOKS LIKE HE'S...IN PAIN?
IT-- IT'S LEAVING?
BUT... WHY?
IT SEEMS... FRIGHTENED. BUT...OF WHAT?
THAT WOULD BE ME.
I ALMOST FORGOT YOU WERE ON THE BOAT...
YOU--?! OF COURSE!

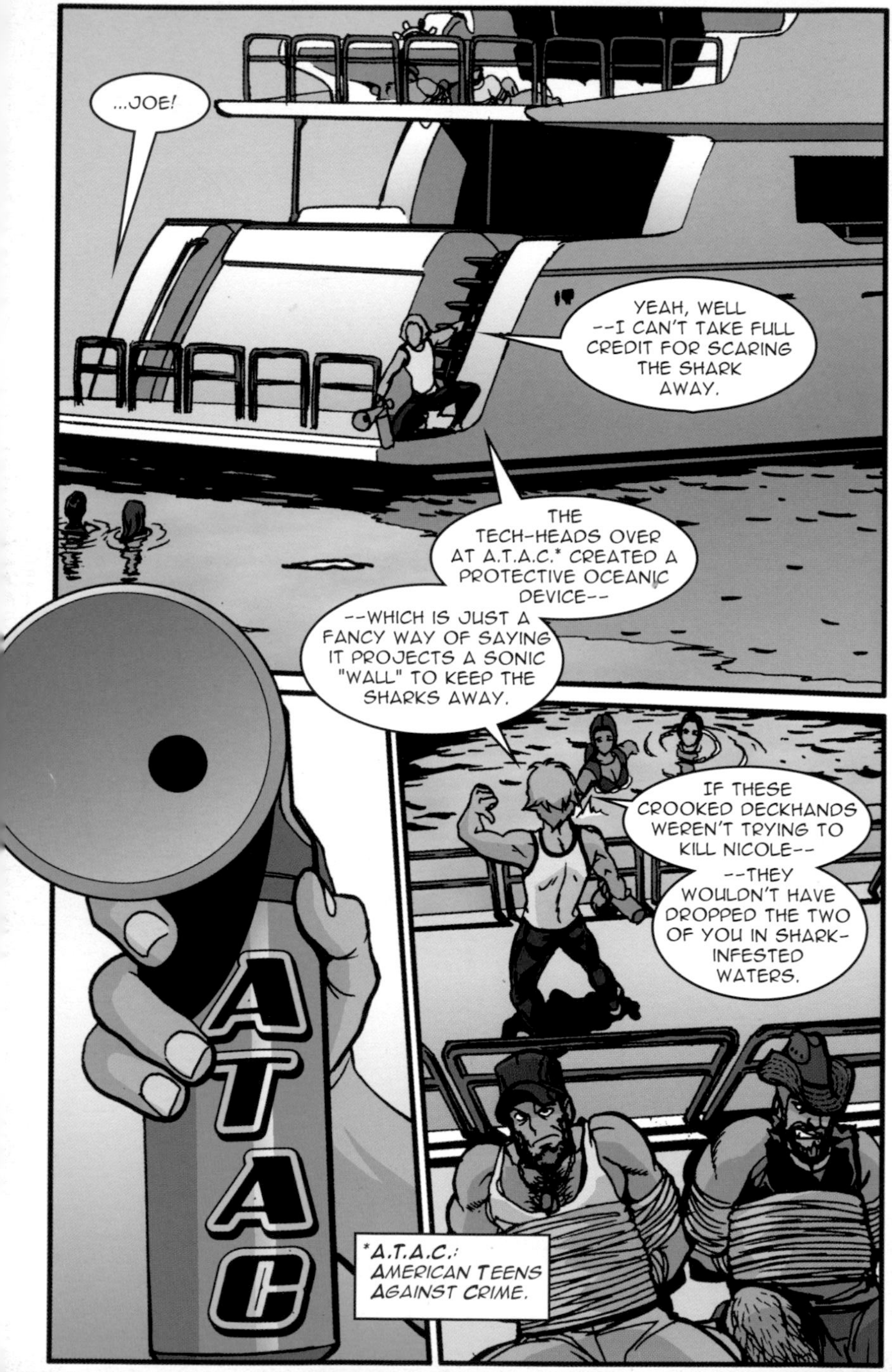
...JOE!
YEAH, WELL --I CAN'T TAKE FULL CREDIT FOR SCARING THE SHARK AWAY.
THE TECH-HEADS OVER AT A.T.A.C.* CREATED A PROTECTIVE OCEANIC DEVICE--
--WHICH IS JUST A FANCY WAY OF SAYING IT PROJECTS A SONIC "WALL" TO KEEP THE SHARKS AWAY.
A.T.A.C
IF THESE CROOKED DECKHANDS WEREN'T TRYING TO KILL NICOLE--
--THEY WOULDN'T HAVE DROPPED THE TWO OF YOU IN SHARK-INFESTED WATERS.
*A.T.A.C.: AMERICAN TEENS AGAINST CRIME.

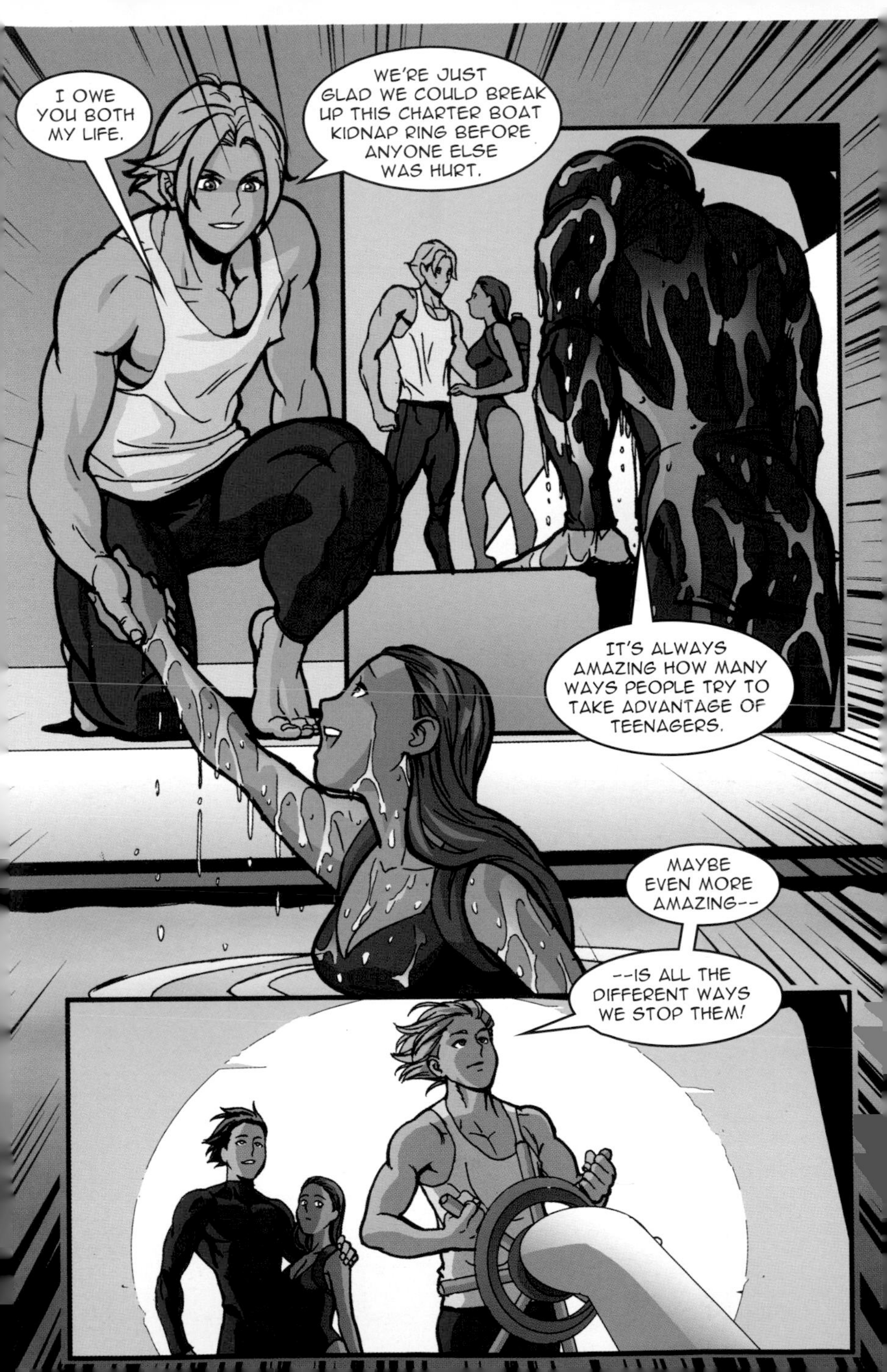
I OWE YOU BOTH MY LIFE.
WE'RE JUST GLAD WE COULD BREAK UP THIS CHARTER BOAT KIDNAP RING BEFORE ANYONE ELSE WAS HURT.
IT'S ALWAYS AMAZING HOW MANY WAYS PEOPLE TRY TO TAKE ADVANTAGE OF TEENAGERS.
MAYBE EVEN MORE AMAZING--
--IS ALL THE DIFFERENT WAYS WE STOP THEM!

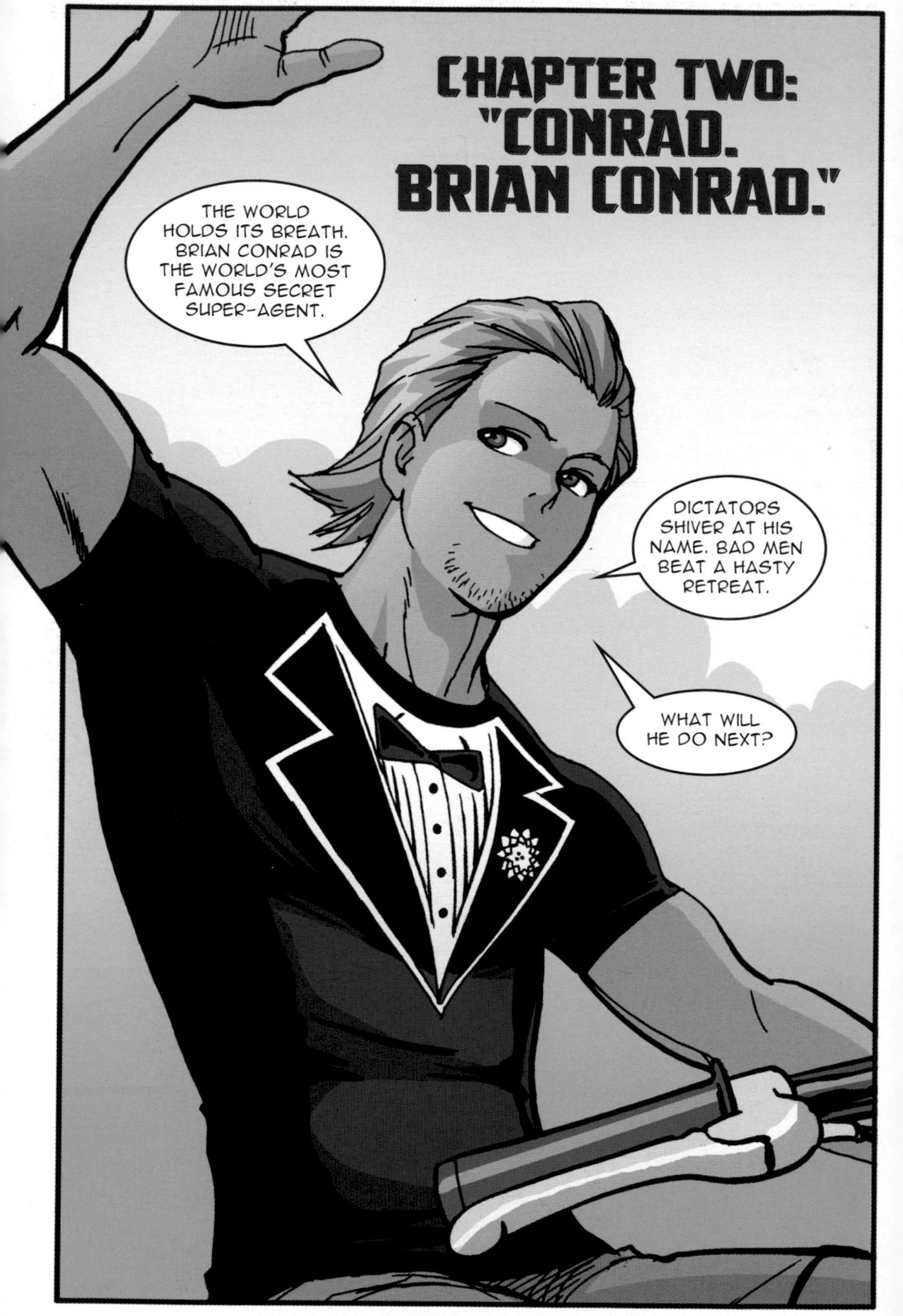
CHAPTER TWO: "CONRAD. BRIAN CONRAD."
THE WORLD HOLDS ITS BREATH. BRIAN CONRAD IS THE WORLD'S MOST FAMOUS SECRET SUPER-AGENT.
DICTATORS SHIVER AT HIS NAME. BAD MEN BEAT A HASTY RETREAT.
WHAT WILL HE DO NEXT?

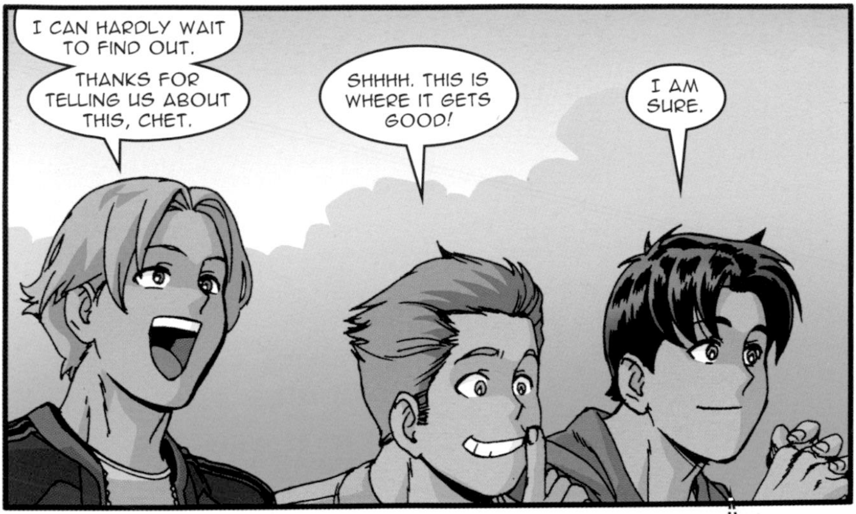
I CAN HARDLY WAIT TO FIND OUT.
THANKS FOR TELLING US ABOUT THIS, CHET.
SHHHH. THIS IS WHERE IT GETS GOOD!
I AM SURE.

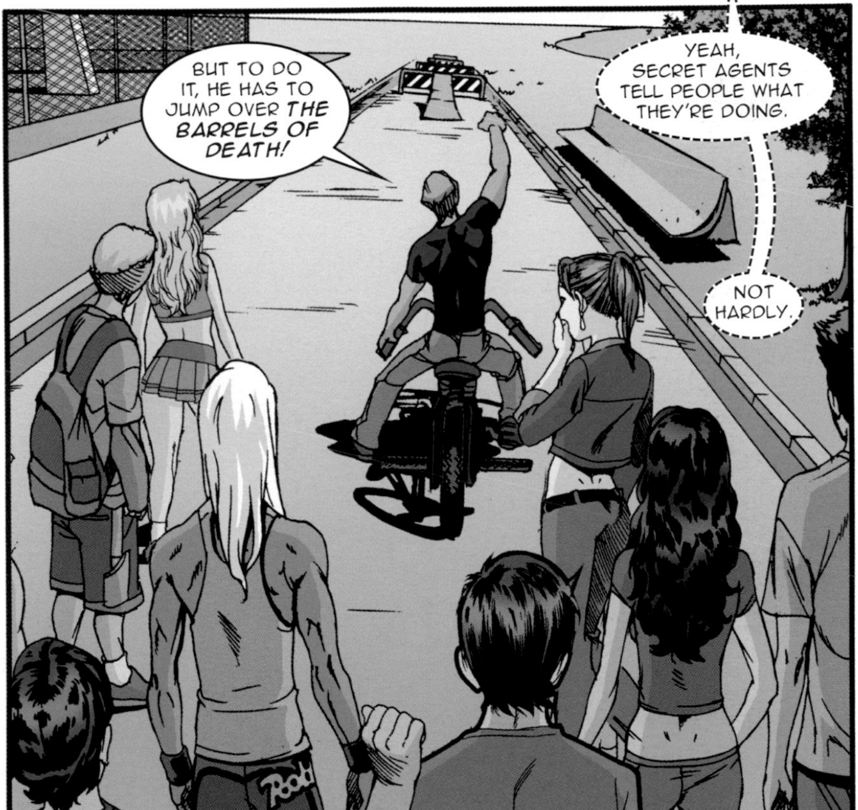
BUT TO DO IT, HE HAS TO JUMP OVER THE BARRELS OF DEATH!
YEAH, SECRET AGENTS TELL PEOPLE WHAT THEY'RE DOING.
NOT HARDLY.

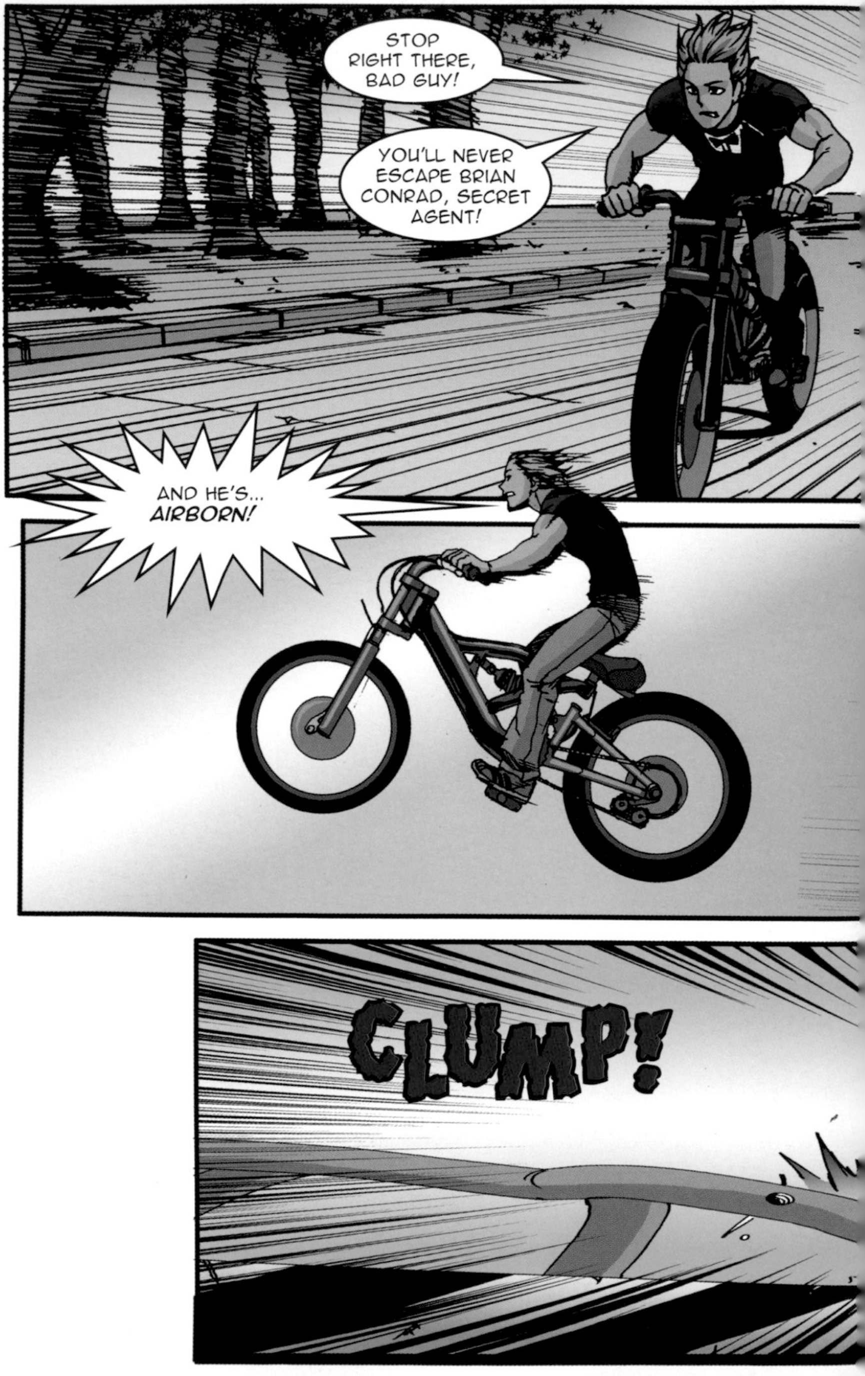
STOP RIGHT THERE, BAD GUY!
YOU'LL NEVER ESCAPE BRIAN CONRAD, SECRET AGENT!
AND HE'S... AIRBORN!
CLUMP!

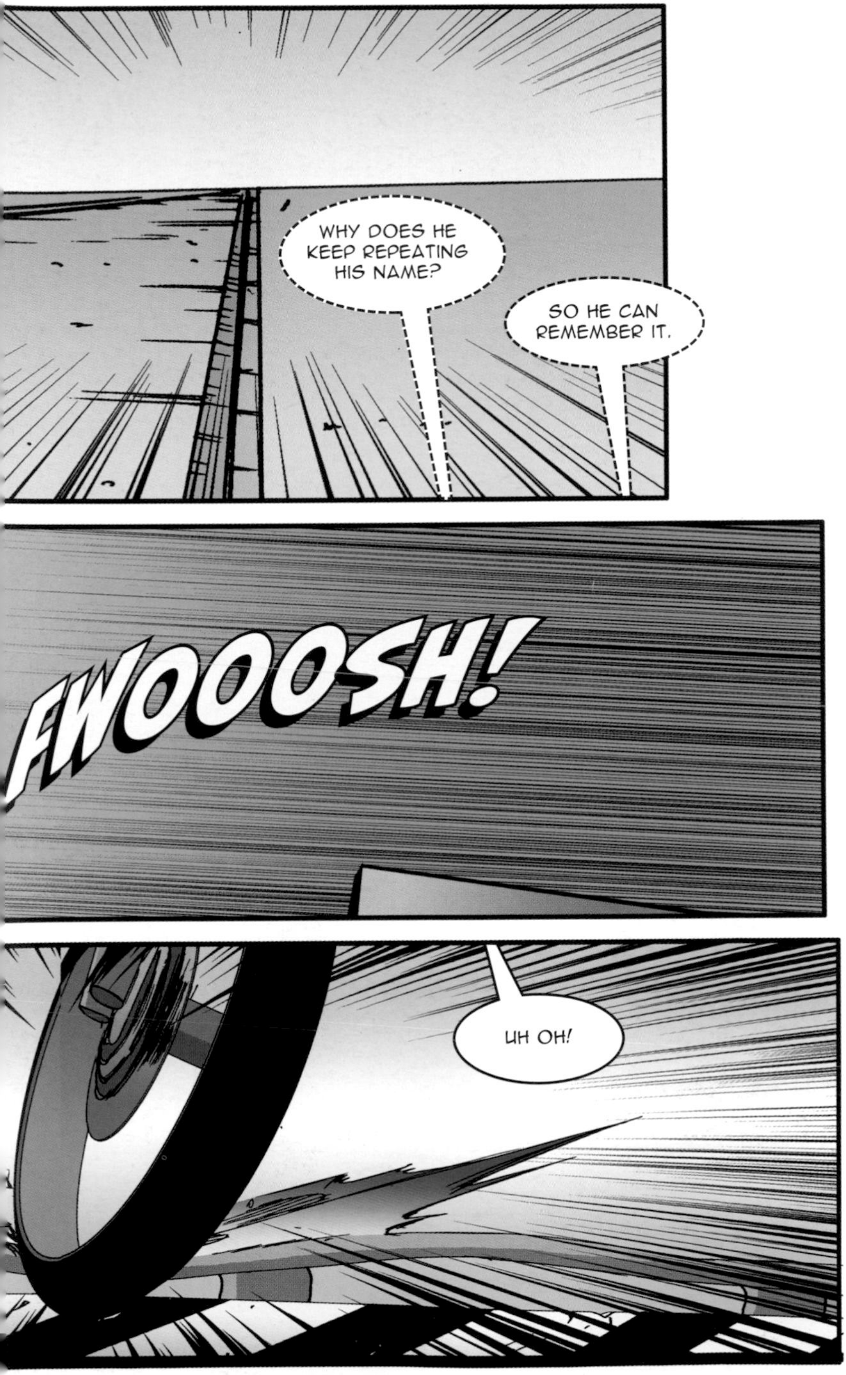
WHY DOES HE KEEP REPEATING HIS NAME?
SO HE CAN REMEMBER IT.
FWOOOSH!
UH OH!

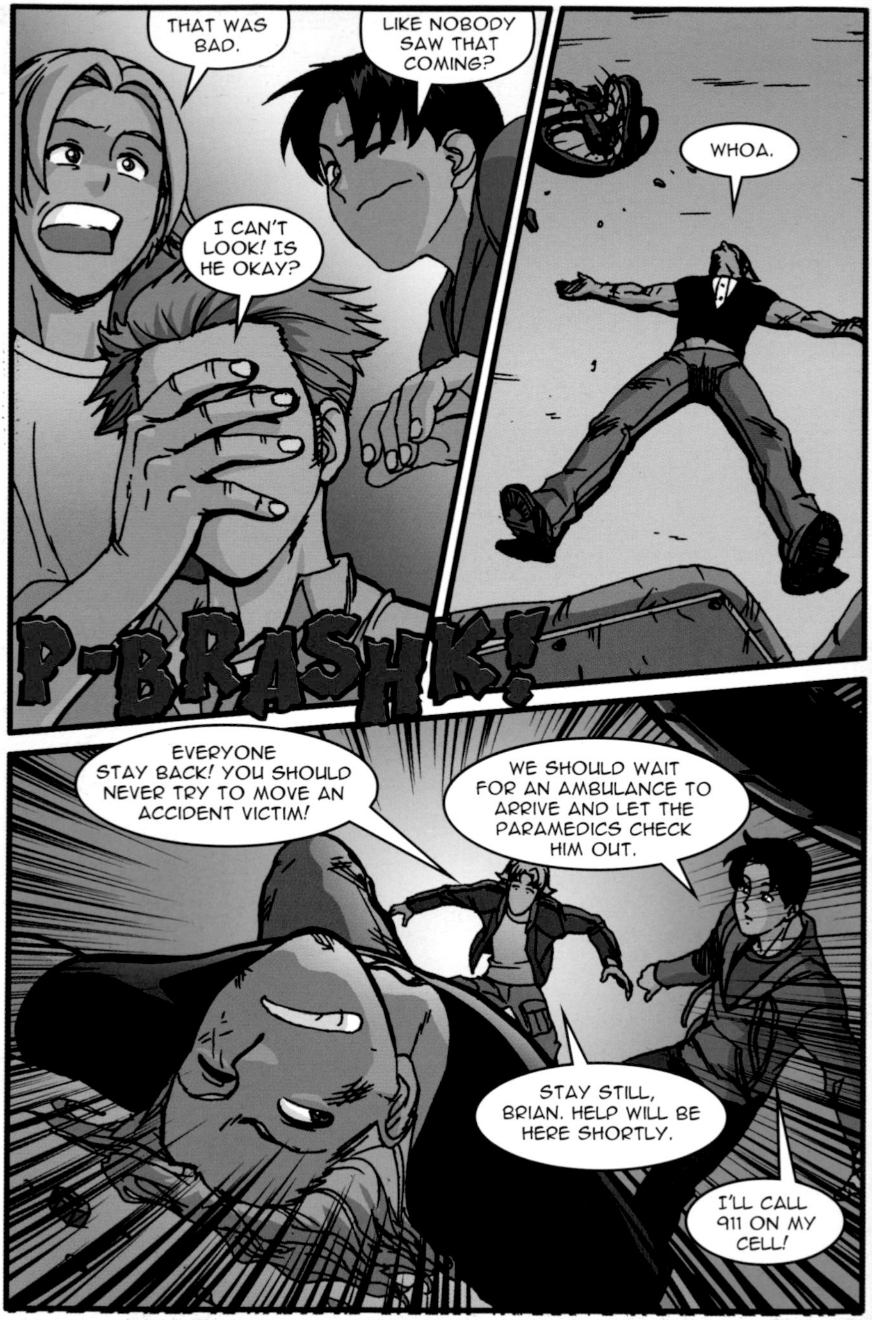
THAT WAS BAD.
LIKE NOBODY SAW THAT COMING?
I CAN'T LOOK! IS HE OKAY?
WHOA.
P-BRASHK!
EVERYONE STAY BACK! YOU SHOULD NEVER TRY TO MOVE AN ACCIDENT VICTIM!
WE SHOULD WAIT FOR AN AMBULANCE TO ARRIVE AND LET THE PARAMEDICS CHECK HIM OUT.
STAY STILL, BRIAN. HELP WILL BE HERE SHORTLY.
I'LL CALL 911 ON MY CELL!

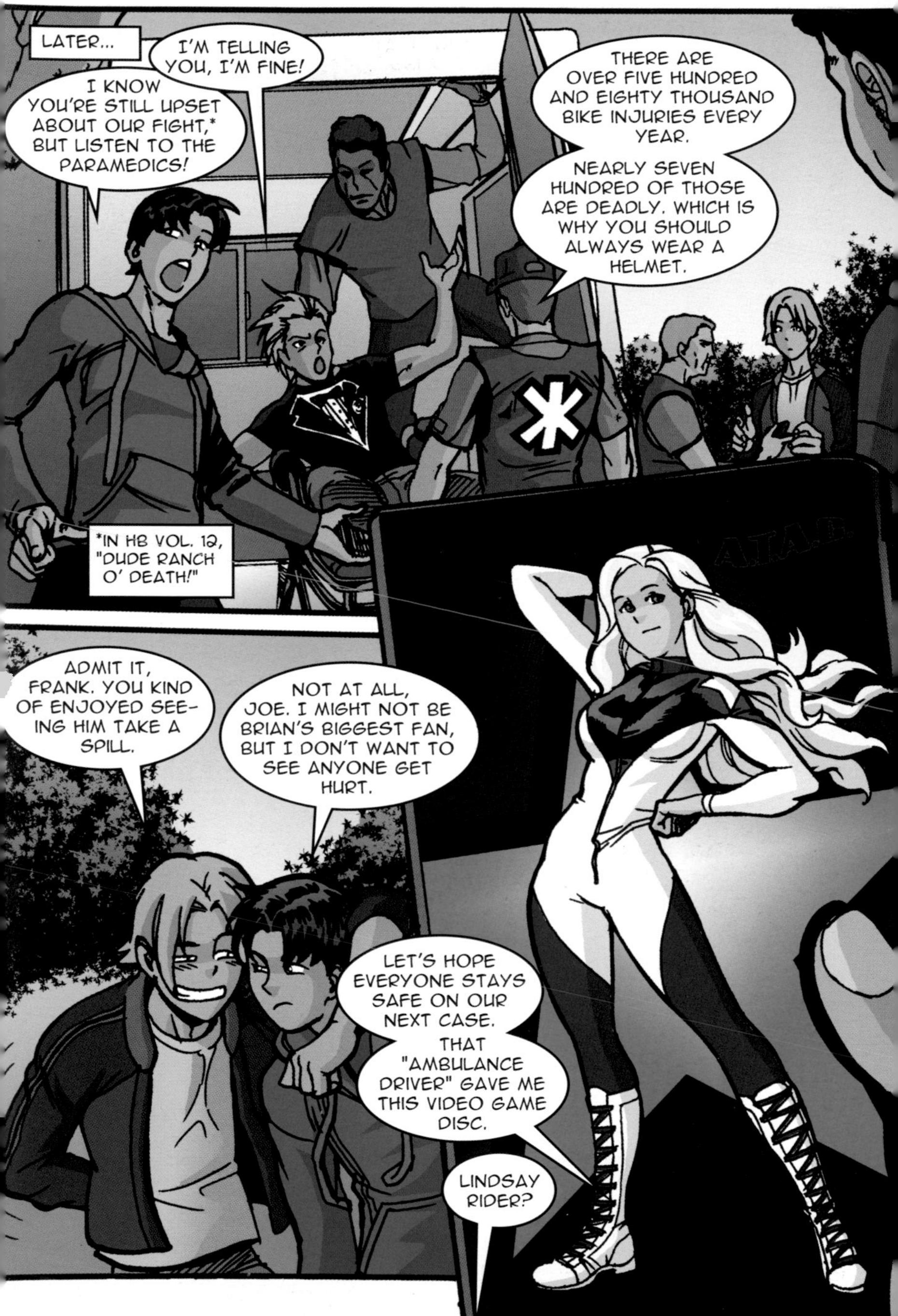
LATER...
I'M TELLING YOU, I'M FINE!
I KNOW YOU'RE STILL UPSET ABOUT OUR FIGHT,* BUT LISTEN TO THE PARAMEDICS!
THERE ARE OVER FIVE HUNDRED AND EIGHTY THOUSAND BIKE INJURIES EVERY YEAR.
NEARLY SEVEN HUNDRED OF THOSE ARE DEADLY. WHICH IS WHY YOU SHOULD ALWAYS WEAR A HELMET.
*IN HB VOL. 12, "DUDE RANCH O' DEATH!"
A.T.A.D.
ADMIT IT, FRANK. YOU KIND OF ENJOYED SEE-ING HIM TAKE A SPILL.
NOT AT ALL, JOE. I MIGHT NOT BE BRIAN'S BIGGEST FAN, BUT I DON'T WANT TO SEE ANYONE GET HURT.
LET'S HOPE EVERYONE STAYS SAFE ON OUR NEXT CASE.
THAT "AMBULANCE DRIVER" GAVE ME THIS VIDEO GAME DISC.
LINDSAY RIDER?

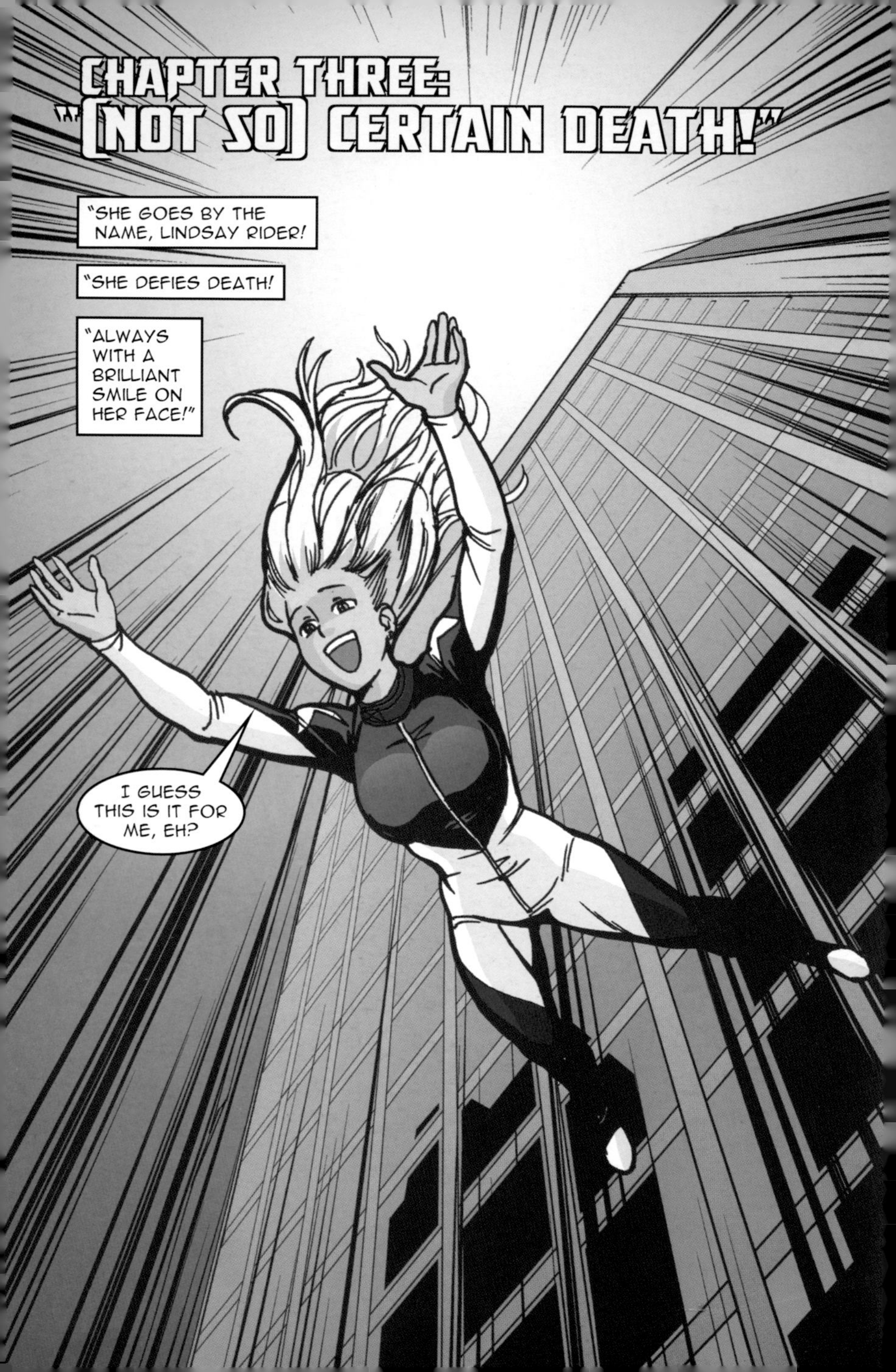
CHAPTER THREE:
"[NOT SO] CERTAIN DEATH!"
"SHE GOES BY THE NAME, LINDSAY RIDER!
"SHE DEFIES DEATH!
"ALWAYS WITH A BRILLIANT SMILE ON HER FACE!"
I GUESS THIS IS IT FOR ME, EH?

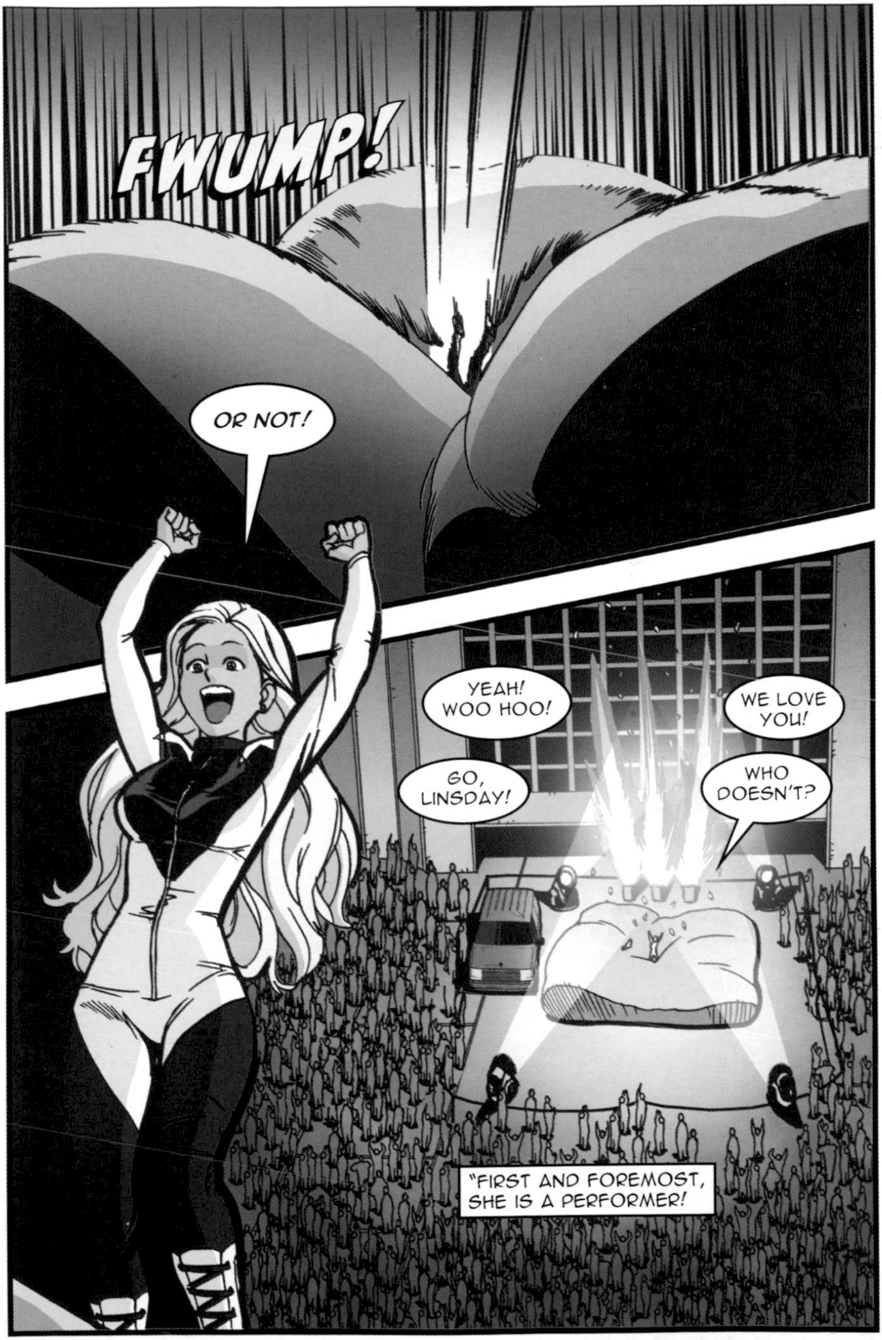
FWUMP!
OR NOT!
YEAH! WOO HOO!
WE LOVE YOU!
GO, LINSDAY!
WHO DOESN'T?
"FIRST AND FOREMOST, SHE IS A PERFORMER!

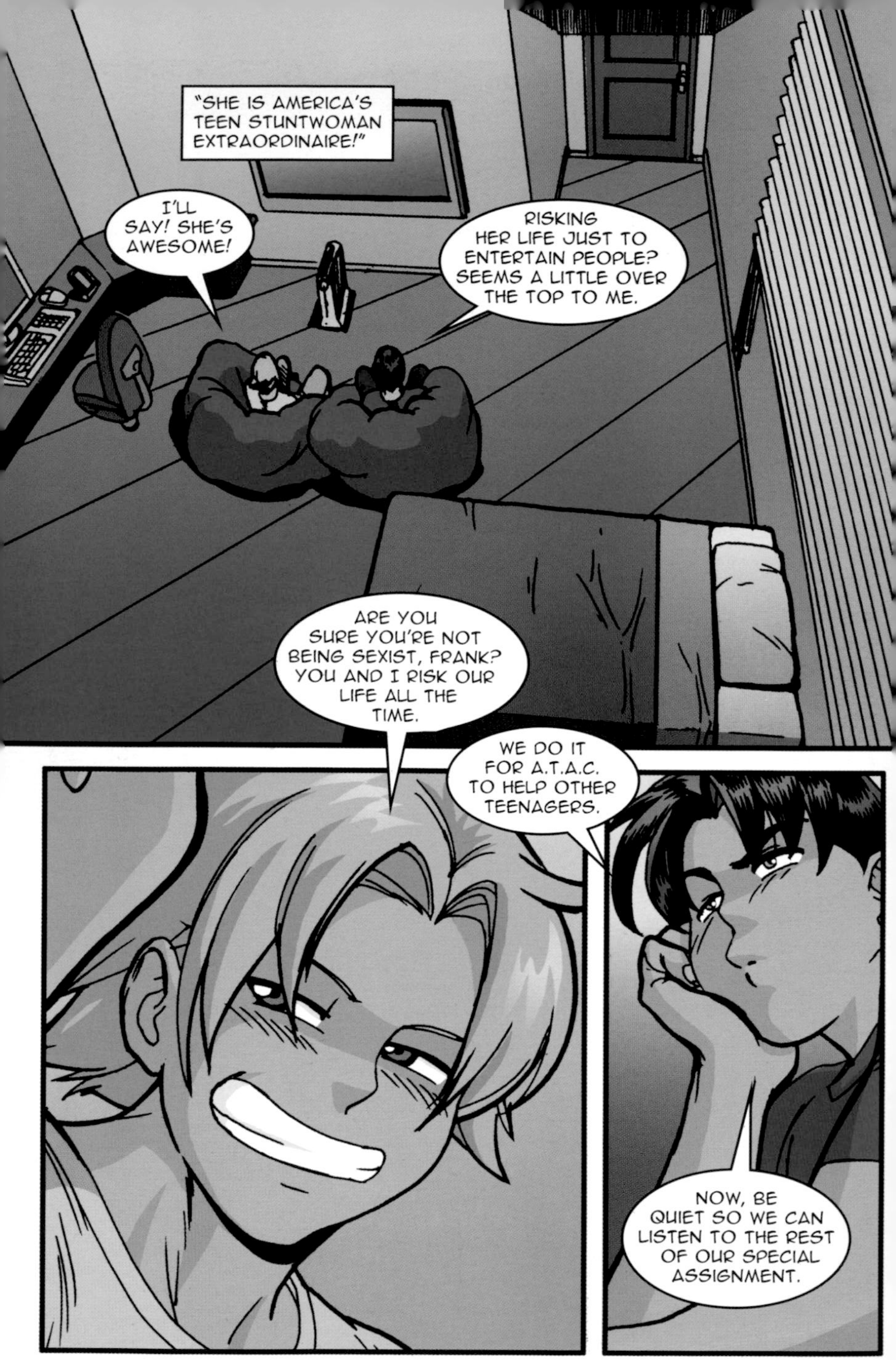
"SHE IS AMERICA'S TEEN STUNTWOMAN EXTRAORDINAIRE!"
I'LL SAY! SHE'S AWESOME!
RISKING HER LIFE JUST TO ENTERTAIN PEOPLE? SEEMS A LITTLE OVER THE TOP TO ME.
ARE YOU SURE YOU'RE NOT BEING SEXIST, FRANK? YOU AND I RISK OUR LIFE ALL THE TIME.
WE DO IT FOR A.T.A.C. TO HELP OTHER TEENAGERS.
NOW, BE QUIET SO WE CAN LISTEN TO THE REST OF OUR SPECIAL ASSIGNMENT.

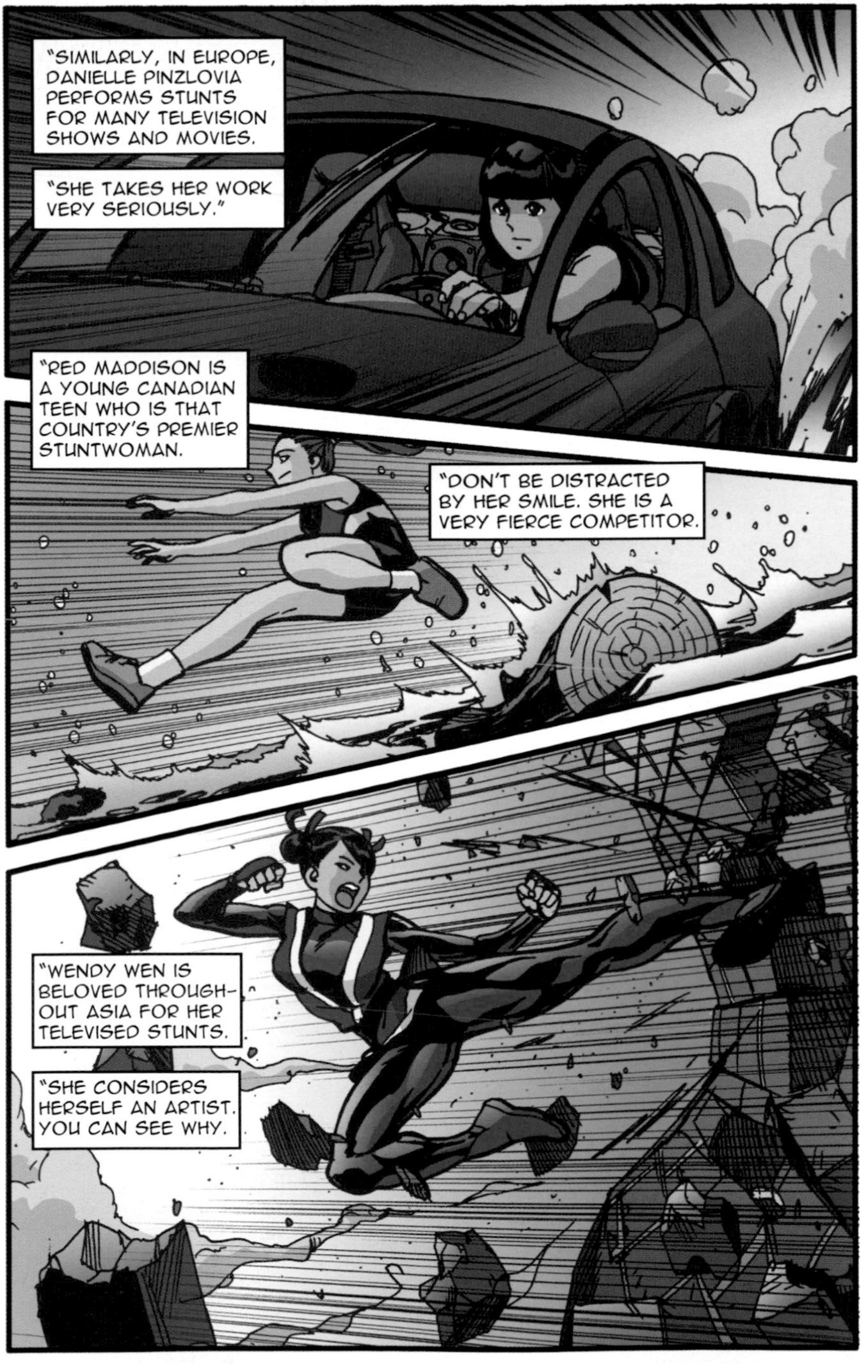
"SIMILARLY, IN EUROPE, DANIELLE PINZLOVIA PERFORMS STUNTS FOR MANY TELEVISION SHOWS AND MOVIES.
"SHE TAKES HER WORK VERY SERIOUSLY."
"RED MADDISON IS A YOUNG CANADIAN TEEN WHO IS THAT COUNTRY'S PREMIER STUNTWOMAN.
"DON'T BE DISTRACTED BY HER SMILE. SHE IS A VERY FIERCE COMPETITOR.
"WENDY WEN IS BELOVED THROUGH-OUT ASIA FOR HER TELEVISED STUNTS.
"SHE CONSIDERS HERSELF AN ARTIST. YOU CAN SEE WHY.

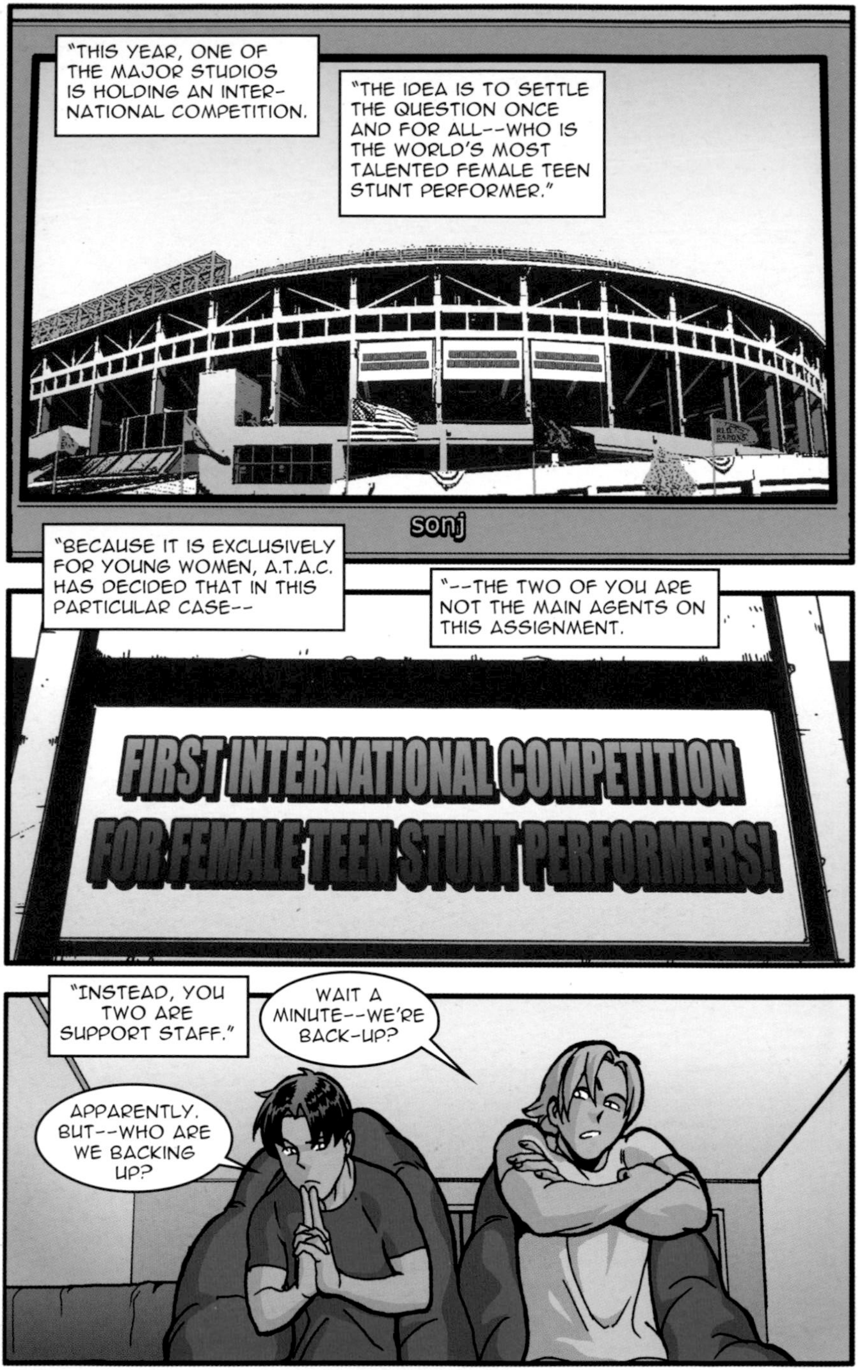
"THIS YEAR, ONE OF THE MAJOR STUDIOS IS HOLDING AN INTER-NATIONAL COMPETITION.
"THE IDEA IS TO SETTLE THE QUESTION ONCE AND FOR ALL--WHO IS THE WORLD'S MOST TALENTED FEMALE TEEN STUNT PERFORMER."
sonj
"BECAUSE IT IS EXCLUSIVELY FOR YOUNG WOMEN, A.T.A.C. HAS DECIDED THAT IN THIS PARTICULAR CASE--
"--THE TWO OF YOU ARE NOT THE MAIN AGENTS ON THIS ASSIGNMENT.
FIRST INTERNATIONAL COMPETITION FOR FEMALE TEEN STUNT PERFORMERS!
"INSTEAD, YOU TWO ARE SUPPORT STAFF."
WAIT A MINUTE--WE'RE BACK-UP?
APPARENTLY. BUT--WHO ARE WE BACKING UP?

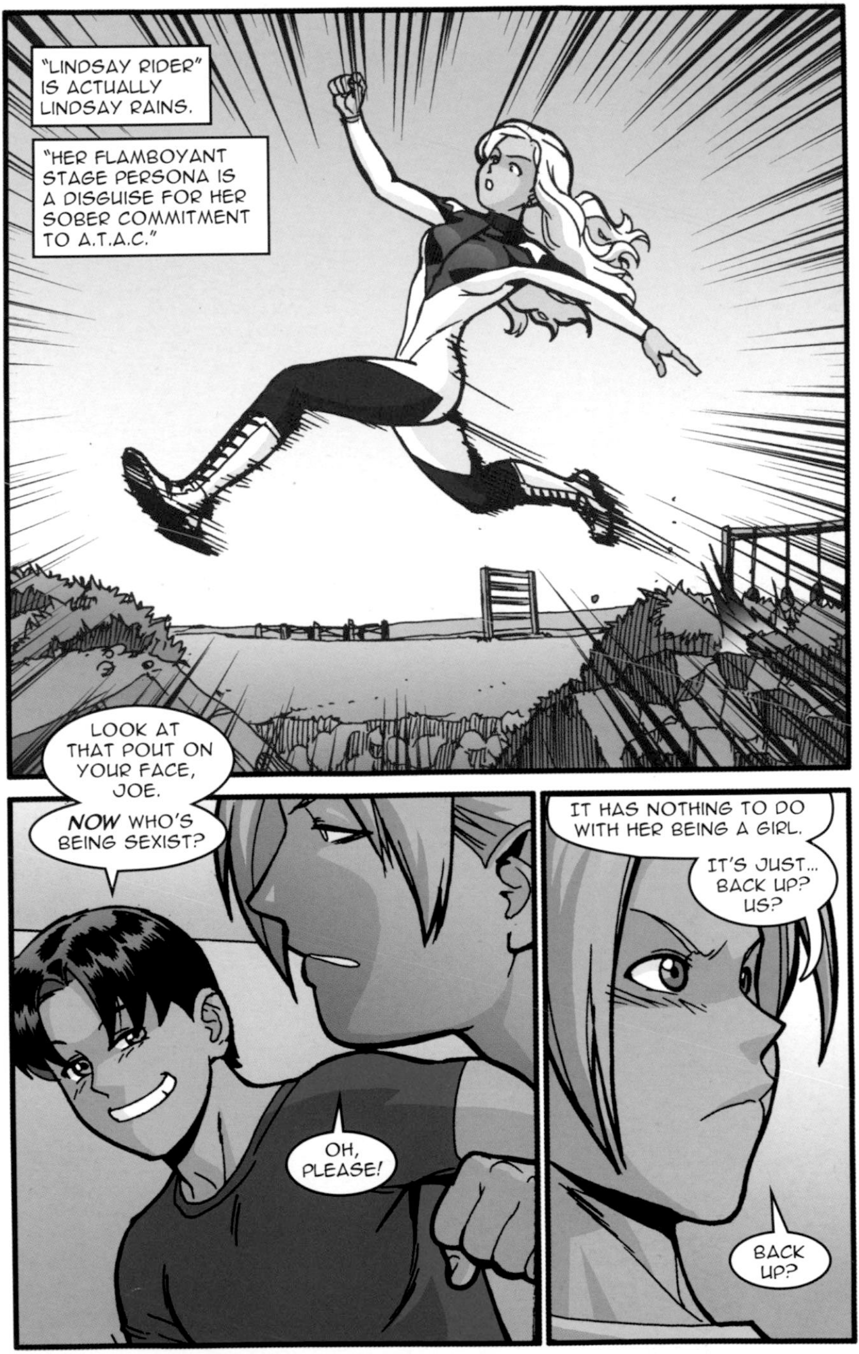

"LINDSAY RIDER" IS ACTUALLY LINDSAY RAINS.
"HER FLAMBOYANT STAGE PERSONA IS A DISGUISE FOR HER SOBER COMMITMENT TO A.T.A.C."
LOOK AT THAT POUT ON YOUR FACE, JOE.
NOW WHO'S BEING SEXIST?
OH, PLEASE!
IT HAS NOTHING TO DO WITH HER BEING A GIRL.
IT'S JUST... BACK UP? US?
BACK UP?

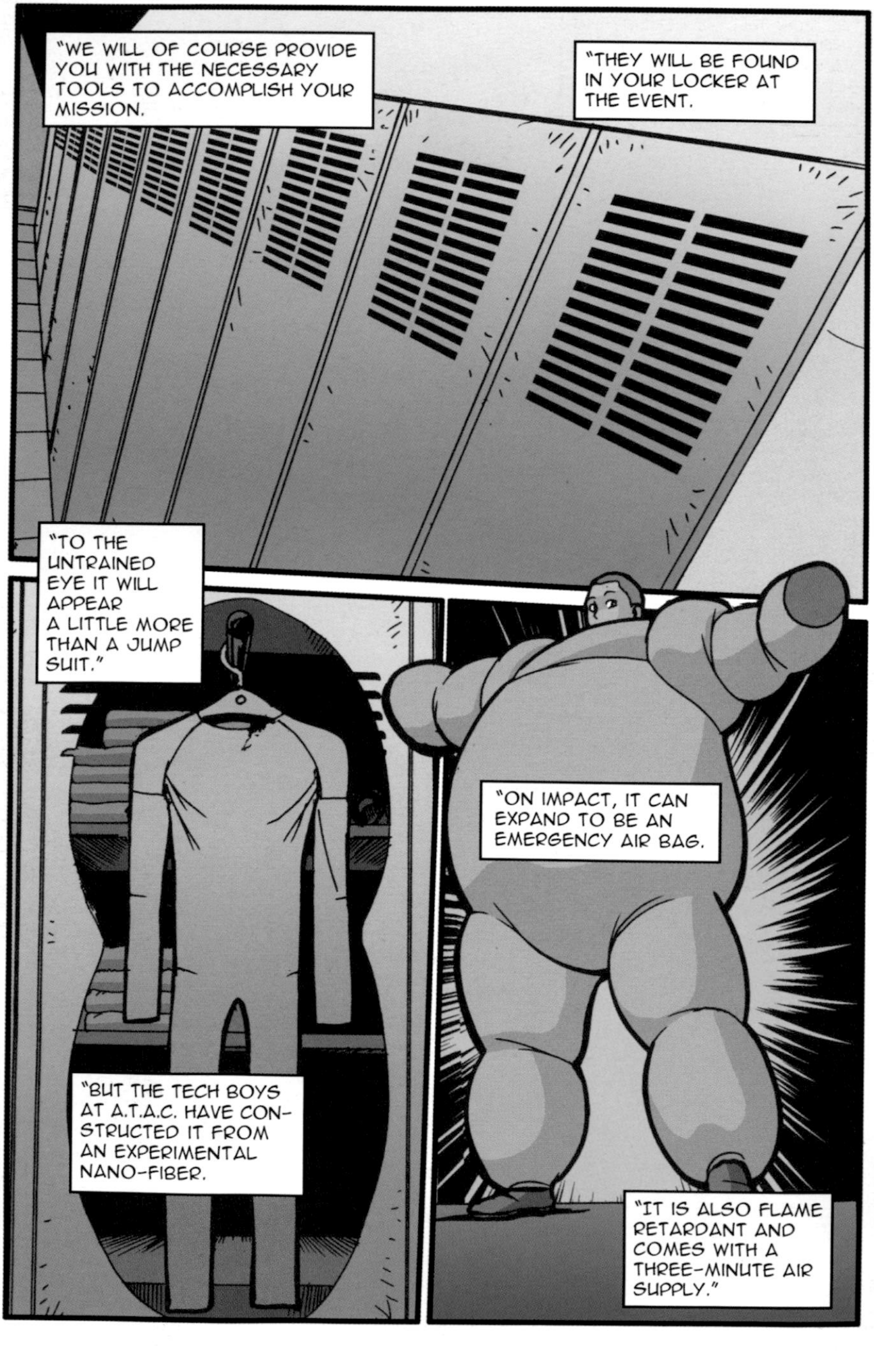
"WE WILL OF COURSE PROVIDE YOU WITH THE NECESSARY TOOLS TO ACCOMPLISH YOUR MISSION.
"THEY WILL BE FOUND IN YOUR LOCKER AT THE EVENT.
"TO THE UNTRAINED EYE IT WILL APPEAR A LITTLE MORE THAN A JUMP SUIT."
"BUT THE TECH BOYS AT A.T.A.C. HAVE CON-STRUCTED IT FROM AN EXPERIMENTAL NANO-FIBER.
"ON IMPACT, IT CAN EXPAND TO BE AN EMERGENCY AIR BAG.
"IT IS ALSO FLAME RETARDANT AND COMES WITH A THREE-MINUTE AIR SUPPLY."

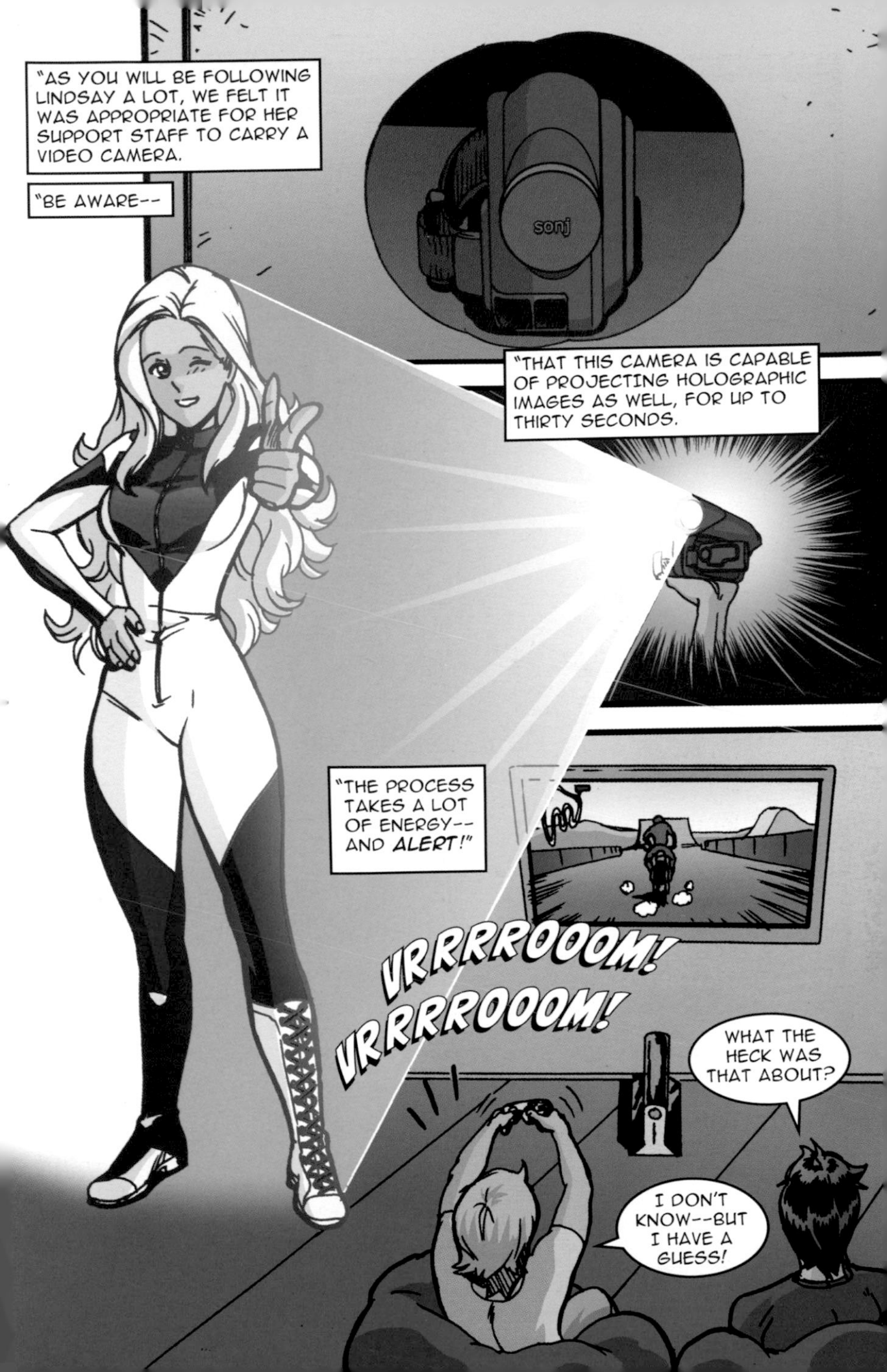
"AS YOU WILL BE FOLLOWING LINDSAY A LOT, WE FELT IT WAS APPROPRIATE FOR HER SUPPORT STAFF TO CARRY A VIDEO CAMERA.
"BE AWARE--
sonj
"THAT THIS CAMERA IS CAPABLE OF PROJECTING HOLOGRAPHIC IMAGES AS WELL, FOR UP TO THIRTY SECONDS.
"THE PROCESS TAKES A LOT OF ENERGY--AND *ALERT*!"
VRRRROOOM!
VRRRROOOM!
WHAT THE HECK WAS THAT ABOUT?
I DON'T KNOW--BUT I HAVE A GUESS!

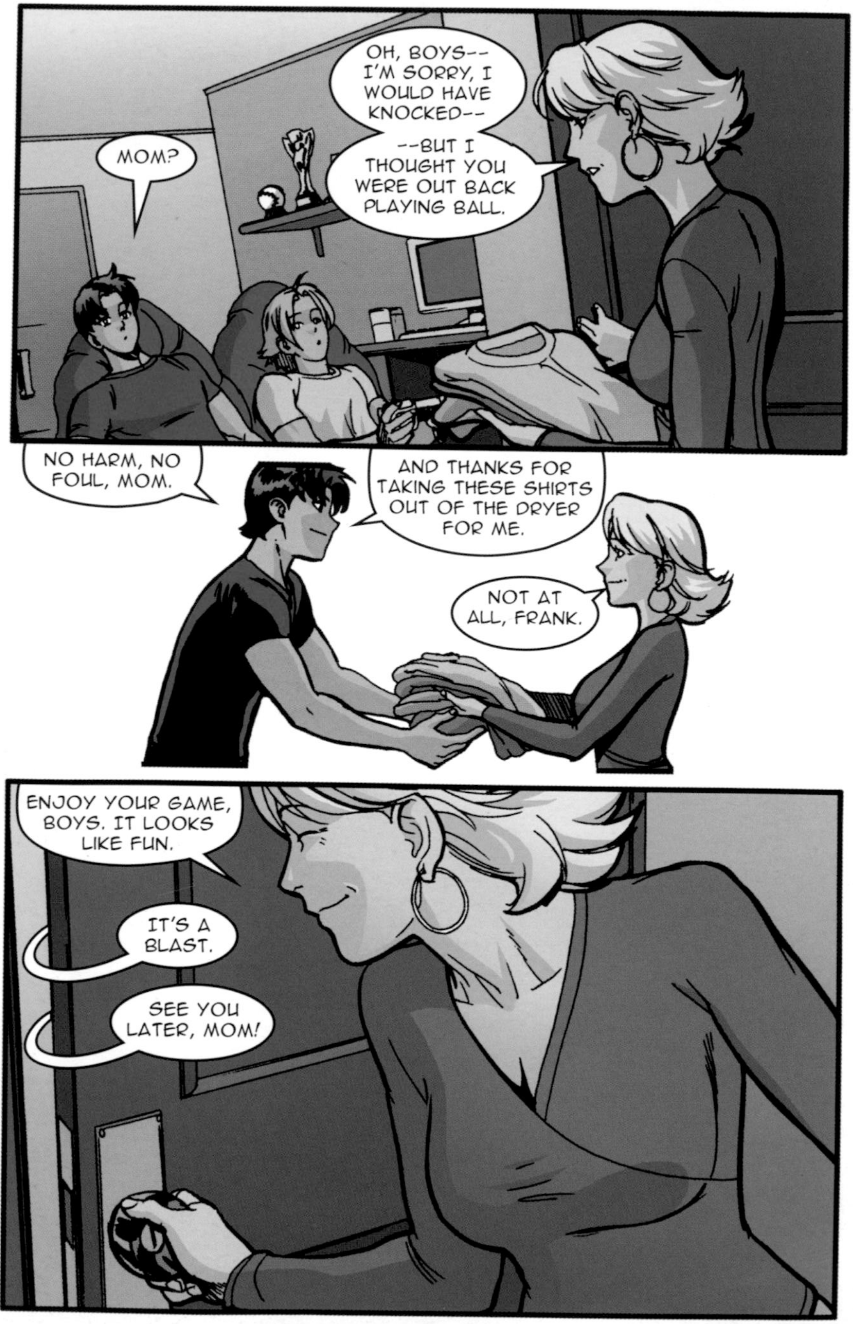
OH, BOYS-- I'M SORRY, I WOULD HAVE KNOCKED--
MOM?
--BUT I THOUGHT YOU WERE OUT BACK PLAYING BALL.
NO HARM, NO FOUL, MOM.
AND THANKS FOR TAKING THESE SHIRTS OUT OF THE DRYER FOR ME.
NOT AT ALL, FRANK.
ENJOY YOUR GAME, BOYS. IT LOOKS LIKE FUN.
IT'S A BLAST.
SEE YOU LATER, MOM!

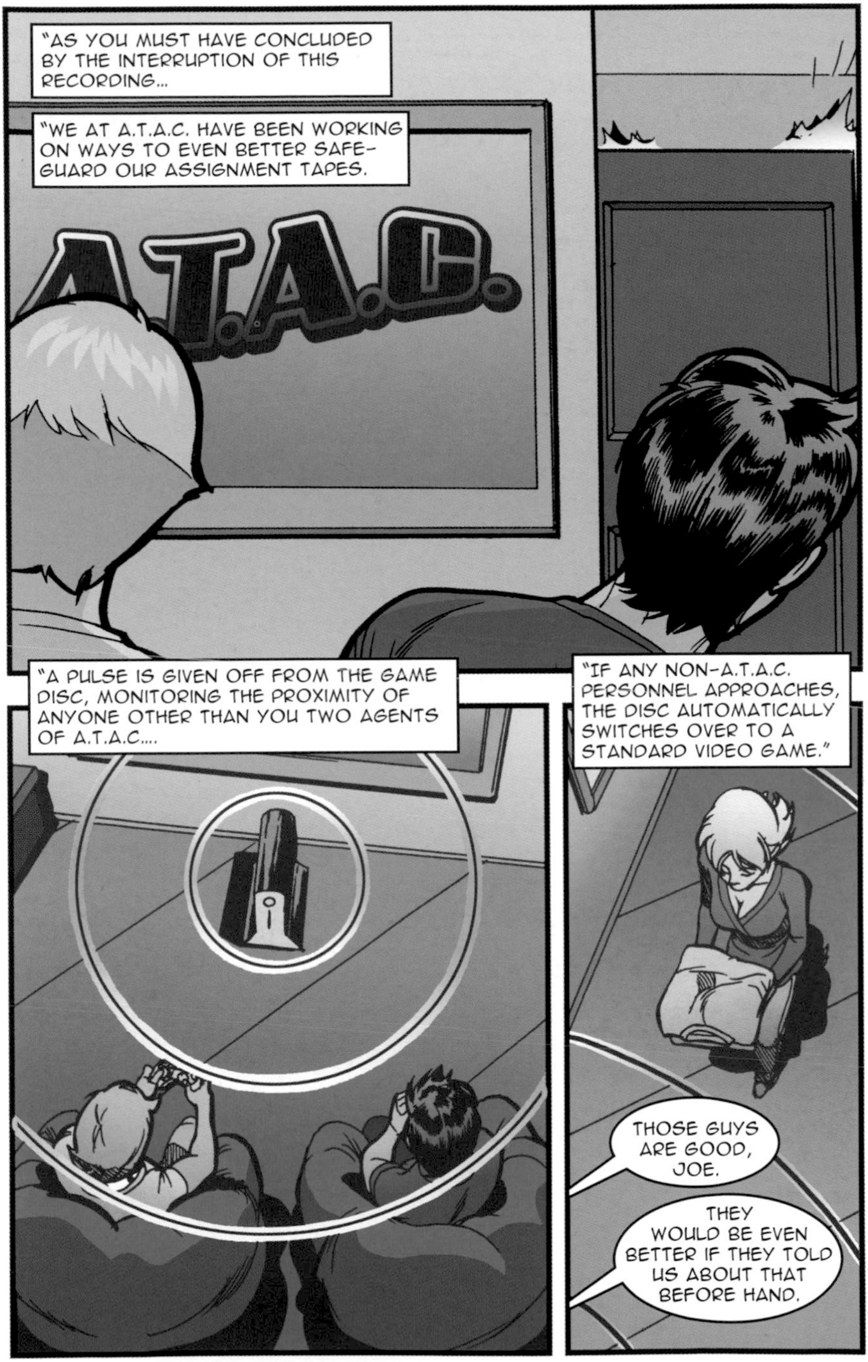
"AS YOU MUST HAVE CONCLUDED BY THE INTERRUPTION OF THIS RECORDING...
"WE AT A.T.A.C. HAVE BEEN WORKING ON WAYS TO EVEN BETTER SAFE-GUARD OUR ASSIGNMENT TAPES.
A.T.A.C.
"A PULSE IS GIVEN OFF FROM THE GAME DISC, MONITORING THE PROXIMITY OF ANYONE OTHER THAN YOU TWO AGENTS OF A.T.A.C....
"IF ANY NON-A.T.A.C. PERSONNEL APPROACHES, THE DISC AUTOMATICALLY SWITCHES OVER TO A STANDARD VIDEO GAME."
THOSE GUYS ARE GOOD, JOE.
THEY WOULD BE EVEN BETTER IF THEY TOLD US ABOUT THAT BEFORE HAND.

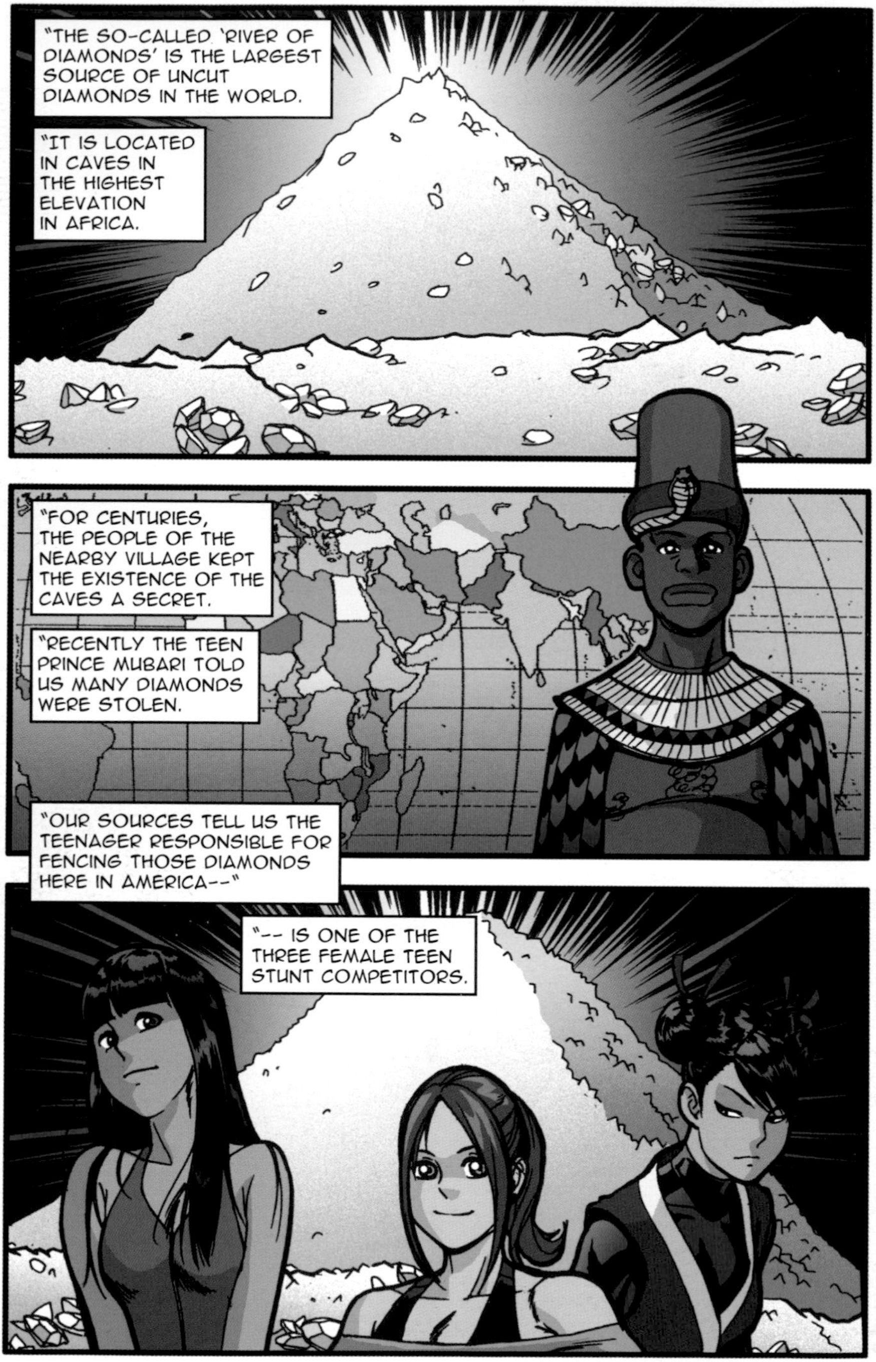
"THE SO-CALLED 'RIVER OF DIAMONDS' IS THE LARGEST SOURCE OF UNCUT DIAMONDS IN THE WORLD.
"IT IS LOCATED IN CAVES IN THE HIGHEST ELEVATION IN AFRICA.
"FOR CENTURIES, THE PEOPLE OF THE NEARBY VILLAGE KEPT THE EXISTENCE OF THE CAVES A SECRET.
"RECENTLY THE TEEN PRINCE MUBARI TOLD US MANY DIAMONDS WERE STOLEN.
"OUR SOURCES TELL US THE TEENAGER RESPONSIBLE FOR FENCING THOSE DIAMONDS HERE IN AMERICA--"
"-- IS ONE OF THE THREE FEMALE TEEN STUNT COMPETITORS.

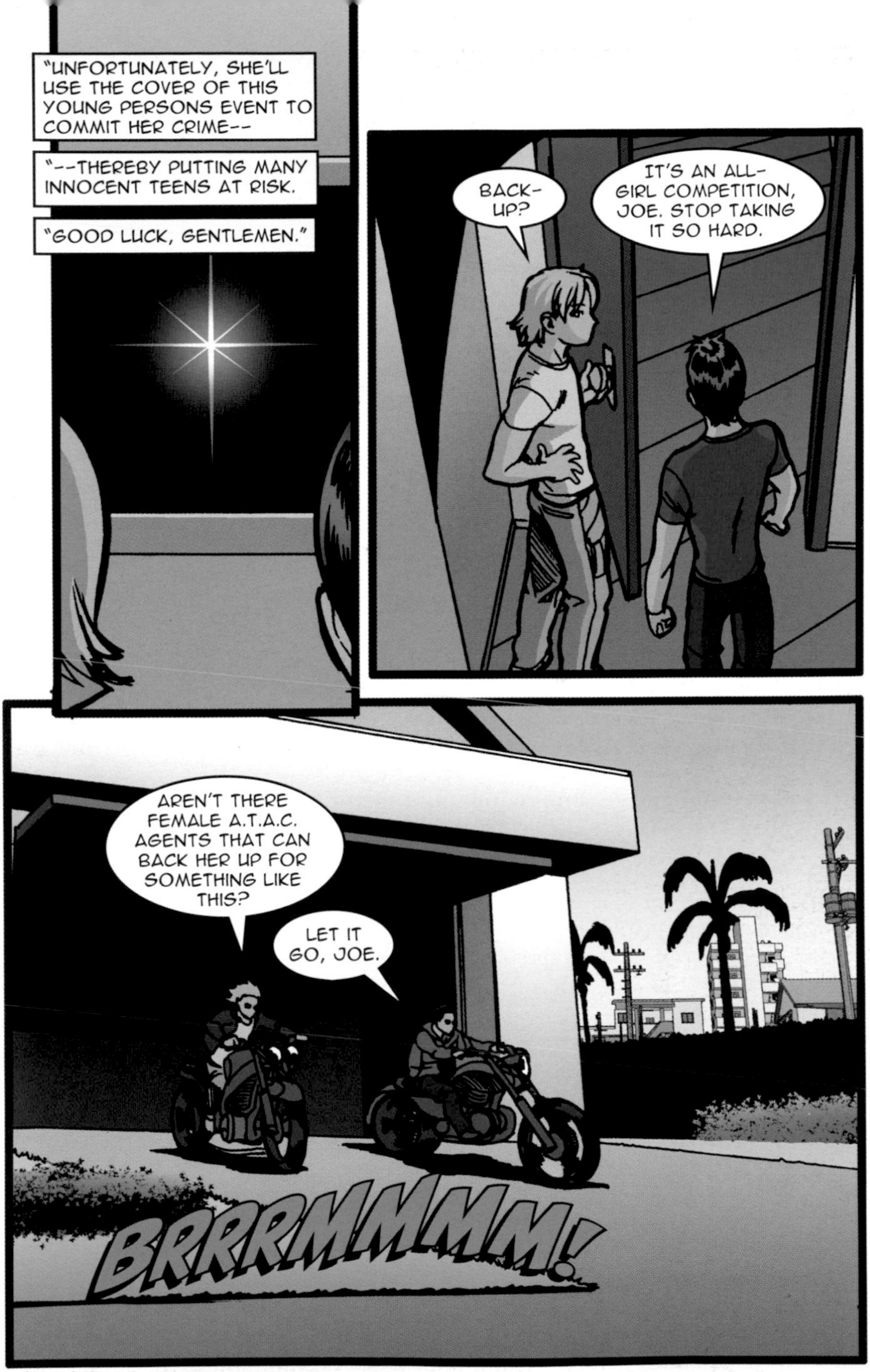
"UNFORTUNATELY, SHE'LL USE THE COVER OF THIS YOUNG PERSONS EVENT TO COMMIT HER CRIME--
"--THEREBY PUTTING MANY INNOCENT TEENS AT RISK.
"GOOD LUCK, GENTLEMEN."
BACK-UP?
IT'S AN ALL-GIRL COMPETITION, JOE. STOP TAKING IT SO HARD.
AREN'T THERE FEMALE A.T.A.C. AGENTS THAT CAN BACK HER UP FOR SOMETHING LIKE THIS?
LET IT GO, JOE.
BRRRMMMMM!

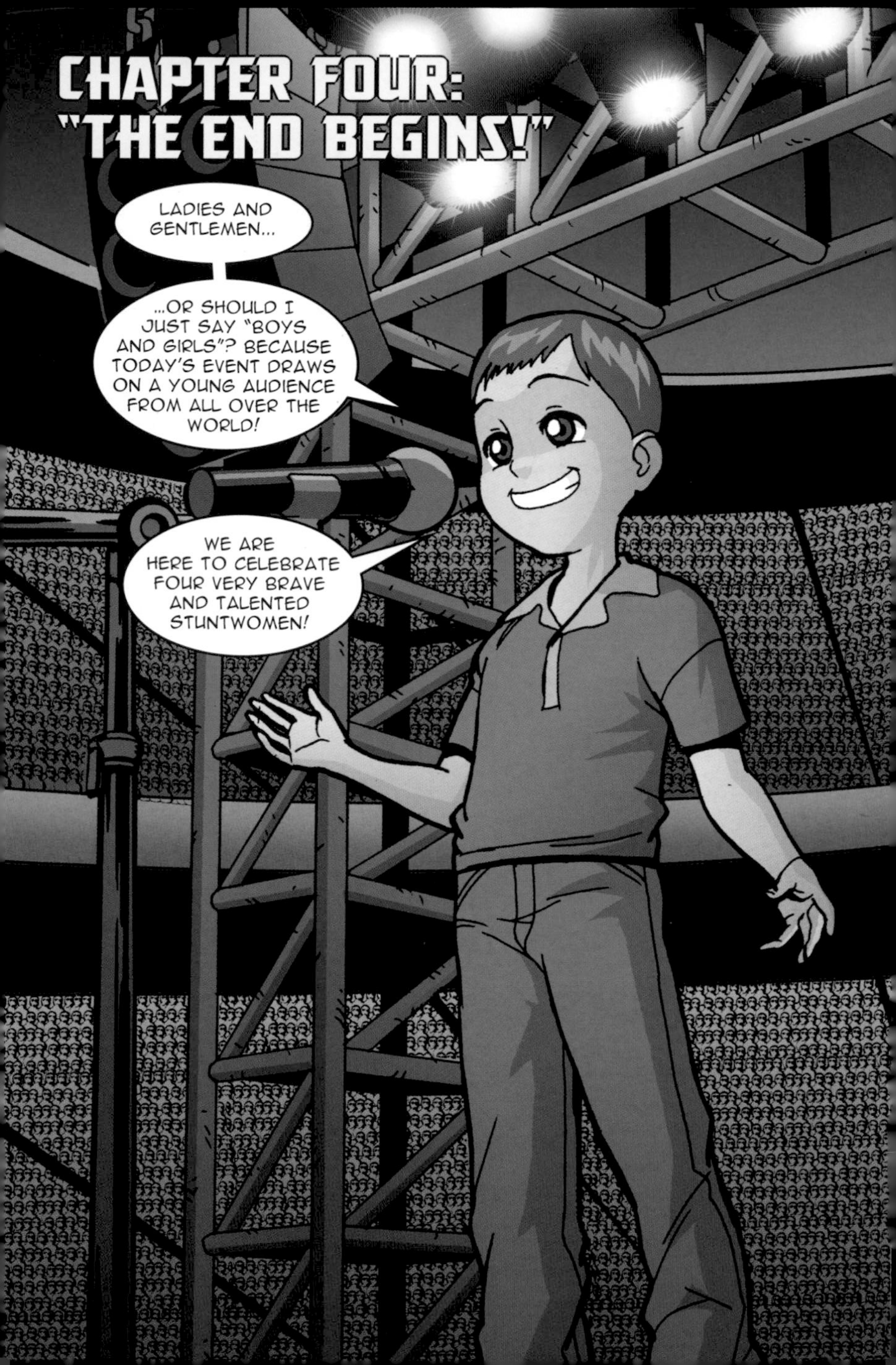
CHAPTER FOUR:
"THE END BEGINS!"
LADIES AND GENTLEMEN...
...OR SHOULD I JUST SAY "BOYS AND GIRLS"? BECAUSE TODAY'S EVENT DRAWS ON A YOUNG AUDIENCE FROM ALL OVER THE WORLD!
WE ARE HERE TO CELEBRATE FOUR VERY BRAVE AND TALENTED STUNTWOMEN!

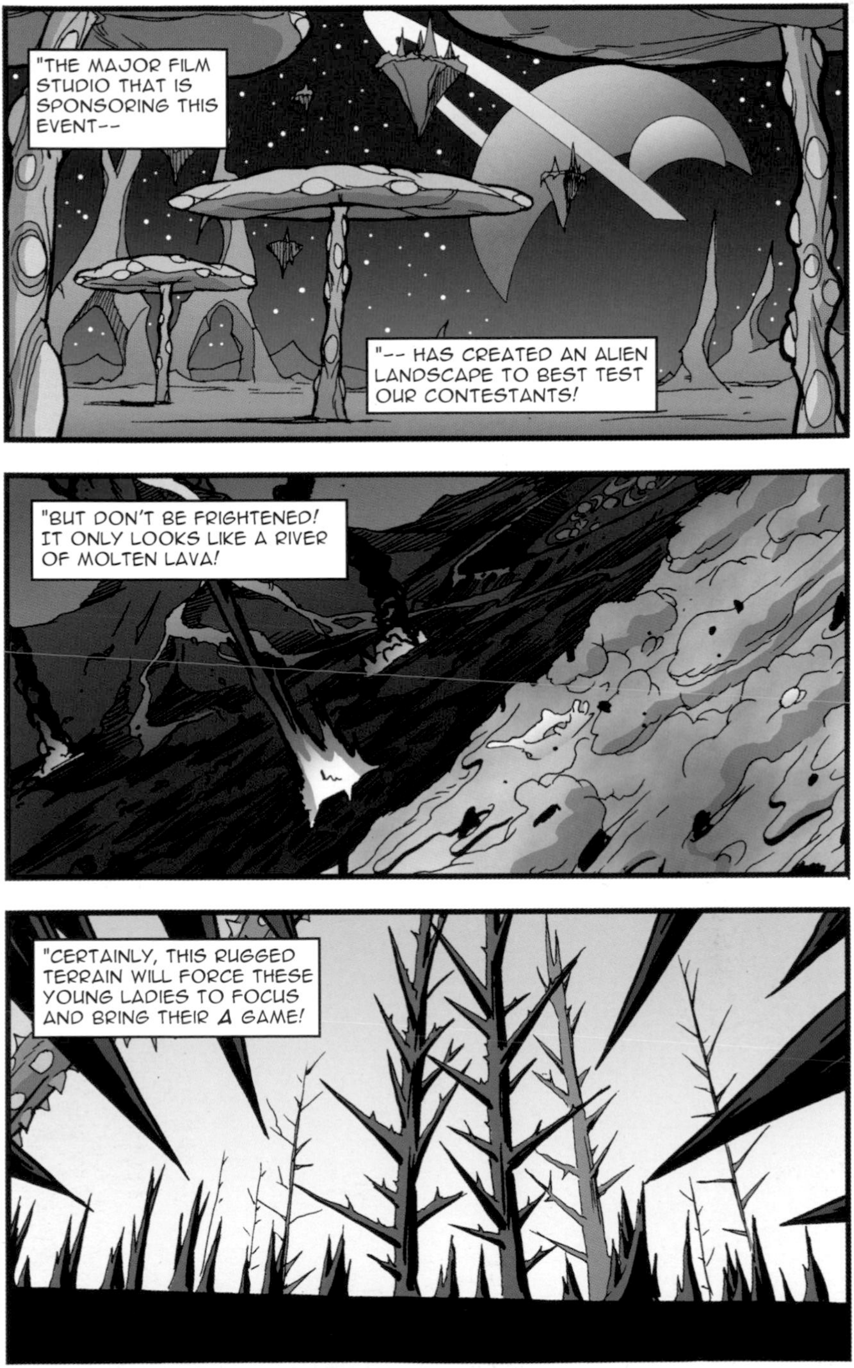
"THE MAJOR FILM STUDIO THAT IS SPONSORING THIS EVENT--
"-- HAS CREATED AN ALIEN LANDSCAPE TO BEST TEST OUR CONTESTANTS!
"BUT DON'T BE FRIGHTENED! IT ONLY LOOKS LIKE A RIVER OF MOLTEN LAVA!
"CERTAINLY, THIS RUGGED TERRAIN WILL FORCE THESE YOUNG LADIES TO FOCUS AND BRING THEIR A GAME!

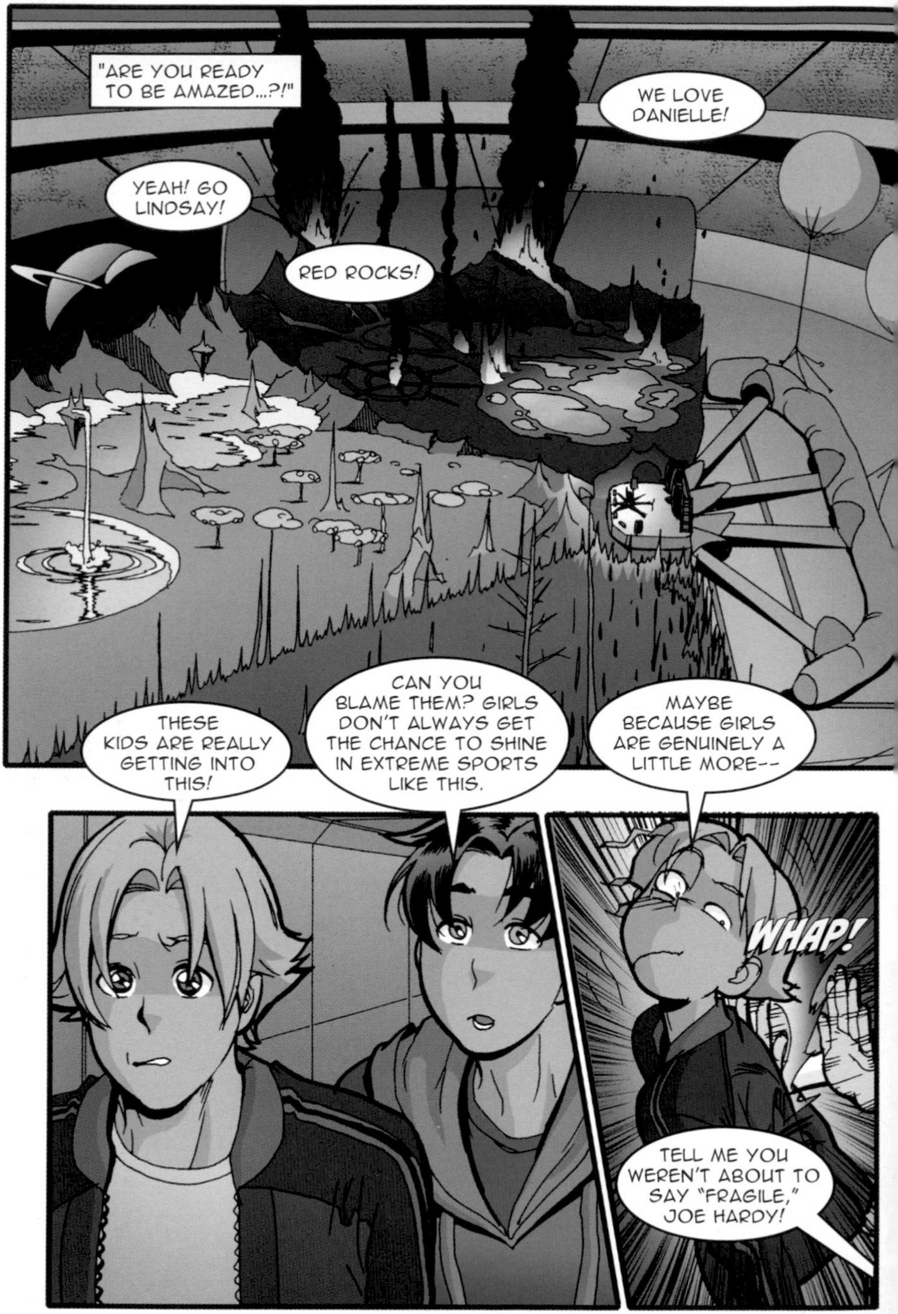
"ARE YOU READY TO BE AMAZED...?!"
WE LOVE DANIELLE!
YEAH! GO LINDSAY!
RED ROCKS!
THESE KIDS ARE REALLY GETTING INTO THIS!
CAN YOU BLAME THEM? GIRLS DON'T ALWAYS GET THE CHANCE TO SHINE IN EXTREME SPORTS LIKE THIS.
MAYBE BECAUSE GIRLS ARE GENUINELY A LITTLE MORE--
WHAP!
TELL ME YOU WEREN'T ABOUT TO SAY "FRAGILE," JOE HARDY!

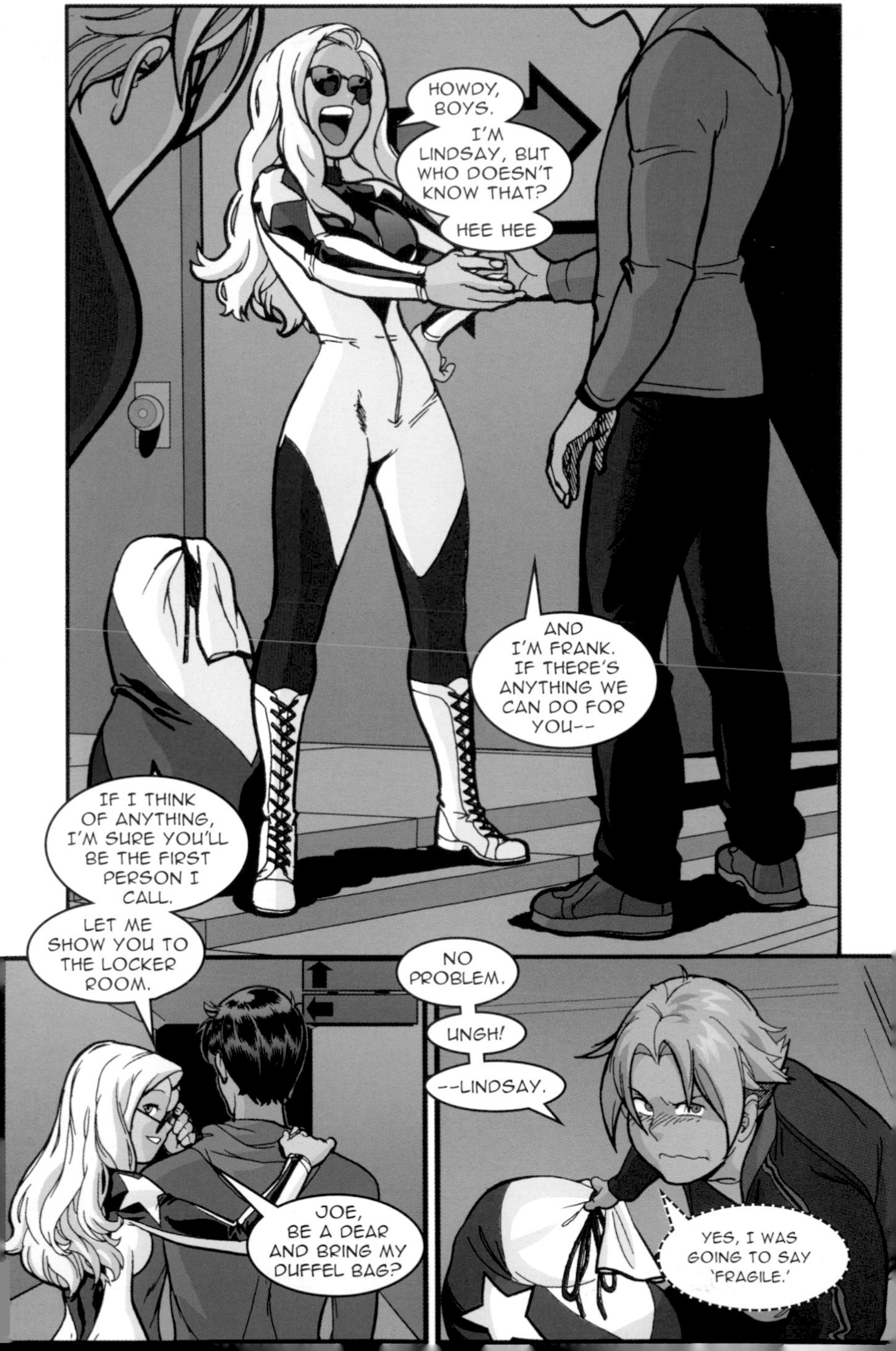
HOWDY, BOYS.
I'M LINDSAY, BUT WHO DOESN'T KNOW THAT?
HEE HEE
AND I'M FRANK. IF THERE'S ANYTHING WE CAN DO FOR YOU--
IF I THINK OF ANYTHING, I'M SURE YOU'LL BE THE FIRST PERSON I CALL.
LET ME SHOW YOU TO THE LOCKER ROOM.
JOE, BE A DEAR AND BRING MY DUFFEL BAG?
NO PROBLEM.
UNGH!
--LINDSAY.
YES, I WAS GOING TO SAY 'FRAGILE.'

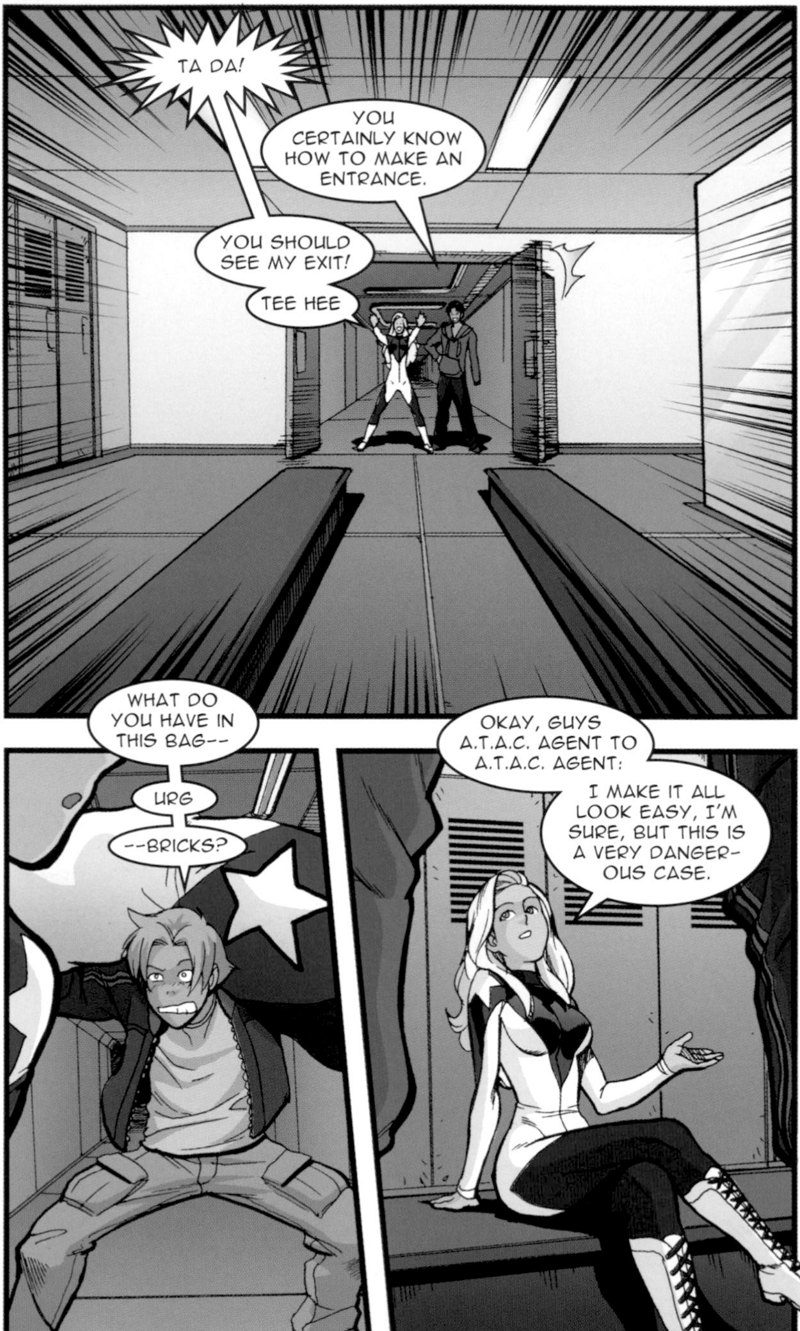
TA DA!
YOU CERTAINLY KNOW HOW TO MAKE AN ENTRANCE.
YOU SHOULD SEE MY EXIT!
TEE HEE
WHAT DO YOU HAVE IN THIS BAG--
URG
--BRICKS?
OKAY, GUYS A.T.A.C. AGENT TO A.T.A.C. AGENT:
I MAKE IT ALL LOOK EASY, I'M SURE, BUT THIS IS A VERY DANGER-OUS CASE.

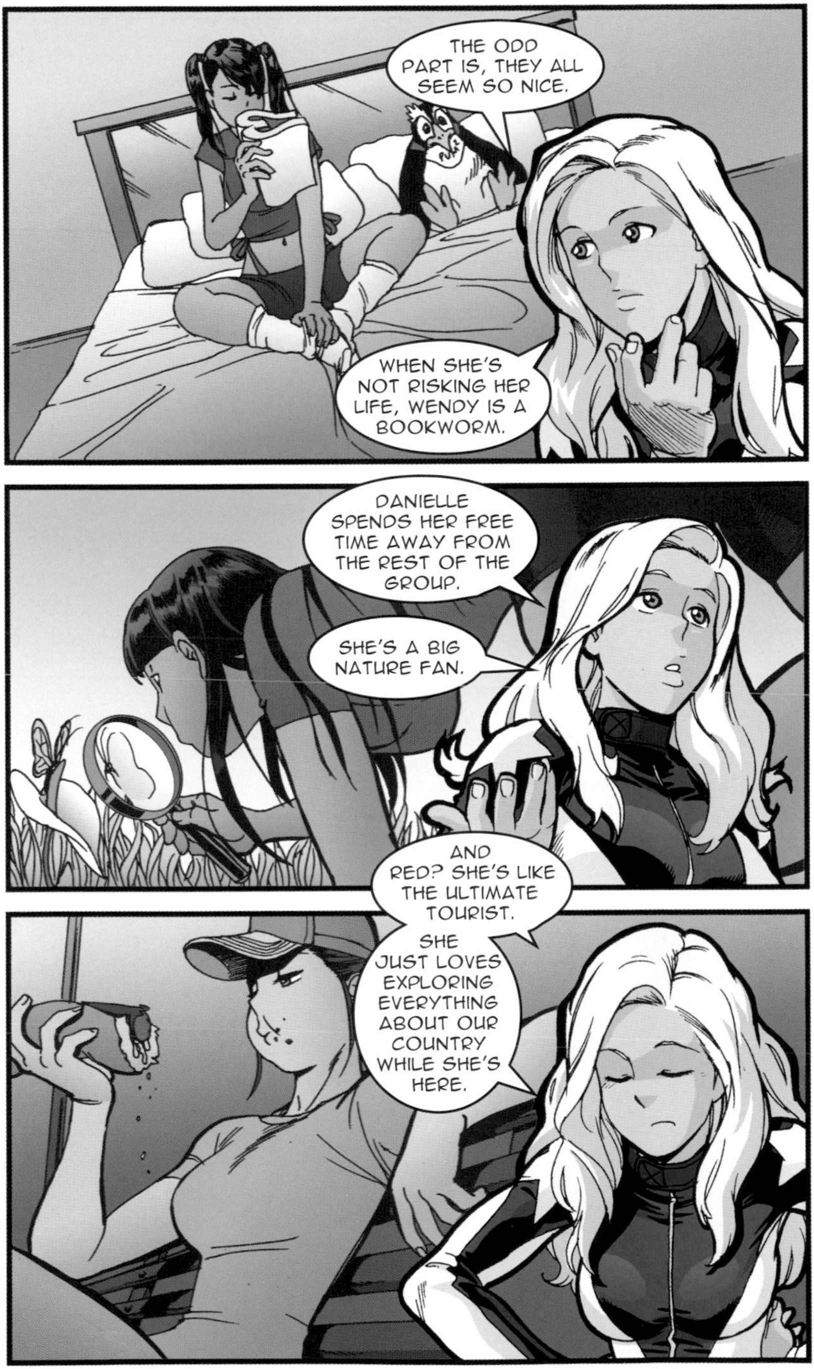
THE ODD PART IS, THEY ALL SEEM SO NICE.
WHEN SHE'S NOT RISKING HER LIFE, WENDY IS A BOOKWORM.
DANIELLE SPENDS HER FREE TIME AWAY FROM THE REST OF THE GROUP.
SHE'S A BIG NATURE FAN.
AND RED? SHE'S LIKE THE ULTIMATE TOURIST.
SHE JUST LOVES EXPLORING EVERYTHING ABOUT OUR COUNTRY WHILE SHE'S HERE.

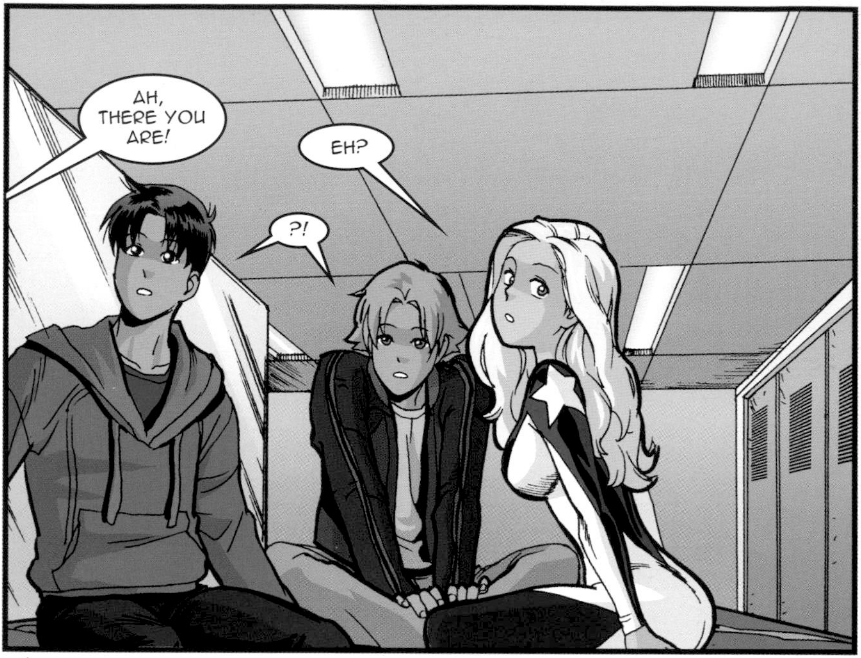
AH, THERE YOU ARE!
EH?
?!

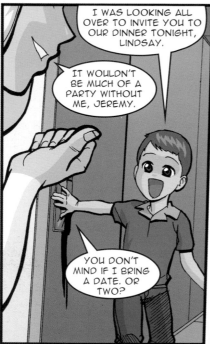

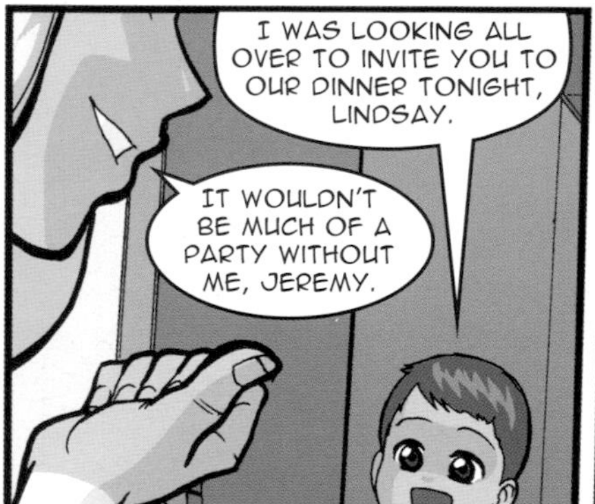
I WAS LOOKING ALL OVER TO INVITE YOU TO OUR DINNER TONIGHT, LINDSAY.
IT WOULDN'T BE MUCH OF A PARTY WITHOUT ME, JEREMY.
YOU DON'T MIND IF I BRING A DATE. OR TWO?

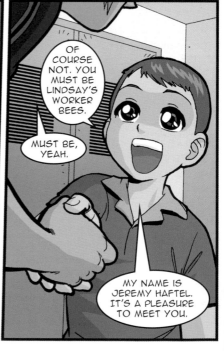

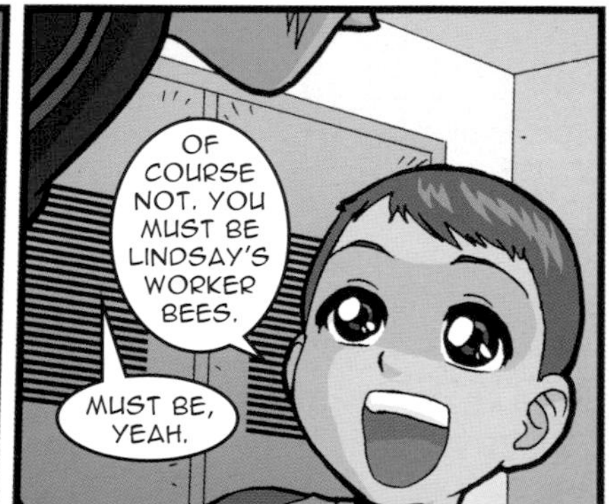
OF COURSE NOT. YOU MUST BE LINDSAY'S WORKER BEES.
MUST BE, YEAH.
MY NAME IS JEREMY HAFTEL. IT'S A PLEASURE TO MEET YOU.

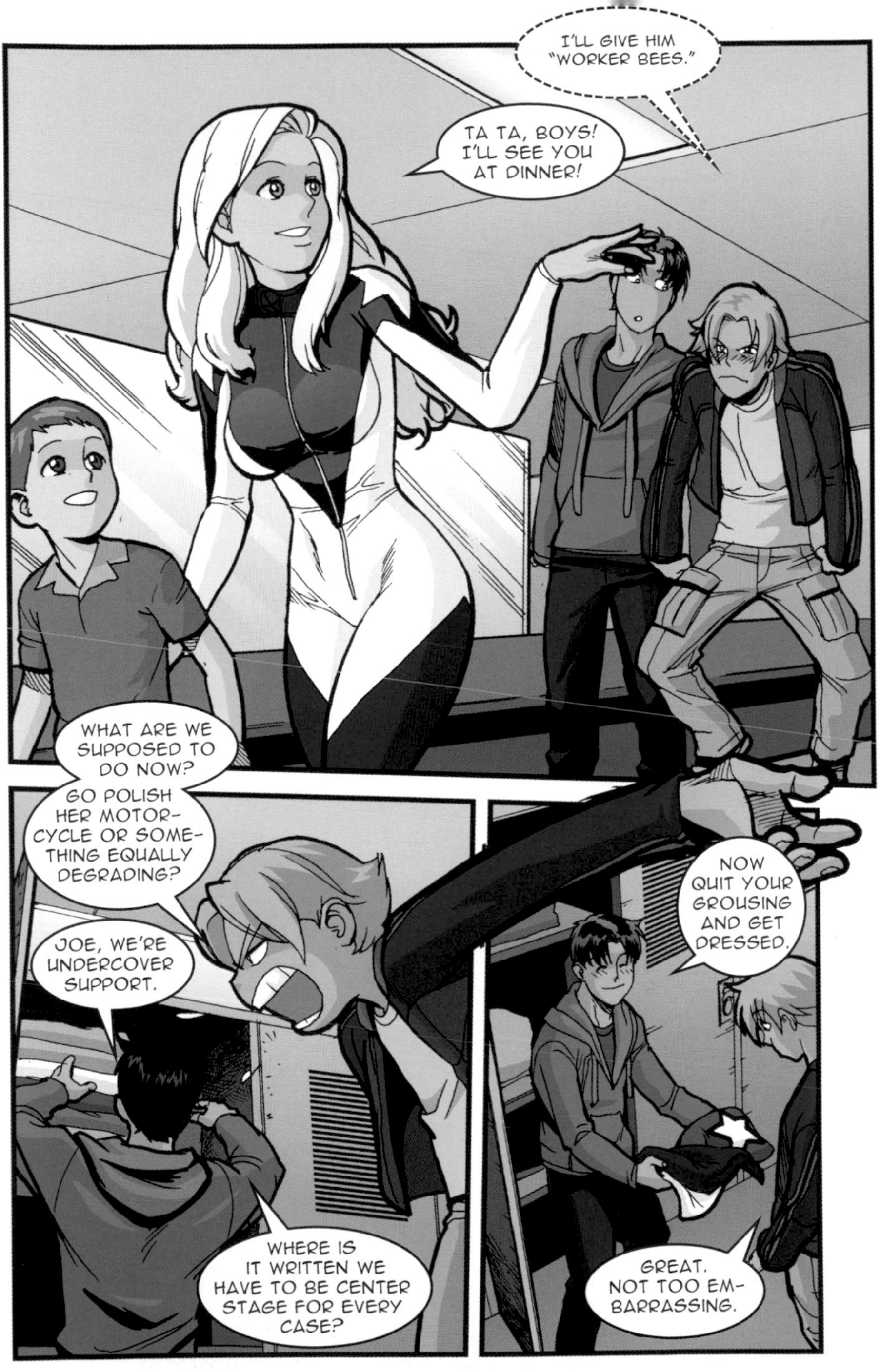
I'LL GIVE HIM "WORKER BEES."
TA TA, BOYS! I'LL SEE YOU AT DINNER!
WHAT ARE WE SUPPOSED TO DO NOW?
GO POLISH HER MOTOR-CYCLE OR SOME-THING EQUALLY DEGRADING?
JOE, WE'RE UNDERCOVER SUPPORT.
WHERE IS IT WRITTEN WE HAVE TO BE CENTER STAGE FOR EVERY CASE?
NOW QUIT YOUR GROUSING AND GET DRESSED.
GREAT. NOT TOO EM-BARRASSING.

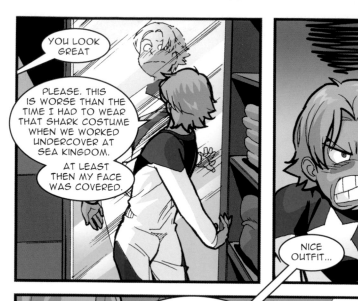

YOU LOOK GREAT

PLEASE. THIS IS WORSE THAN THE TIME I HAD TO WEAR THAT SHARK COSTUME WHEN WE WORKED UNDERCOVER AT SEA KINGDOM.

AT LEAST THEN MY FACE WAS COVERED.

NICE OUTFIT...

...BUT LOOKING LIKE A BOY SCOUT WRAPPED IN FLAG ISN'T GOING TO DISTRACT ME.

I'M STILL GOING TO BURY YOUR BOSS LINDSAY.

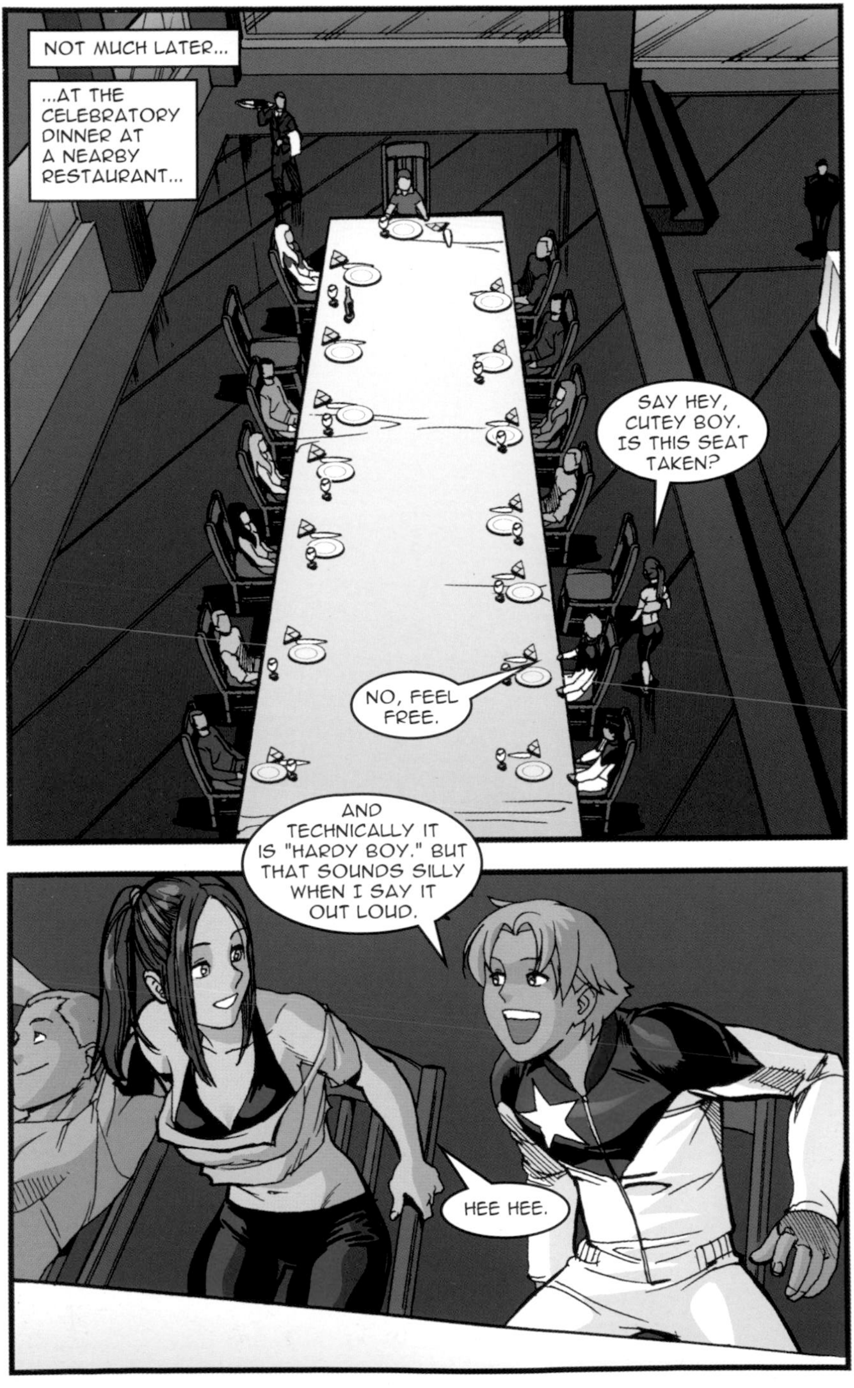
NOT MUCH LATER...
...AT THE CELEBRATORY DINNER AT A NEARBY RESTAURANT...
SAY HEY, CUTEY BOY. IS THIS SEAT TAKEN?
NO, FEEL FREE.
AND TECHNICALLY IT IS "HARDY BOY." BUT THAT SOUNDS SILLY WHEN I SAY IT OUT LOUD.
HEE HEE.

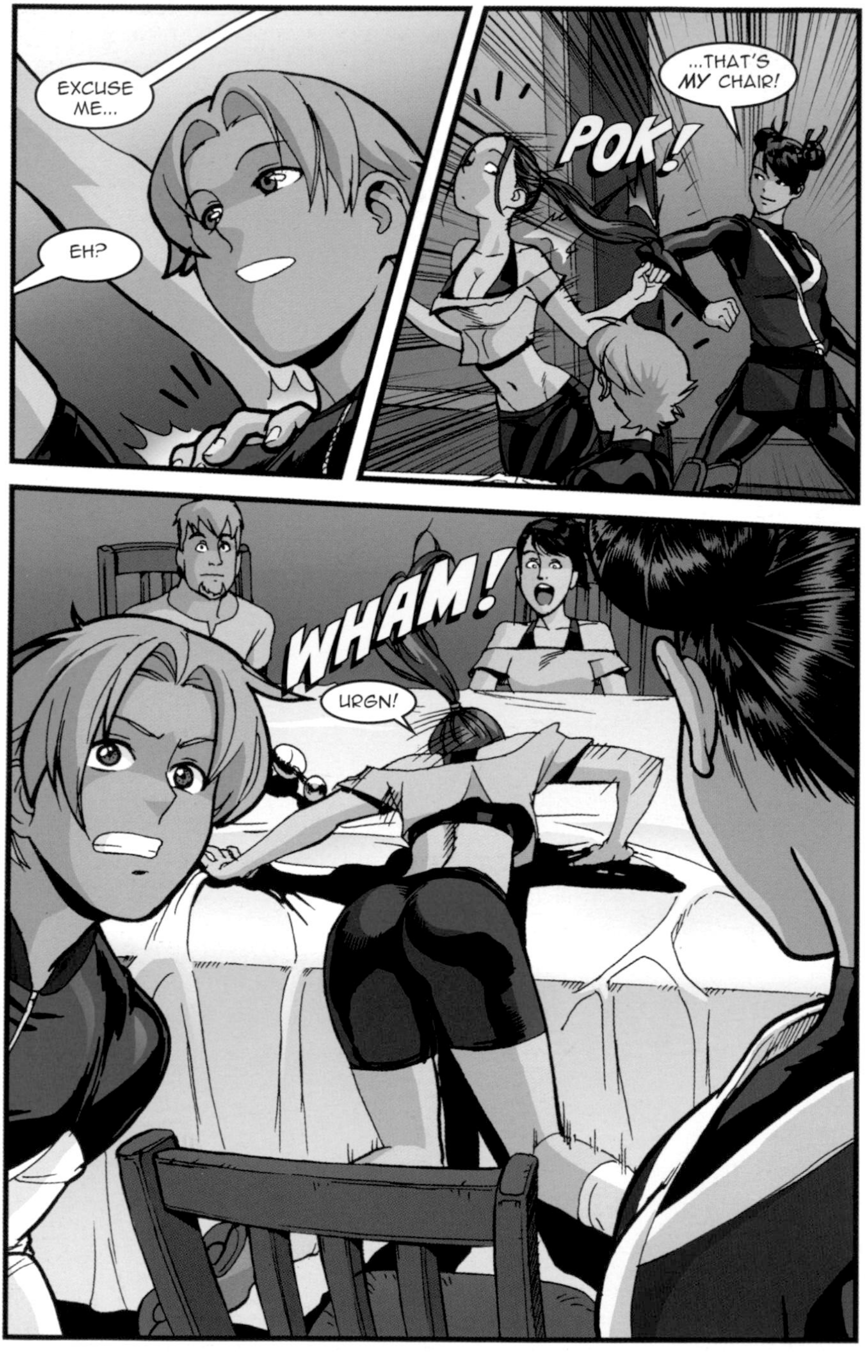
EXCUSE ME...
EH?
...THAT'S MY CHAIR!
POK!
WHAM!
URGN!

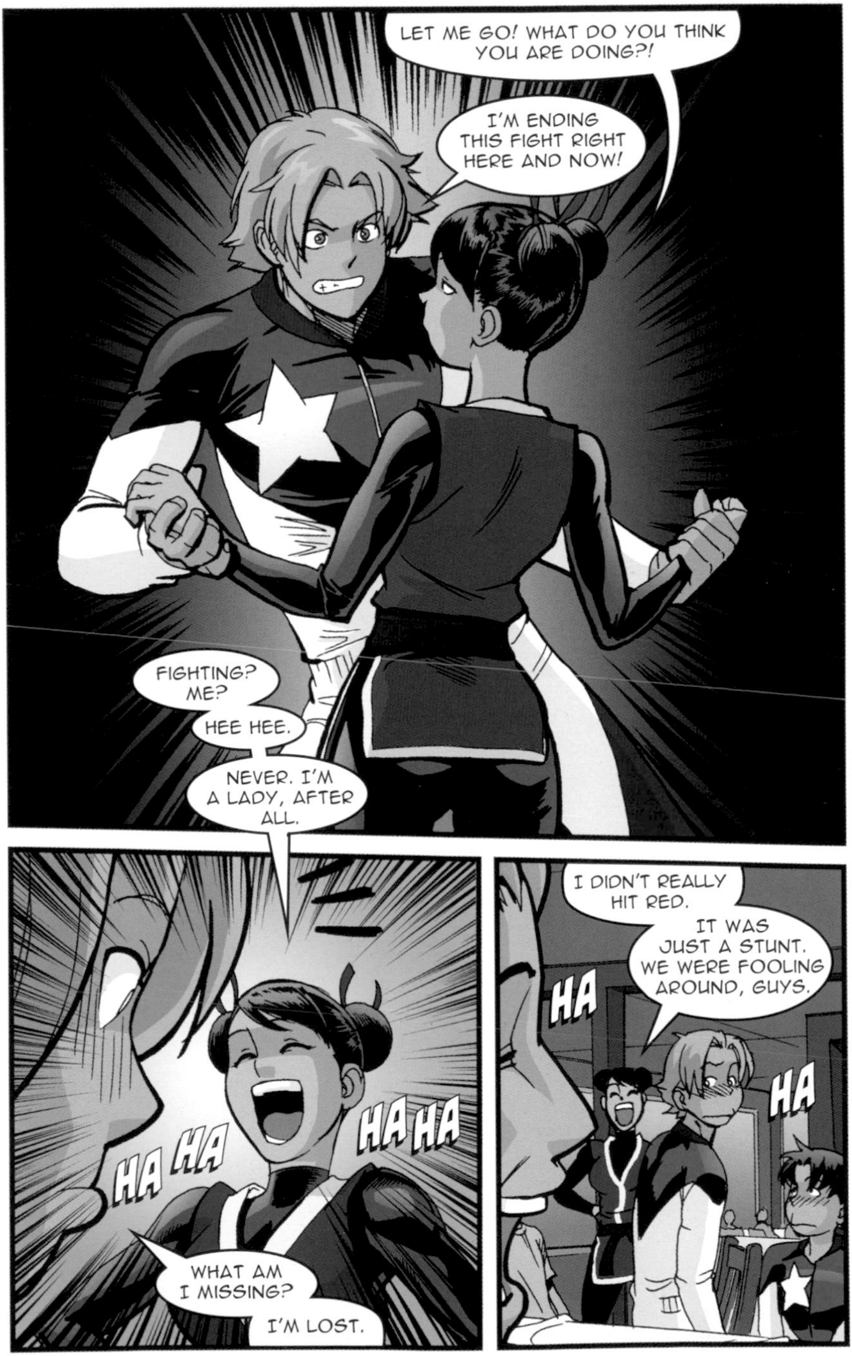
LET ME GO! WHAT DO YOU THINK YOU ARE DOING?!
I'M ENDING THIS FIGHT RIGHT HERE AND NOW!
FIGHTING? ME?
HEE HEE.
NEVER. I'M A LADY, AFTER ALL.
HA HA
HA HA
WHAT AM I MISSING?
I'M LOST.
I DIDN'T REALLY HIT RED.
IT WAS JUST A STUNT. WE WERE FOOLING AROUND, GUYS.
HA
HA

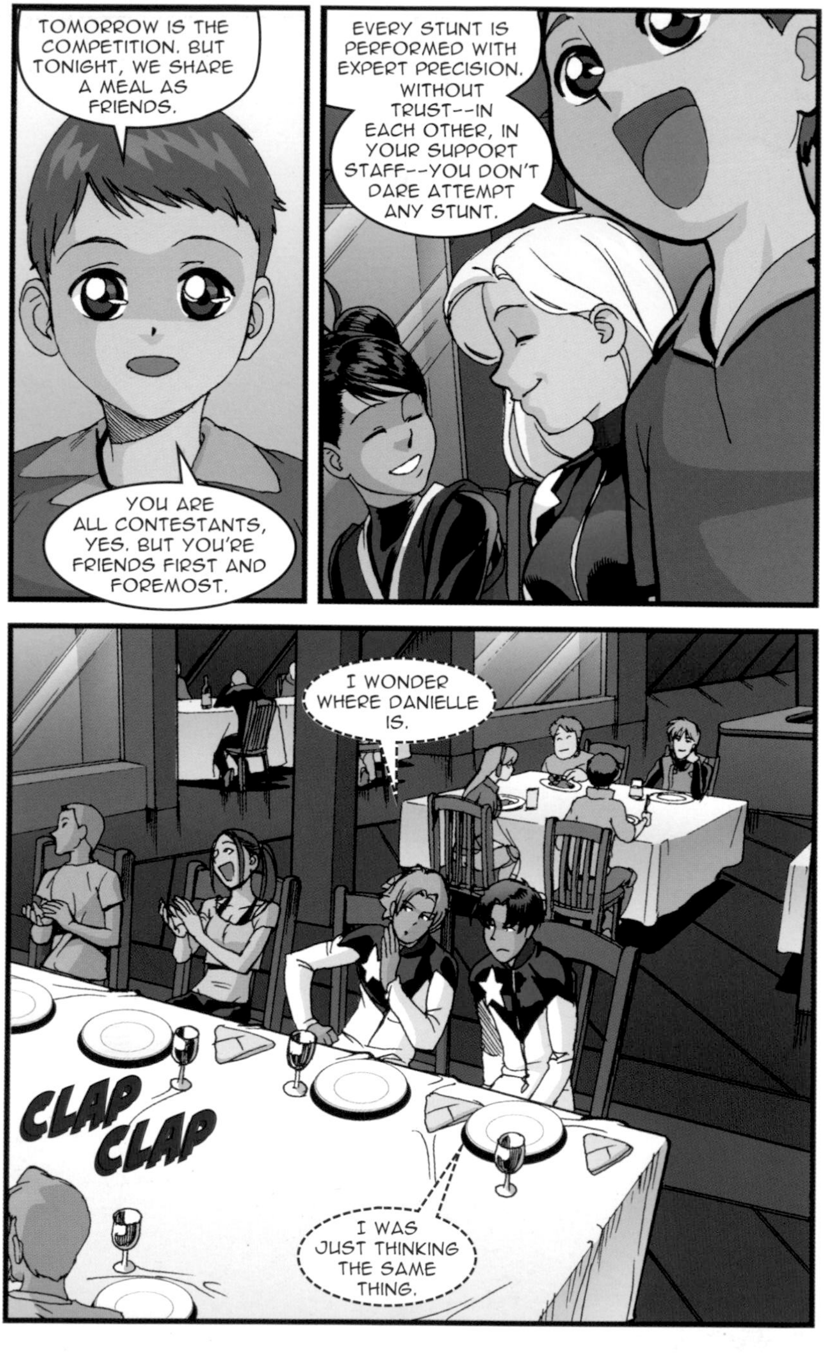
TOMORROW IS THE COMPETITION. BUT TONIGHT, WE SHARE A MEAL AS FRIENDS.
YOU ARE ALL CONTESTANTS, YES. BUT YOU'RE FRIENDS FIRST AND FOREMOST.
EVERY STUNT IS PERFORMED WITH EXPERT PRECISION.
WITHOUT TRUST--IN EACH OTHER, IN YOUR SUPPORT STAFF--YOU DON'T DARE ATTEMPT ANY STUNT.
I WONDER WHERE DANIELLE IS.
CLAP CLAP
I WAS JUST THINKING THE SAME THING.

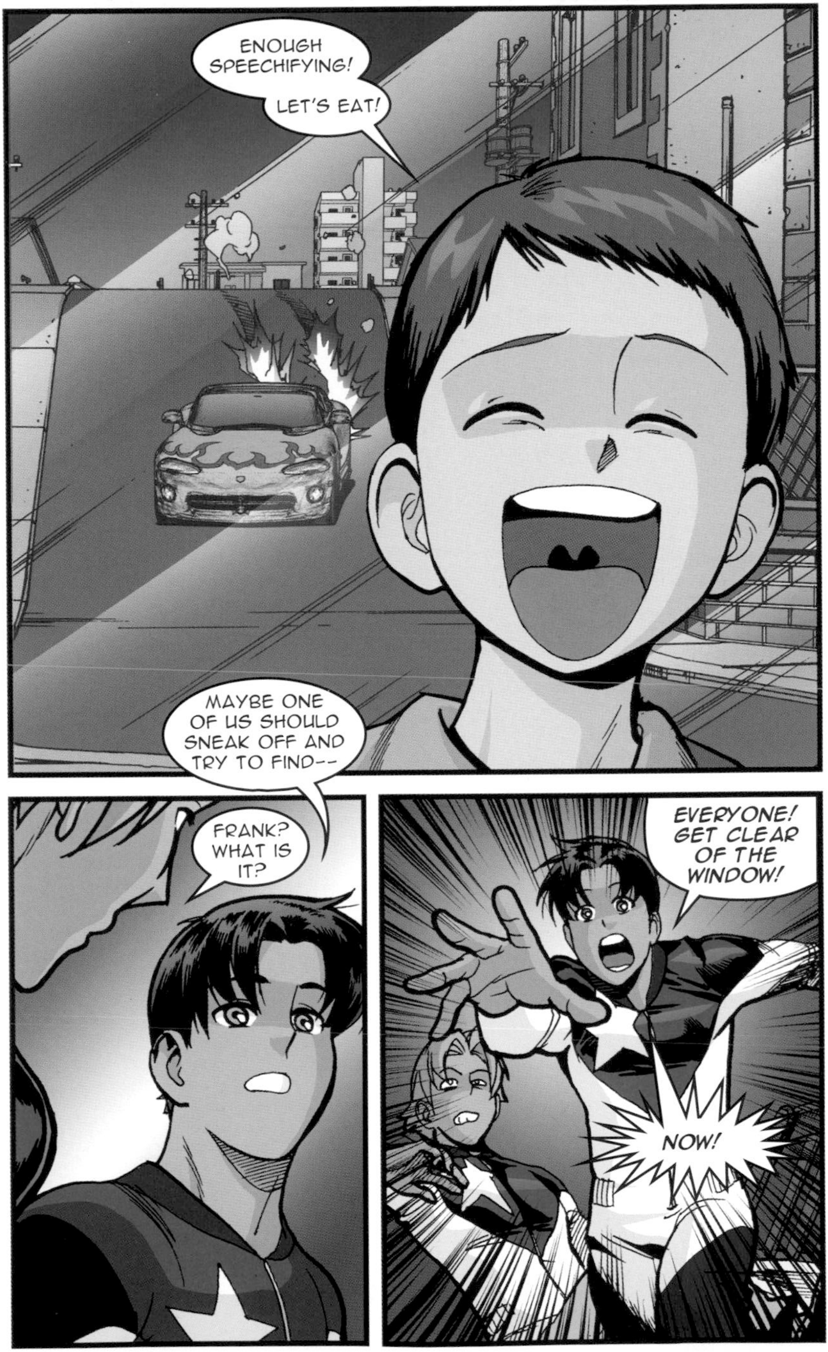
ENOUGH SPEECHIFYING!
LET'S EAT!
MAYBE ONE OF US SHOULD SNEAK OFF AND TRY TO FIND--
FRANK? WHAT IS IT?
EVERYONE! GET CLEAR OF THE WINDOW!
NOW!

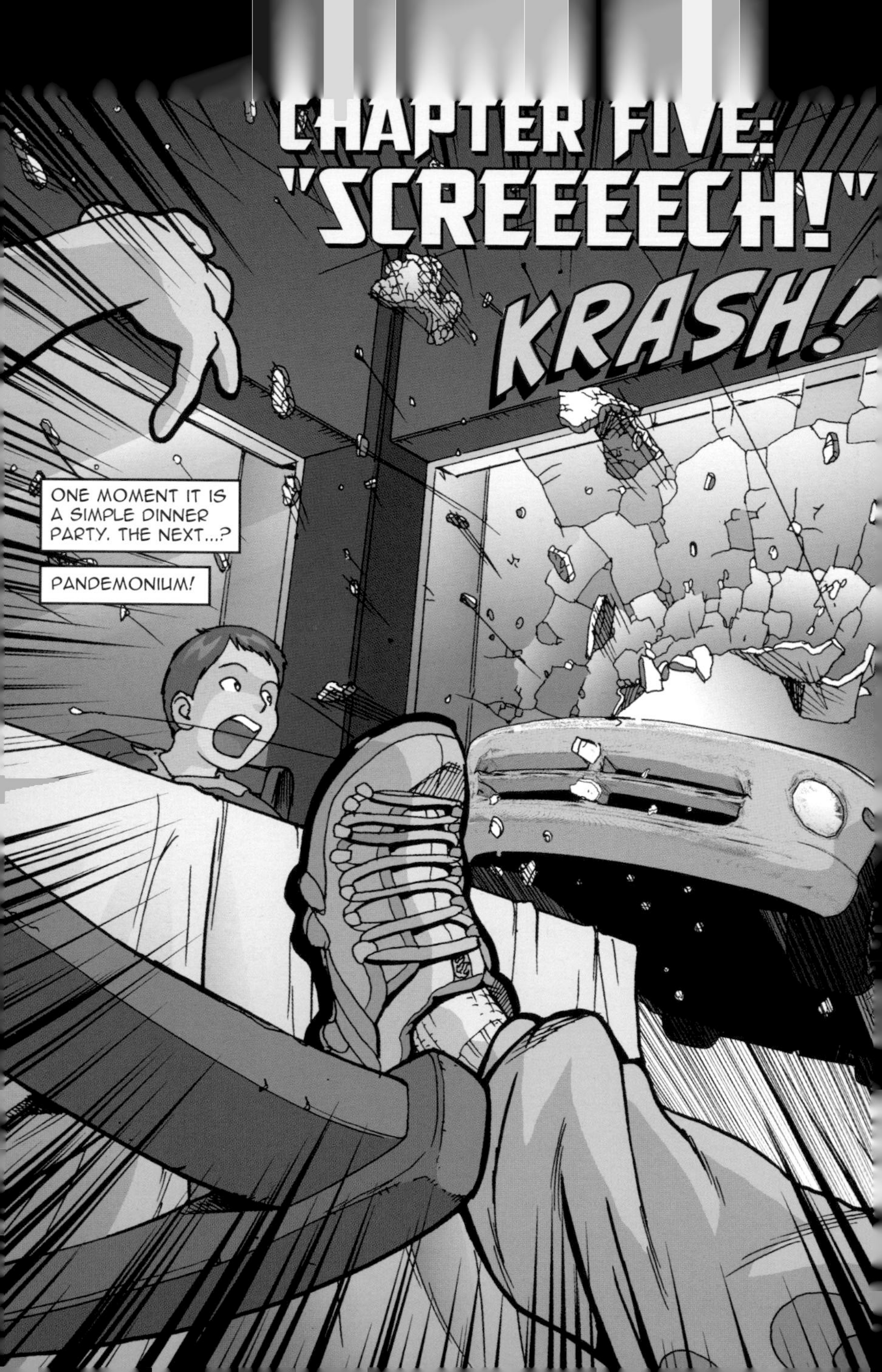

CHAPTER FIVE:
"SCREEEECH!"
KRASH!
ONE MOMENT IT IS A SIMPLE DINNER PARTY. THE NEXT...?
PANDEMONIUM!

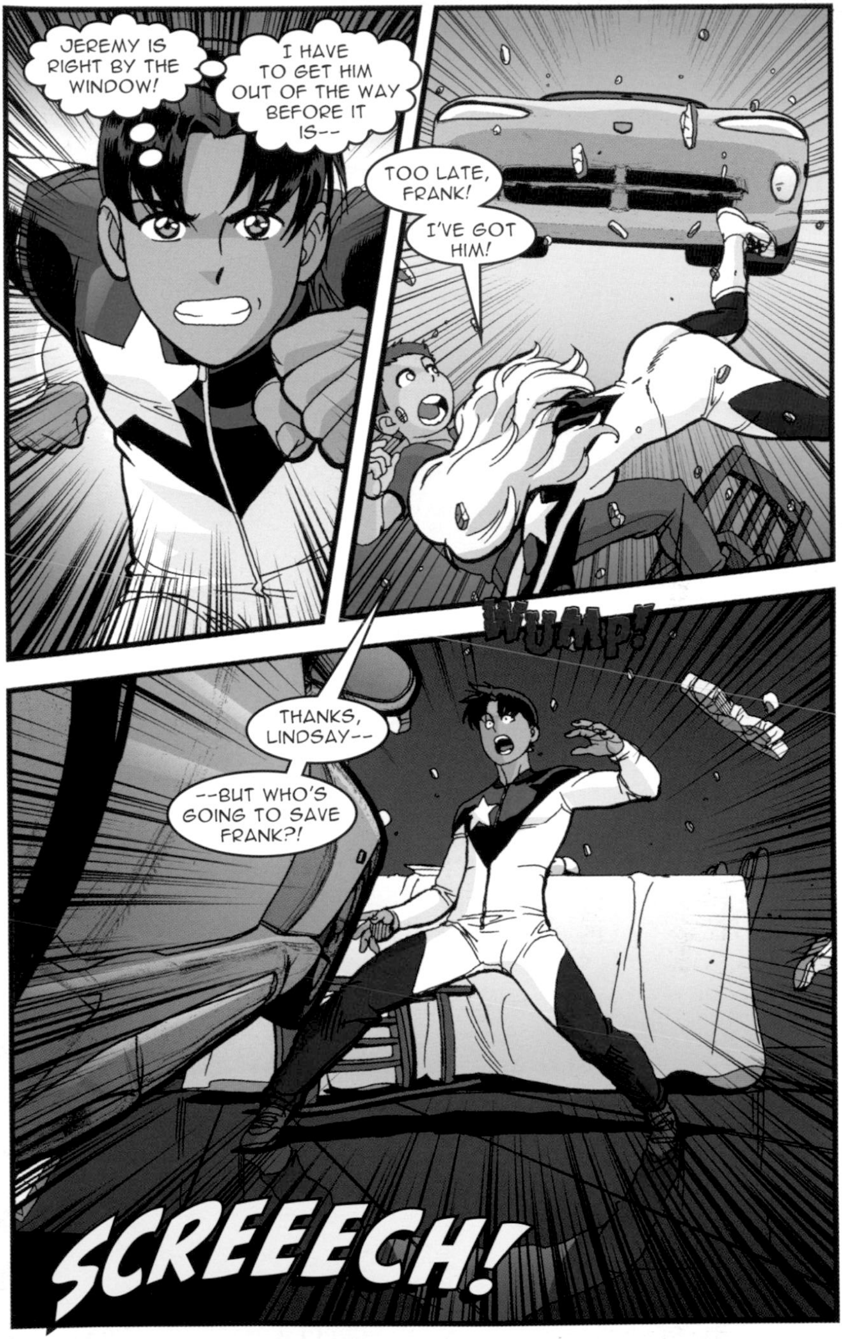
JEREMY IS RIGHT BY THE WINDOW!
I HAVE TO GET HIM OUT OF THE WAY BEFORE IT IS--
TOO LATE, FRANK!
I'VE GOT HIM!
WUMP!
THANKS, LINDSAY--
--BUT WHO'S GOING TO SAVE FRANK?!
SCREEECH!

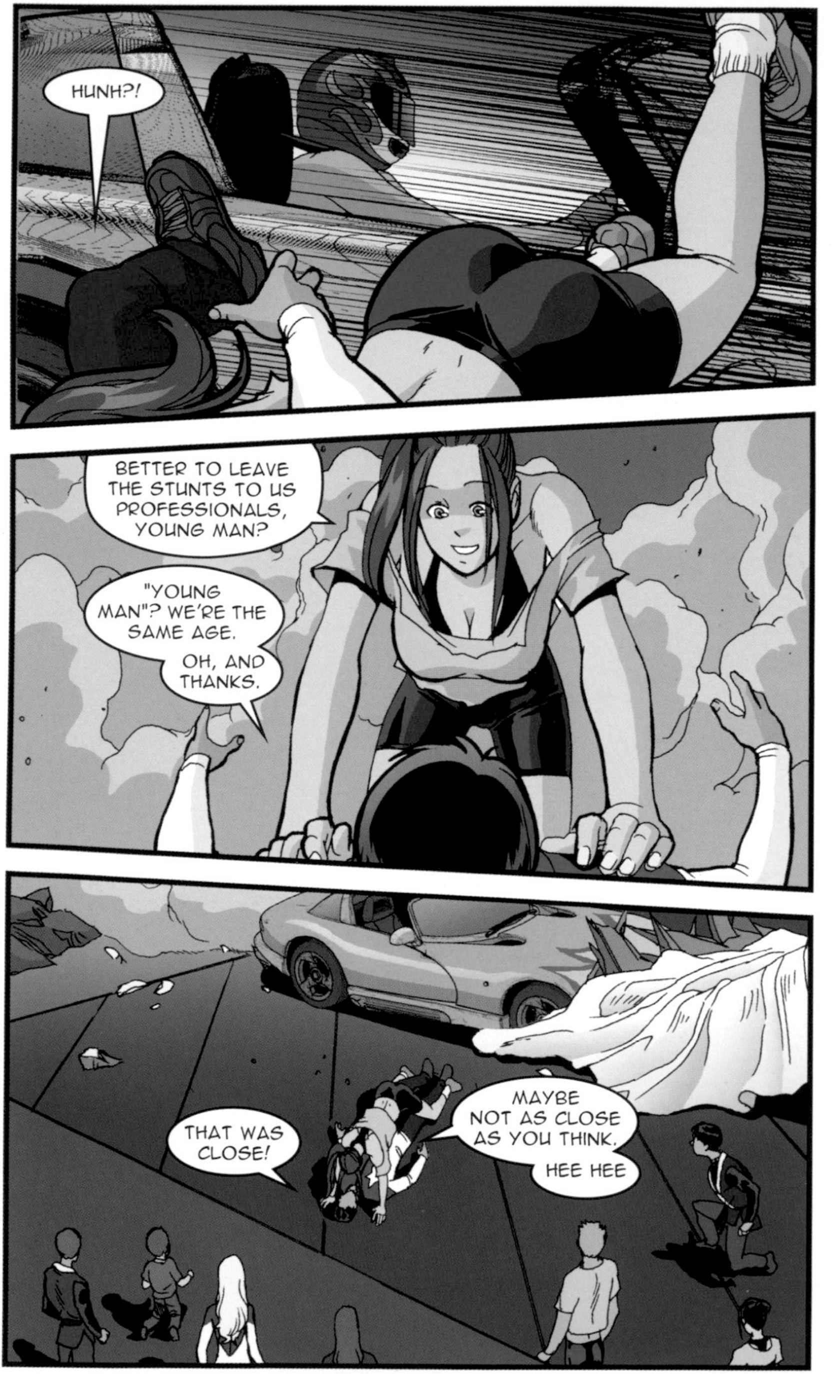
HUNH?!
BETTER TO LEAVE THE STUNTS TO US PROFESSIONALS, YOUNG MAN?
"YOUNG MAN"? WE'RE THE SAME AGE.
OH, AND THANKS.
THAT WAS CLOSE!
MAYBE NOT AS CLOSE AS YOU THINK.
HEE HEE

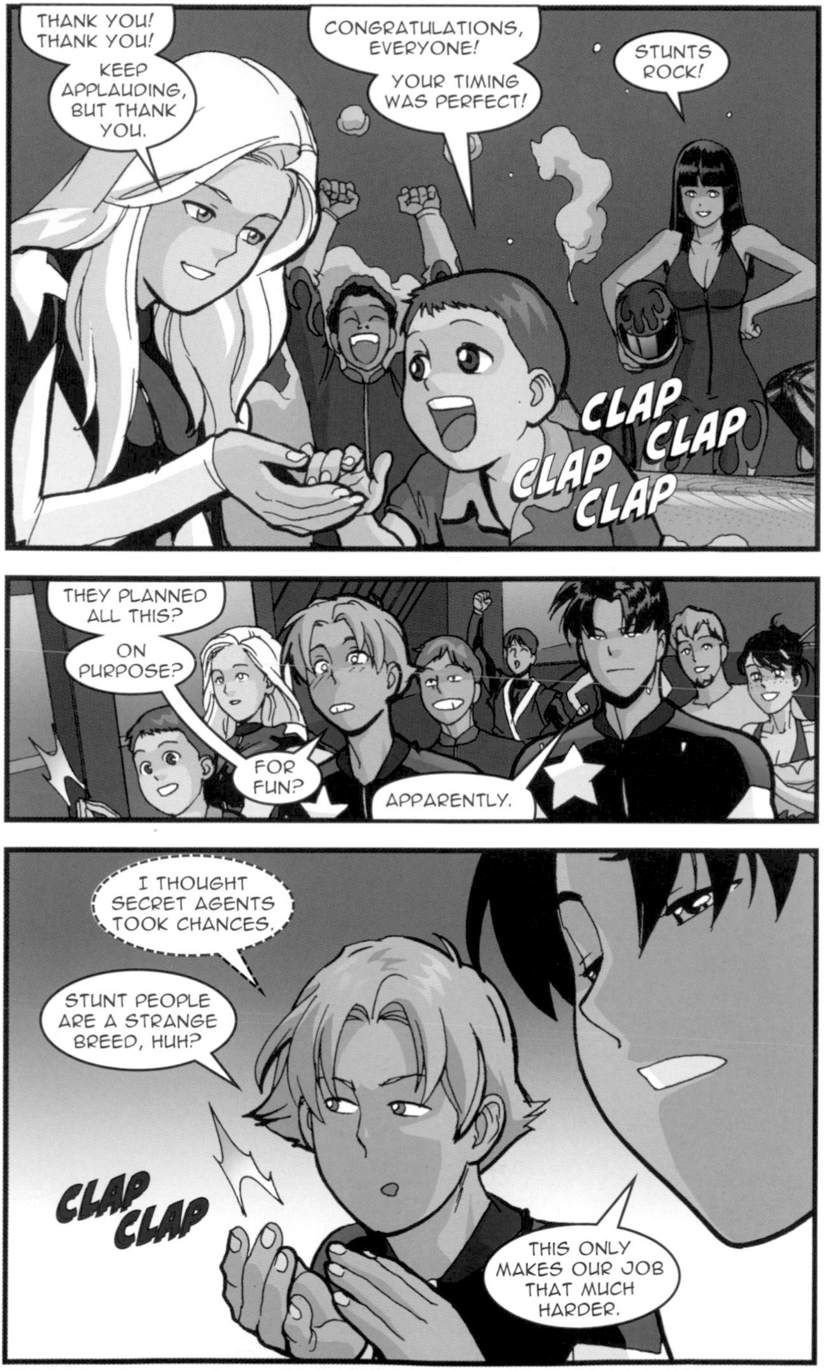
THANK YOU! THANK YOU!
KEEP APPLAUDING, BUT THANK YOU.
CONGRATULATIONS, EVERYONE!
YOUR TIMING WAS PERFECT!
STUNTS ROCK!
CLAP CLAP CLAP CLAP
THEY PLANNED ALL THIS?
ON PURPOSE?
FOR FUN?
APPARENTLY.
I THOUGHT SECRET AGENTS TOOK CHANCES.
STUNT PEOPLE ARE A STRANGE BREED, HUH?
CLAP CLAP
THIS ONLY MAKES OUR JOB THAT MUCH HARDER.

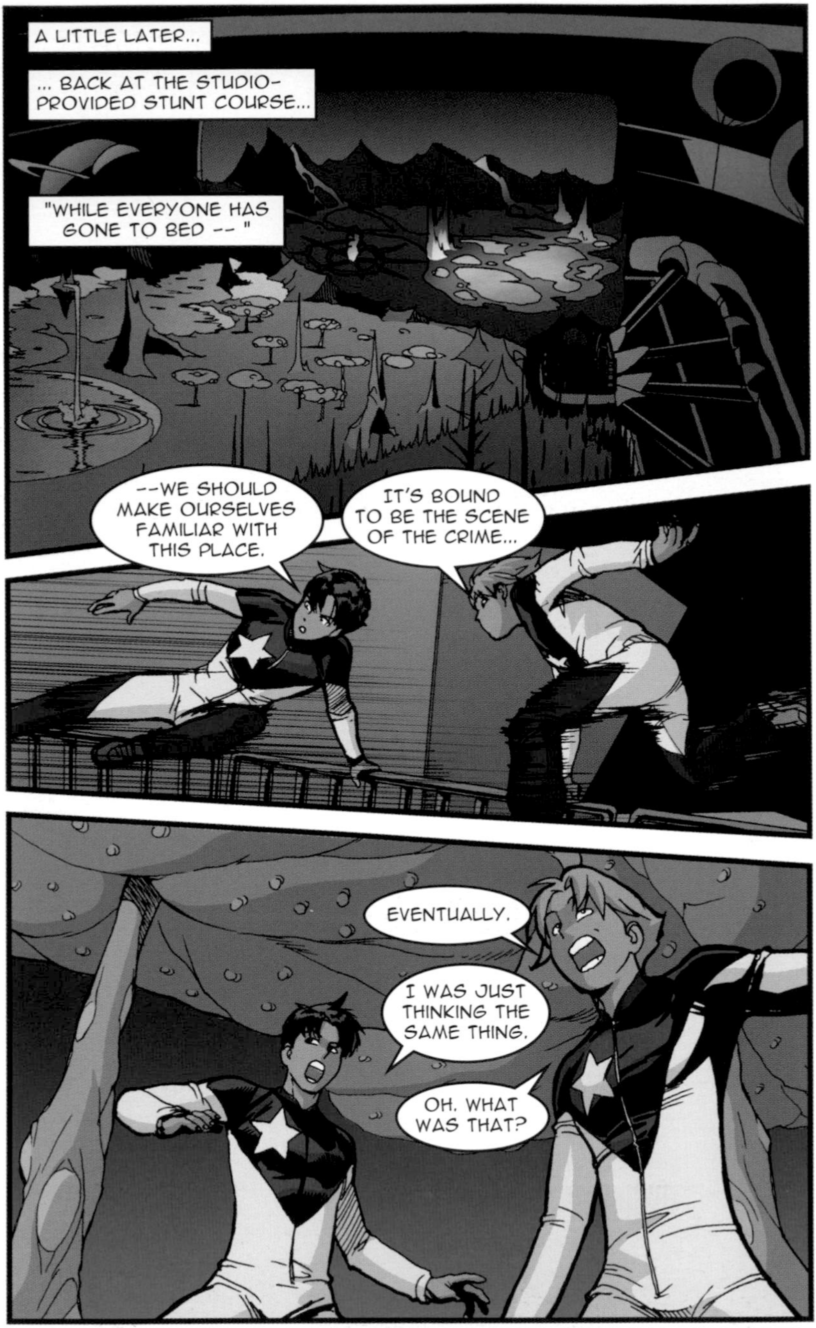
A LITTLE LATER...
... BACK AT THE STUDIO-PROVIDED STUNT COURSE...
"WHILE EVERYONE HAS GONE TO BED -- "
--WE SHOULD MAKE OURSELVES FAMILIAR WITH THIS PLACE.
IT'S BOUND TO BE THE SCENE OF THE CRIME...
EVENTUALLY.
I WAS JUST THINKING THE SAME THING.
OH. WHAT WAS THAT?

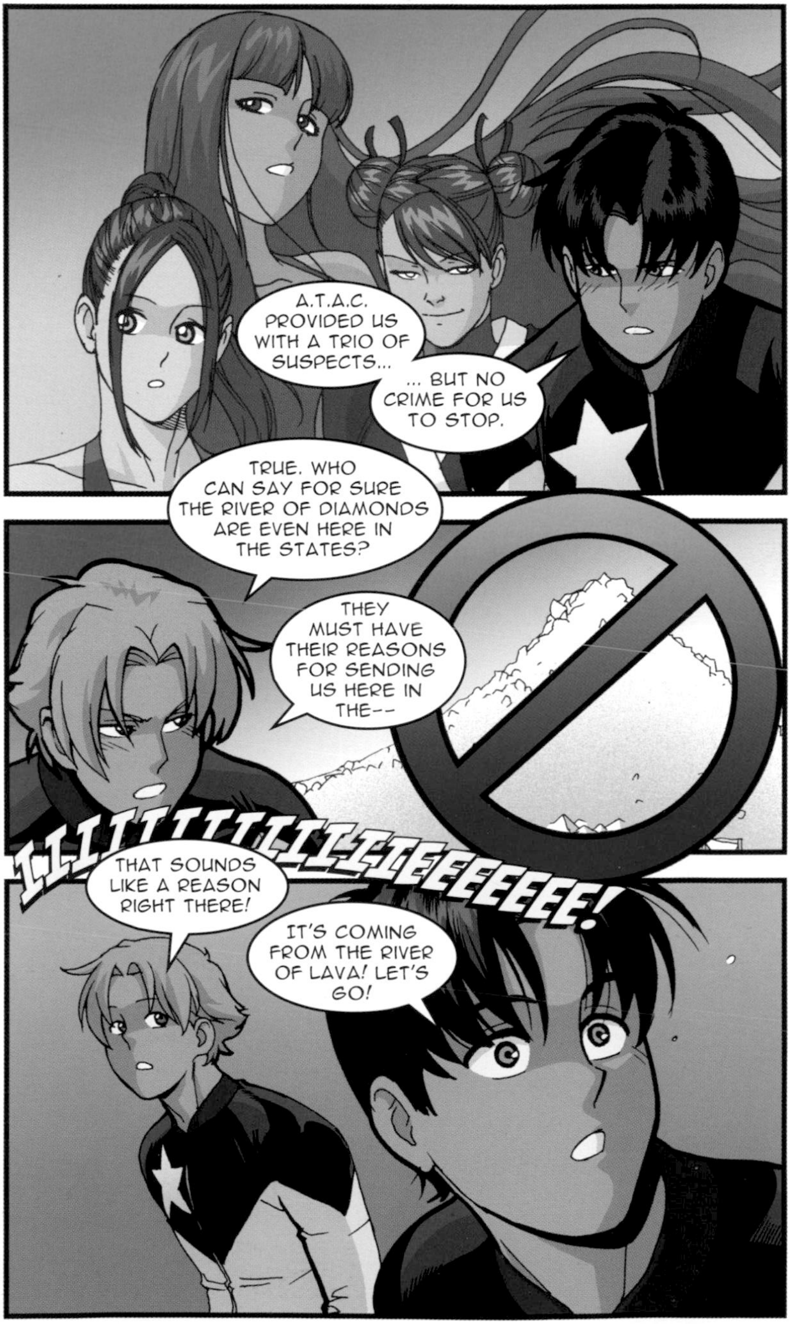
A.T.A.C. PROVIDED US WITH A TRIO OF SUSPECTS...
... BUT NO CRIME FOR US TO STOP.
TRUE. WHO CAN SAY FOR SURE THE RIVER OF DIAMONDS ARE EVEN HERE IN THE STATES?
THEY MUST HAVE THEIR REASONS FOR SENDING US HERE IN THE--
IIIIIIIIIIIIIEEEEEEEE!
THAT SOUNDS LIKE A REASON RIGHT THERE!
IT'S COMING FROM THE RIVER OF LAVA! LET'S GO!

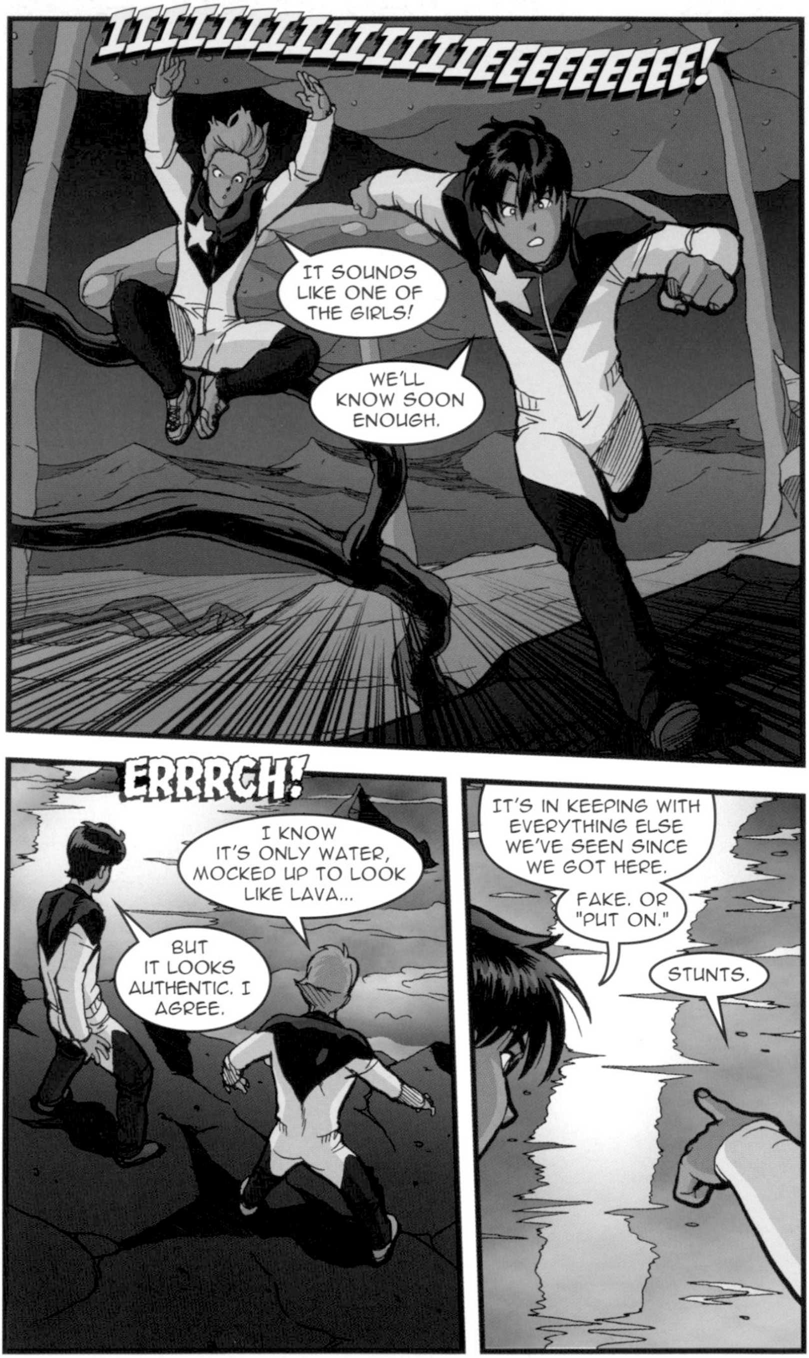
IIIIIIIIIIIIIIIIEEEEEEEEEE!
IT SOUNDS LIKE ONE OF THE GIRLS!
WE'LL KNOW SOON ENOUGH.
ERRRCH!
I KNOW IT'S ONLY WATER, MOCKED UP TO LOOK LIKE LAVA...
BUT IT LOOKS AUTHENTIC. I AGREE.
IT'S IN KEEPING WITH EVERYTHING ELSE WE'VE SEEN SINCE WE GOT HERE.
FAKE. OR "PUT ON."
STUNTS.

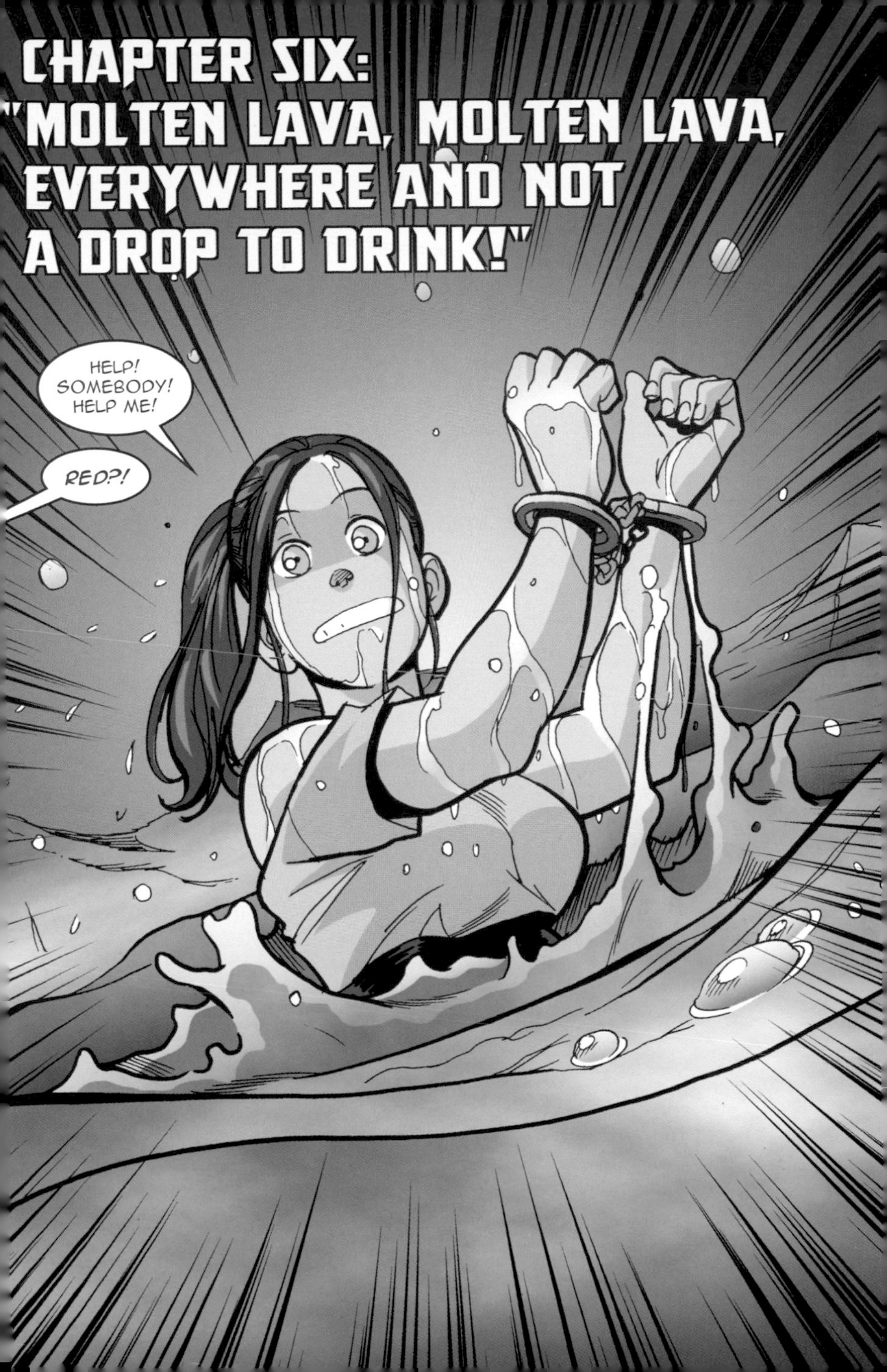
CHAPTER SIX:
"MOLTEN LAVA, MOLTEN LAVA, EVERYWHERE AND NOT A DROP TO DRINK!"
HELP! SOMEBODY! HELP ME!
RED?!

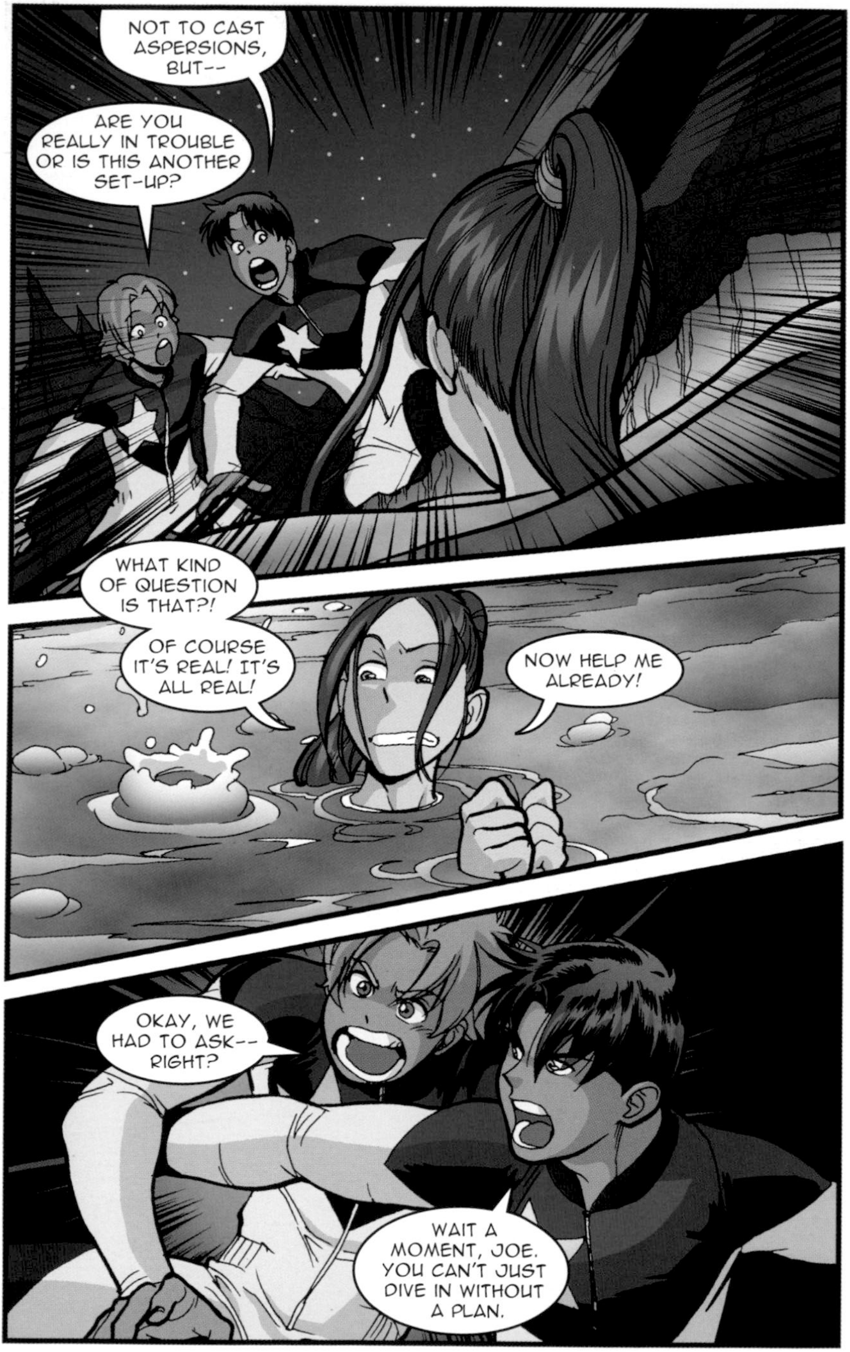
NOT TO CAST ASPERSIONS, BUT--
ARE YOU REALLY IN TROUBLE OR IS THIS ANOTHER SET-UP?
WHAT KIND OF QUESTION IS THAT?!
OF COURSE IT'S REAL! IT'S ALL REAL!
NOW HELP ME ALREADY!
OKAY, WE HAD TO ASK-- RIGHT?
WAIT A MOMENT, JOE. YOU CAN'T JUST DIVE IN WITHOUT A PLAN.

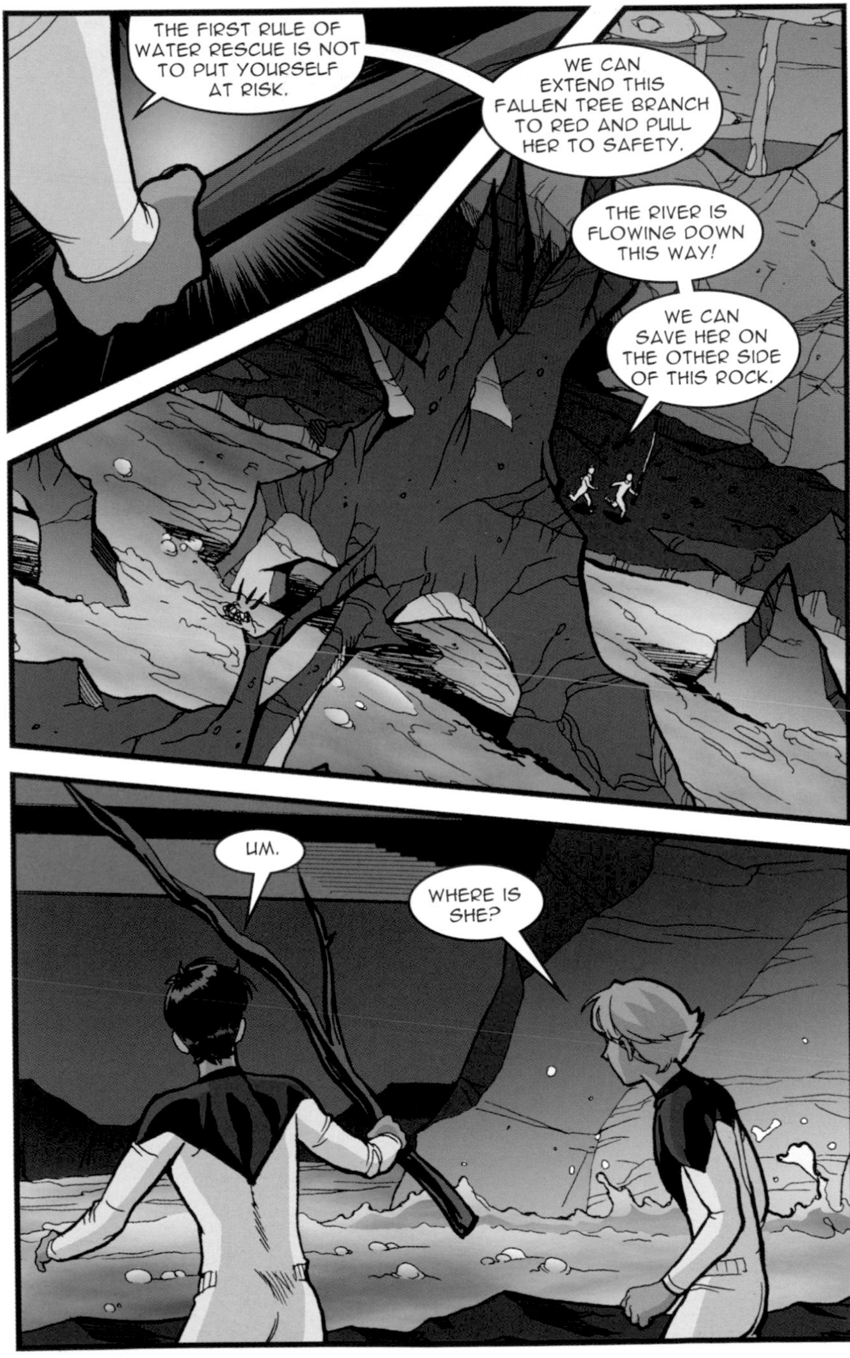
THE FIRST RULE OF WATER RESCUE IS NOT TO PUT YOURSELF AT RISK.
WE CAN EXTEND THIS FALLEN TREE BRANCH TO RED AND PULL HER TO SAFETY.
THE RIVER IS FLOWING DOWN THIS WAY!
WE CAN SAVE HER ON THE OTHER SIDE OF THIS ROCK.
UM.
WHERE IS SHE?

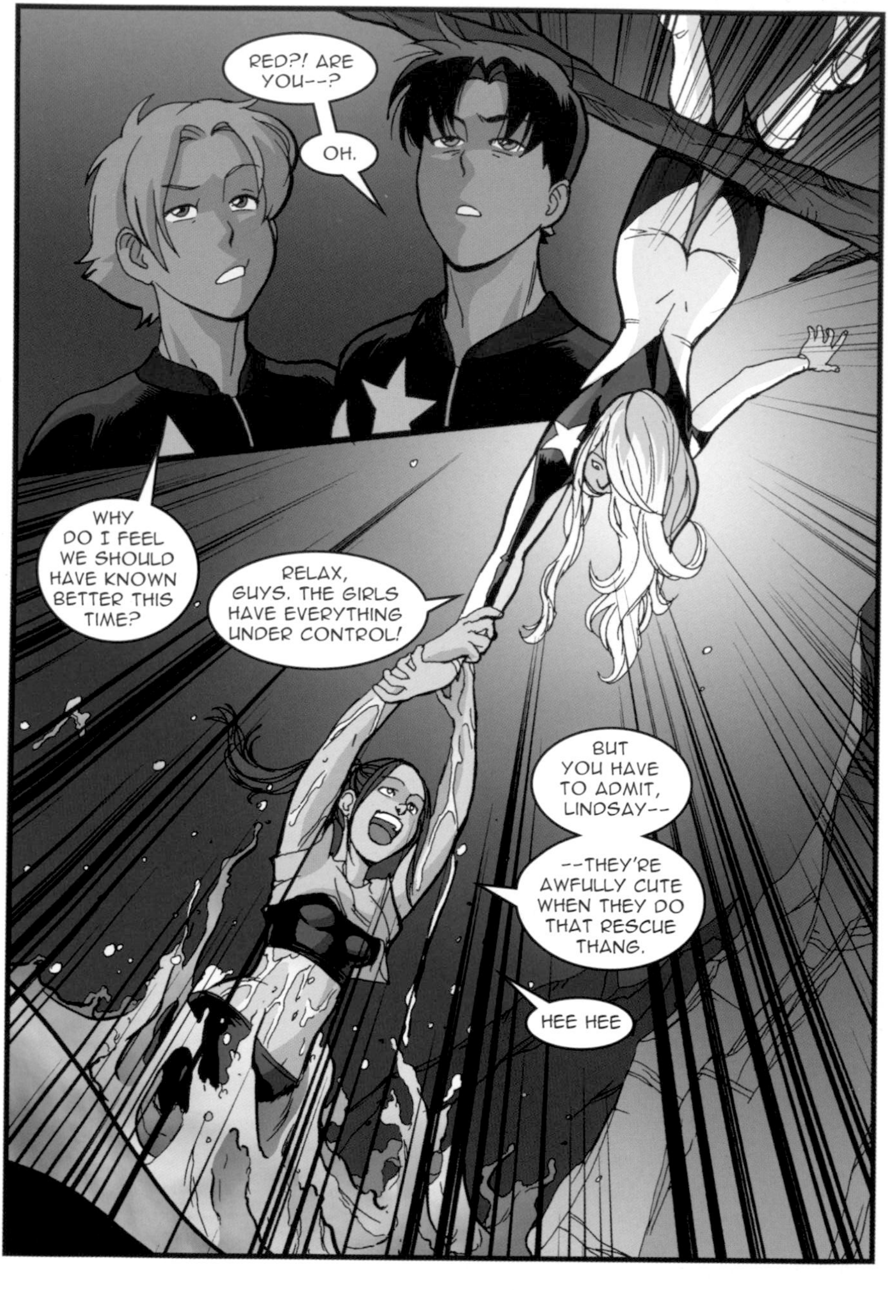
RED?! ARE YOU--?
OH.
WHY DO I FEEL WE SHOULD HAVE KNOWN BETTER THIS TIME?
RELAX, GUYS. THE GIRLS HAVE EVERYTHING UNDER CONTROL!
BUT YOU HAVE TO ADMIT, LINDSAY--
--THEY'RE AWFULLY CUTE WHEN THEY DO THAT RESCUE THANG.
HEE HEE

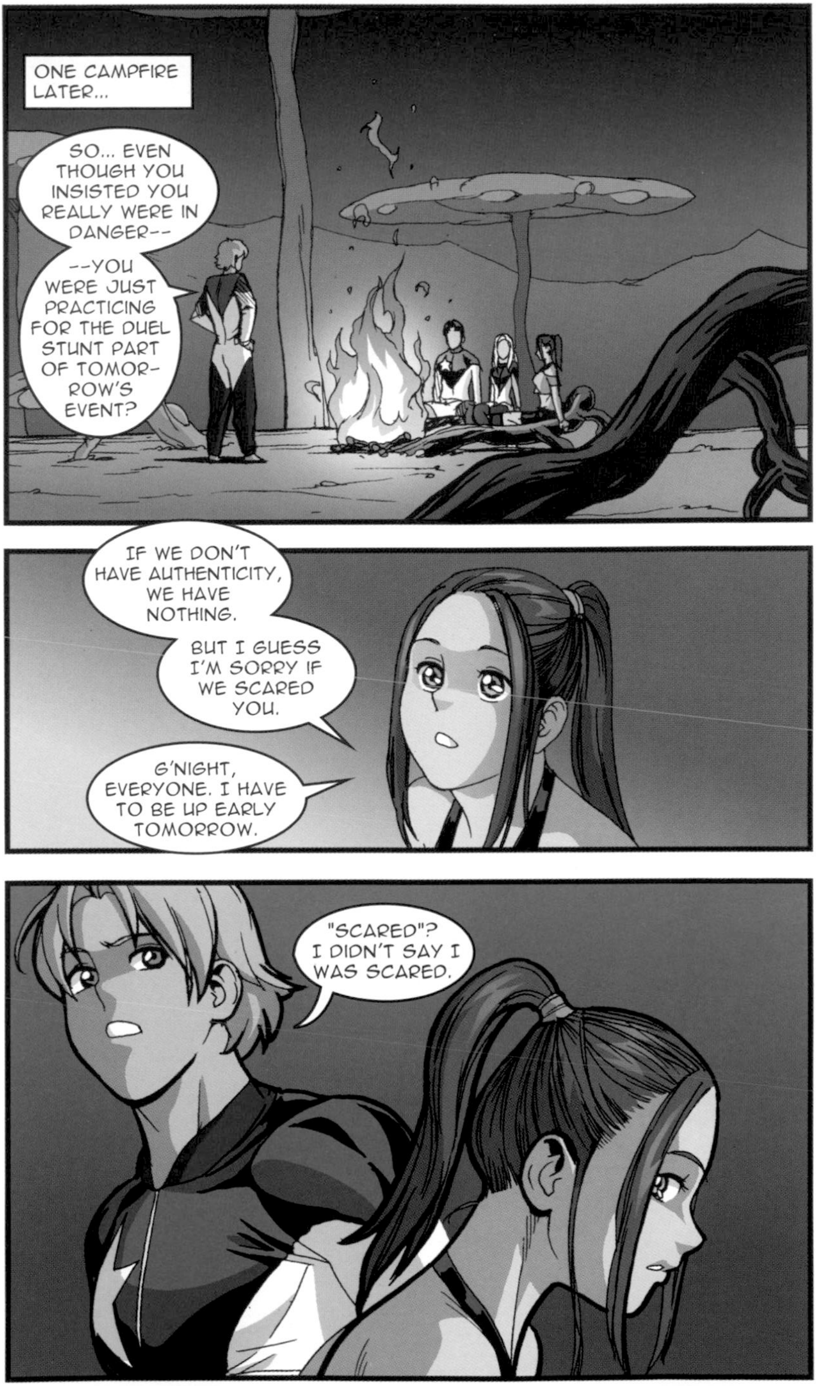
ONE CAMPFIRE LATER...
SO... EVEN THOUGH YOU INSISTED YOU REALLY WERE IN DANGER--
--YOU WERE JUST PRACTICING FOR THE DUEL STUNT PART OF TOMOR-ROW'S EVENT?
IF WE DON'T HAVE AUTHENTICITY, WE HAVE NOTHING.
BUT I GUESS I'M SORRY IF WE SCARED YOU.
G'NIGHT, EVERYONE. I HAVE TO BE UP EARLY TOMORROW.
"SCARED"? I DIDN'T SAY I WAS SCARED.

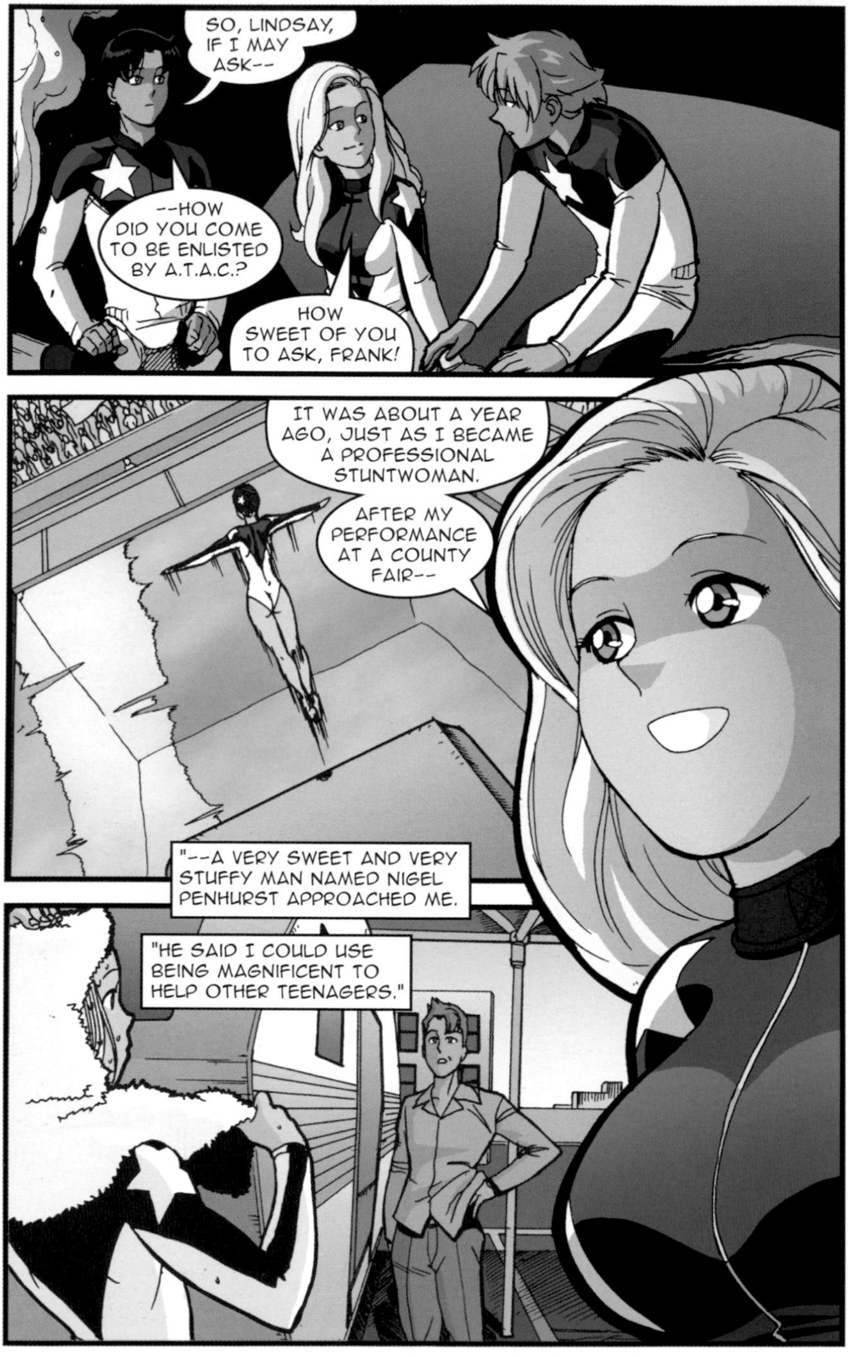
SO, LINDSAY, IF I MAY ASK--
--HOW DID YOU COME TO BE ENLISTED BY A.T.A.C.?
HOW SWEET OF YOU TO ASK, FRANK!
IT WAS ABOUT A YEAR AGO, JUST AS I BECAME A PROFESSIONAL STUNTWOMAN.
AFTER MY PERFORMANCE AT A COUNTY FAIR--
"--A VERY SWEET AND VERY STUFFY MAN NAMED NIGEL PENHURST APPROACHED ME.
"HE SAID I COULD USE BEING MAGNIFICENT TO HELP OTHER TEENAGERS."

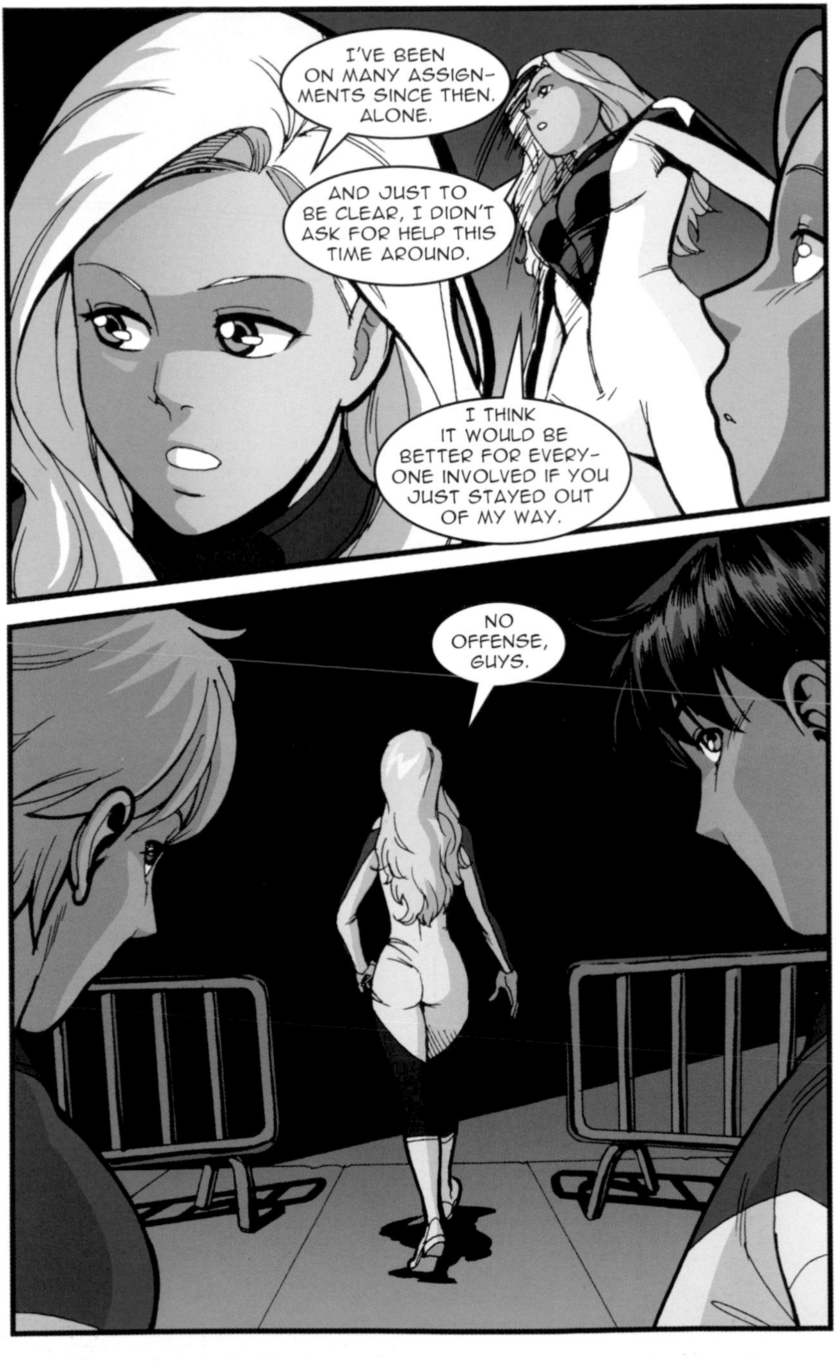
I'VE BEEN ON MANY ASSIGNMENTS SINCE THEN. ALONE.
AND JUST TO BE CLEAR, I DIDN'T ASK FOR HELP THIS TIME AROUND.
I THINK IT WOULD BE BETTER FOR EVERYONE INVOLVED IF YOU JUST STAYED OUT OF MY WAY.
NO OFFENSE, GUYS.

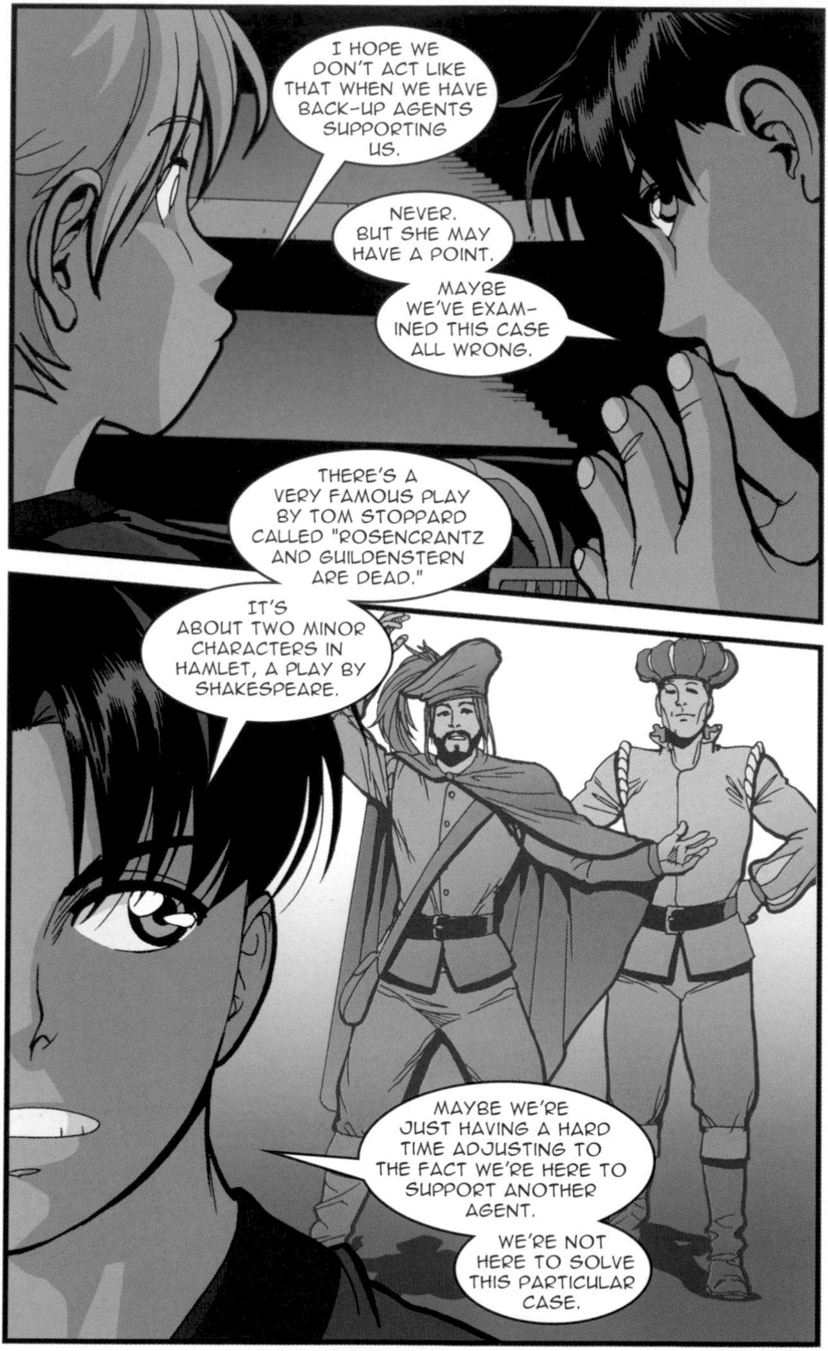
I HOPE WE DON'T ACT LIKE THAT WHEN WE HAVE BACK-UP AGENTS SUPPORTING US.
NEVER. BUT SHE MAY HAVE A POINT.
MAYBE WE'VE EXAMINED THIS CASE ALL WRONG.
THERE'S A VERY FAMOUS PLAY BY TOM STOPPARD CALLED "ROSENCRANTZ AND GUILDENSTERN ARE DEAD."
IT'S ABOUT TWO MINOR CHARACTERS IN HAMLET, A PLAY BY SHAKESPEARE.
MAYBE WE'RE JUST HAVING A HARD TIME ADJUSTING TO THE FACT WE'RE HERE TO SUPPORT ANOTHER AGENT.
WE'RE NOT HERE TO SOLVE THIS PARTICULAR CASE.

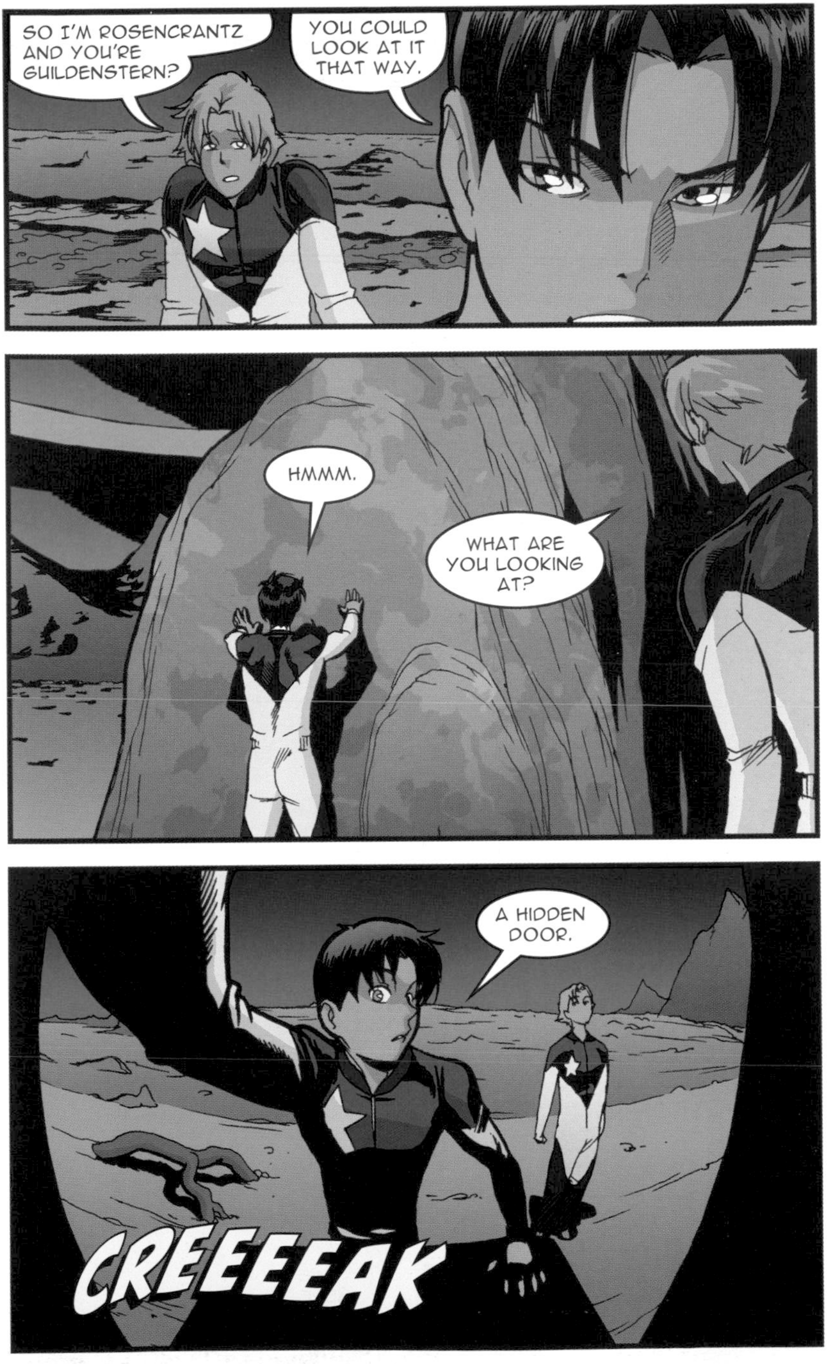
SO I'M ROSENCRANTZ AND YOU'RE GUILDENSTERN?
YOU COULD LOOK AT IT THAT WAY.
HMMM.
WHAT ARE YOU LOOKING AT?
A HIDDEN DOOR.
CREEEEAK

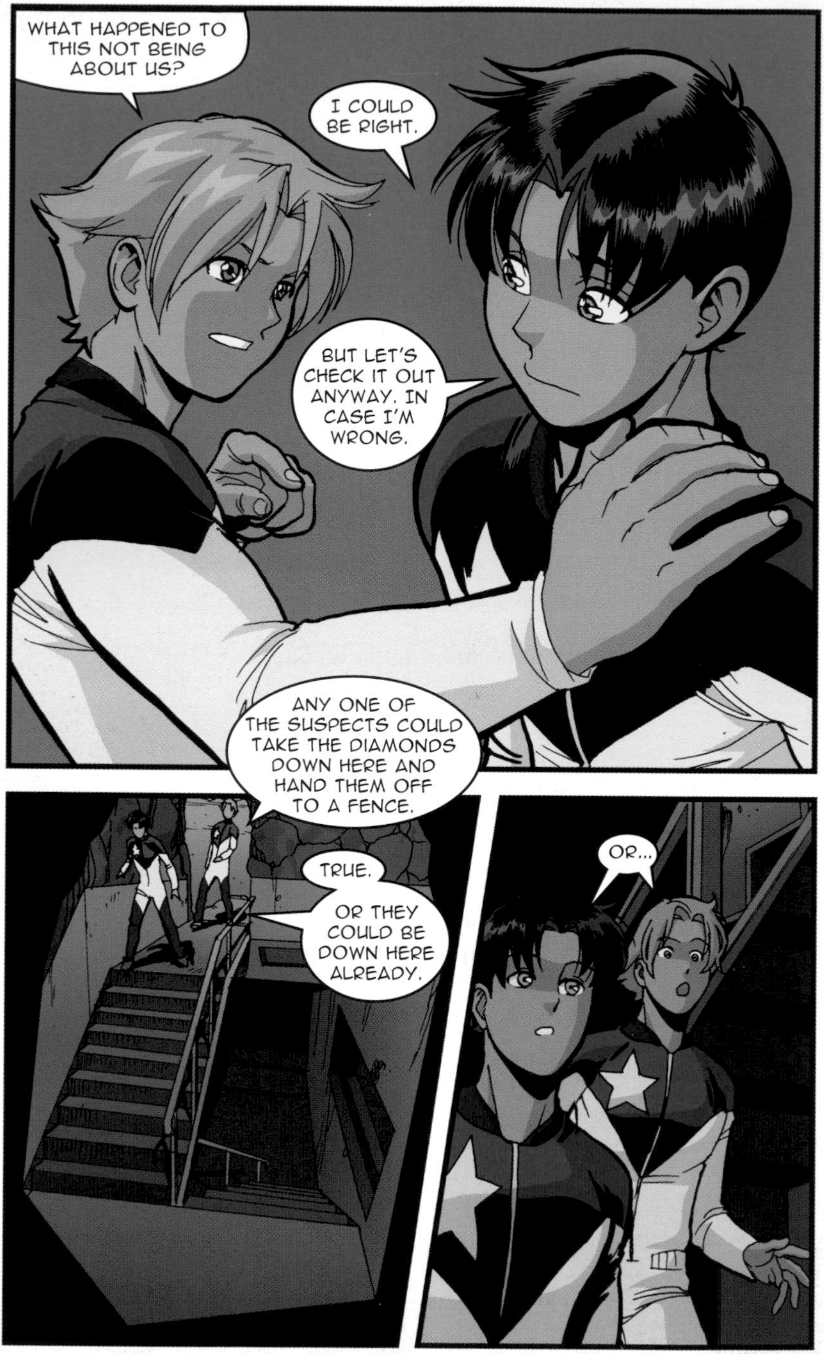
WHAT HAPPENED TO THIS NOT BEING ABOUT US?
I COULD BE RIGHT.
BUT LET'S CHECK IT OUT ANYWAY. IN CASE I'M WRONG.
ANY ONE OF THE SUSPECTS COULD TAKE THE DIAMONDS DOWN HERE AND HAND THEM OFF TO A FENCE.
TRUE.
OR THEY COULD BE DOWN HERE ALREADY.
OR...

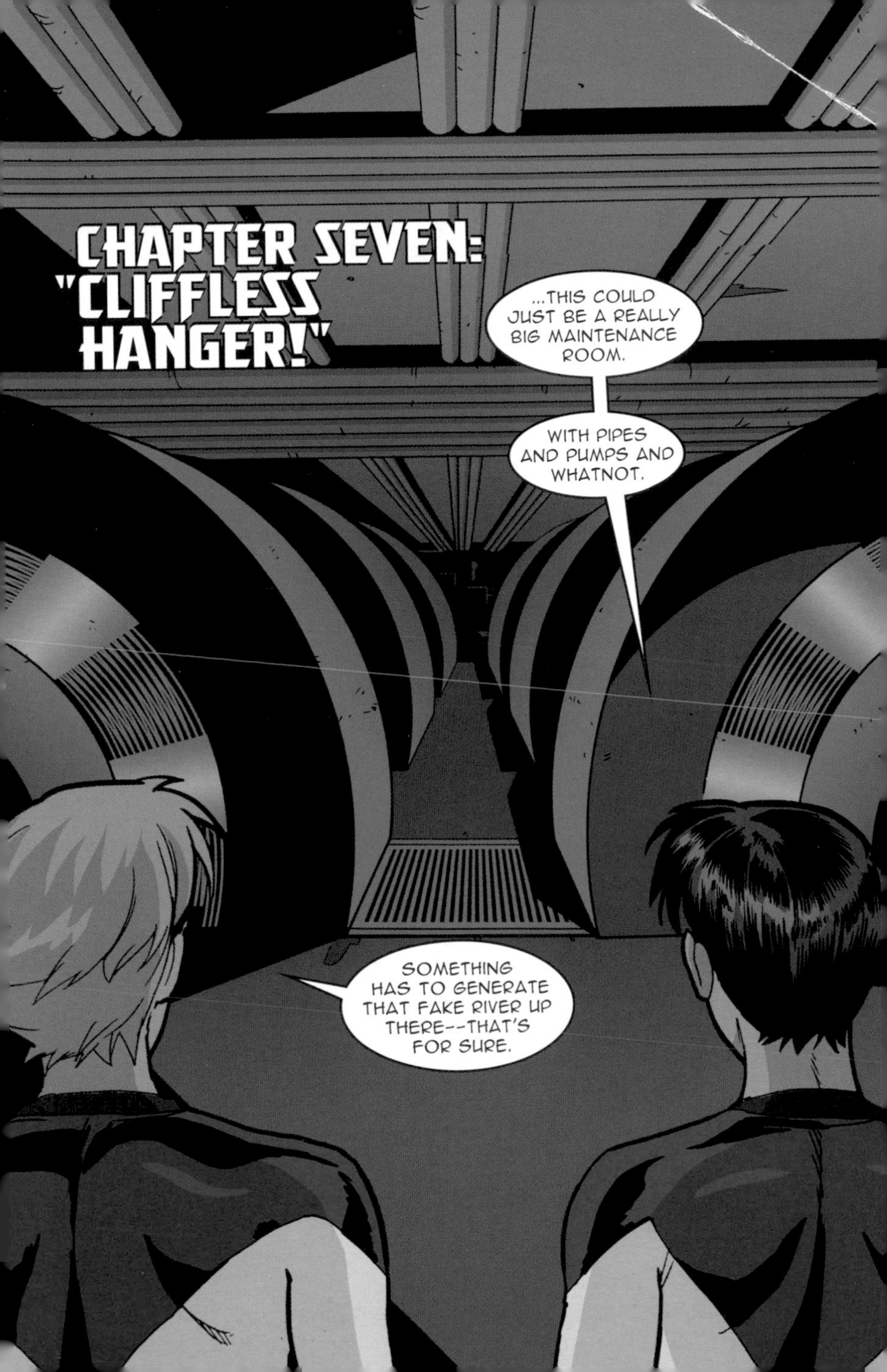
CHAPTER SEVEN: "CLIFFLESS HANGER!"
...THIS COULD JUST BE A REALLY BIG MAINTENANCE ROOM.
WITH PIPES AND PUMPS AND WHATNOT.
SOMETHING HAS TO GENERATE THAT FAKE RIVER UP THERE--THAT'S FOR SURE.

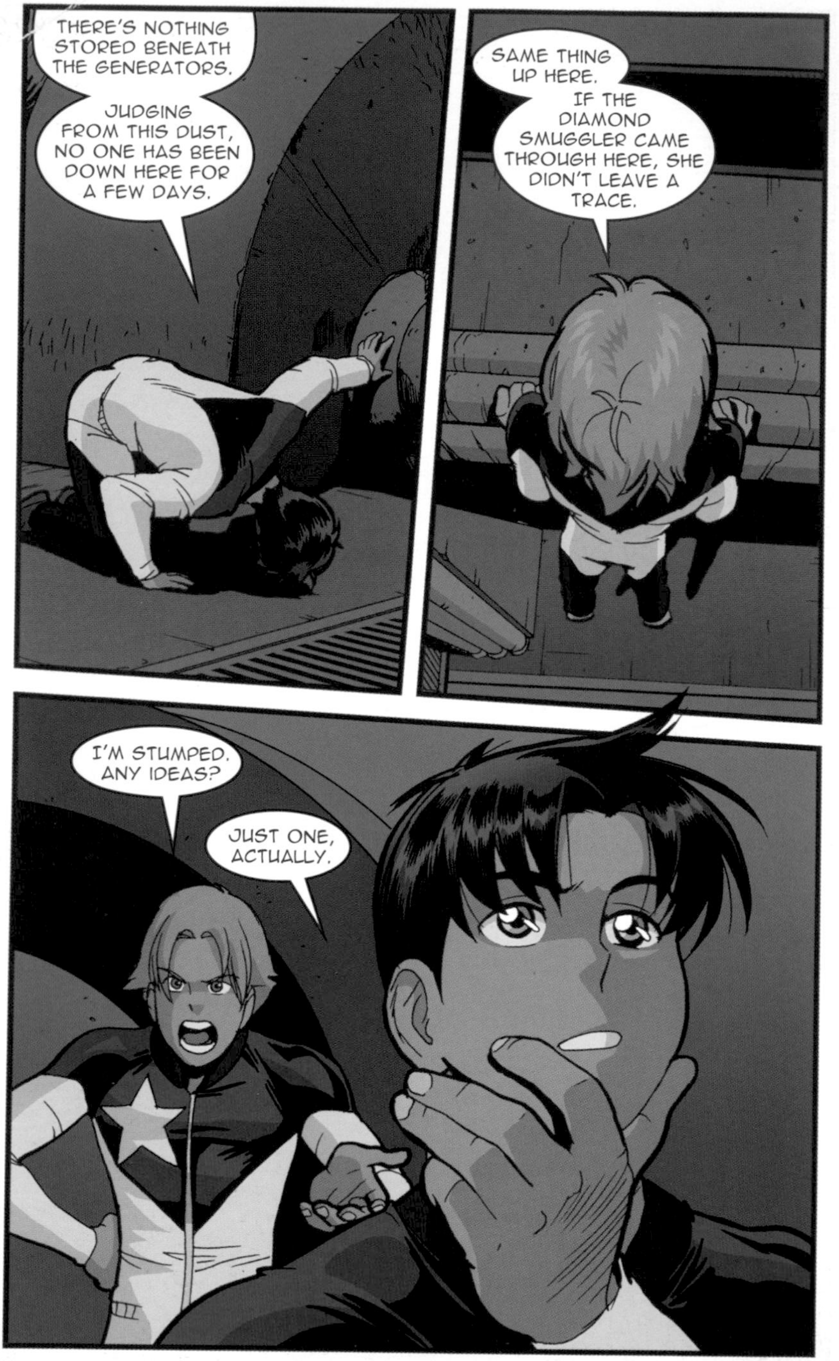
THERE'S NOTHING STORED BENEATH THE GENERATORS.
JUDGING FROM THIS DUST, NO ONE HAS BEEN DOWN HERE FOR A FEW DAYS.
SAME THING UP HERE.
IF THE DIAMOND SMUGGLER CAME THROUGH HERE, SHE DIDN'T LEAVE A TRACE.
I'M STUMPED. ANY IDEAS?
JUST ONE, ACTUALLY.

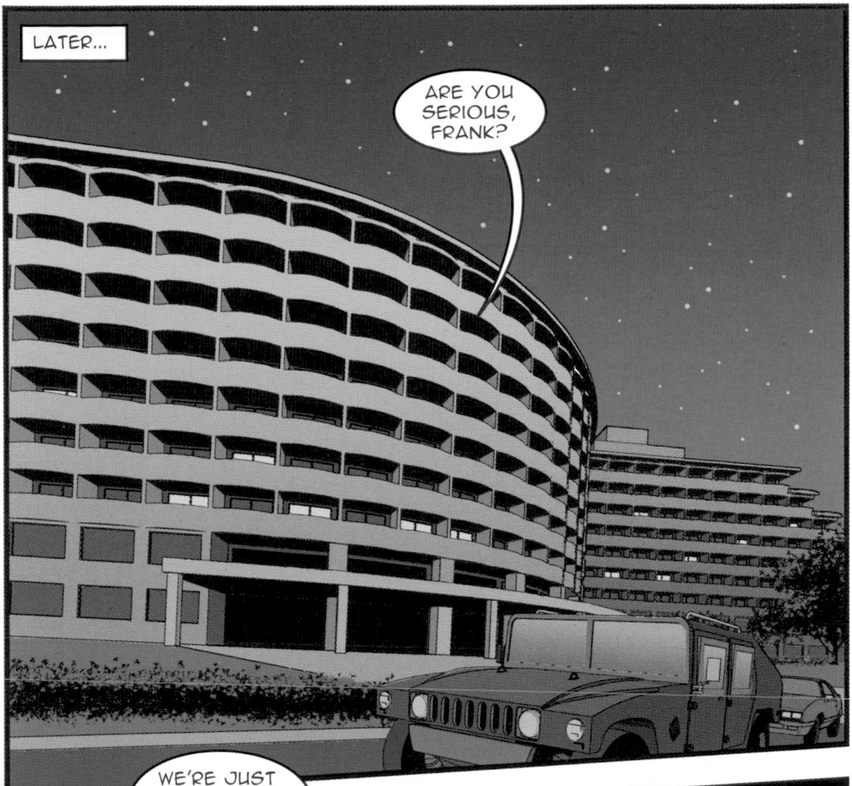
LATER...
ARE YOU SERIOUS, FRANK?

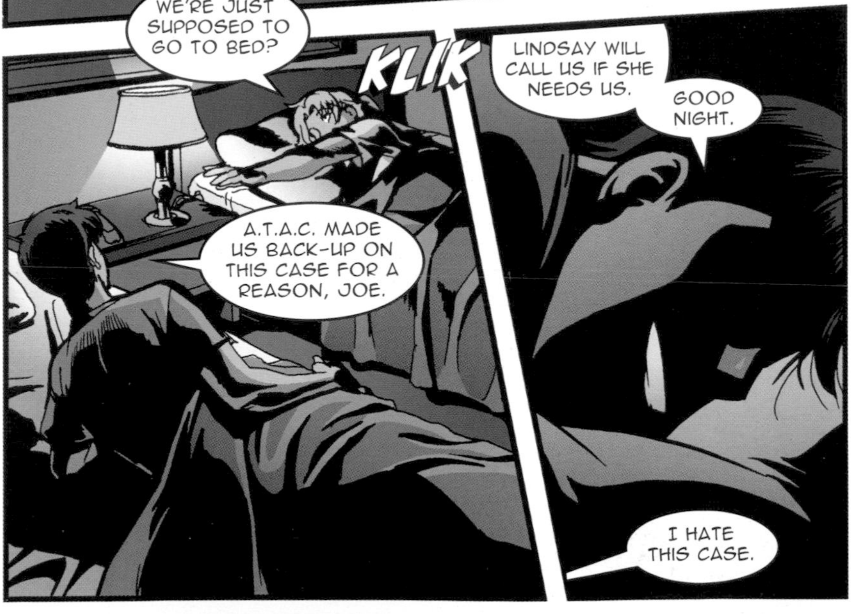
WE'RE JUST SUPPOSED TO GO TO BED?
KLIK
LINDSAY WILL CALL US IF SHE NEEDS US.
GOOD NIGHT.
A.T.A.C. MADE US BACK-UP ON THIS CASE FOR A REASON, JOE.
I HATE THIS CASE.

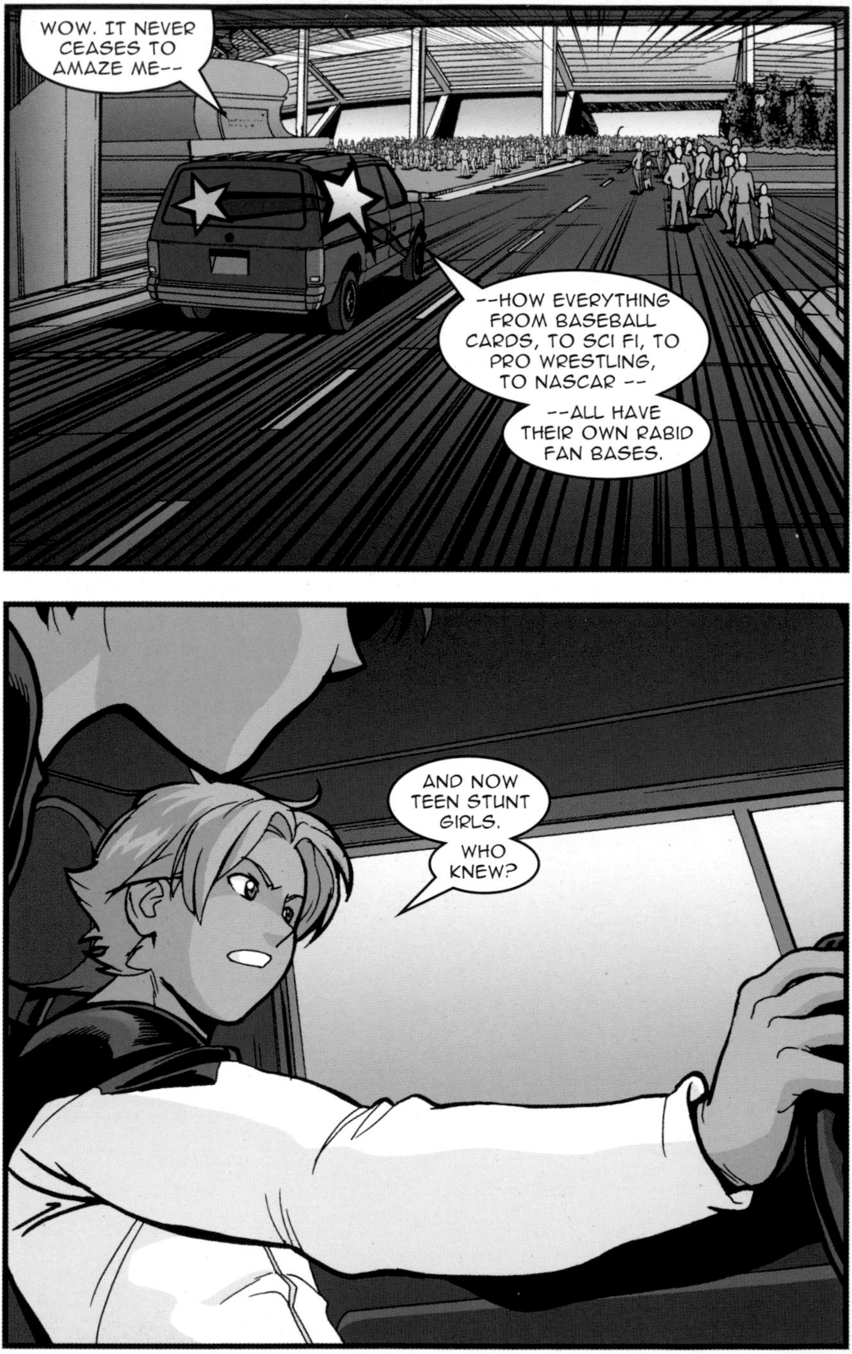
WOW. IT NEVER CEASES TO AMAZE ME--
--HOW EVERYTHING FROM BASEBALL CARDS, TO SCI FI, TO PRO WRESTLING, TO NASCAR --
--ALL HAVE THEIR OWN RABID FAN BASES.
AND NOW TEEN STUNT GIRLS.
WHO KNEW?

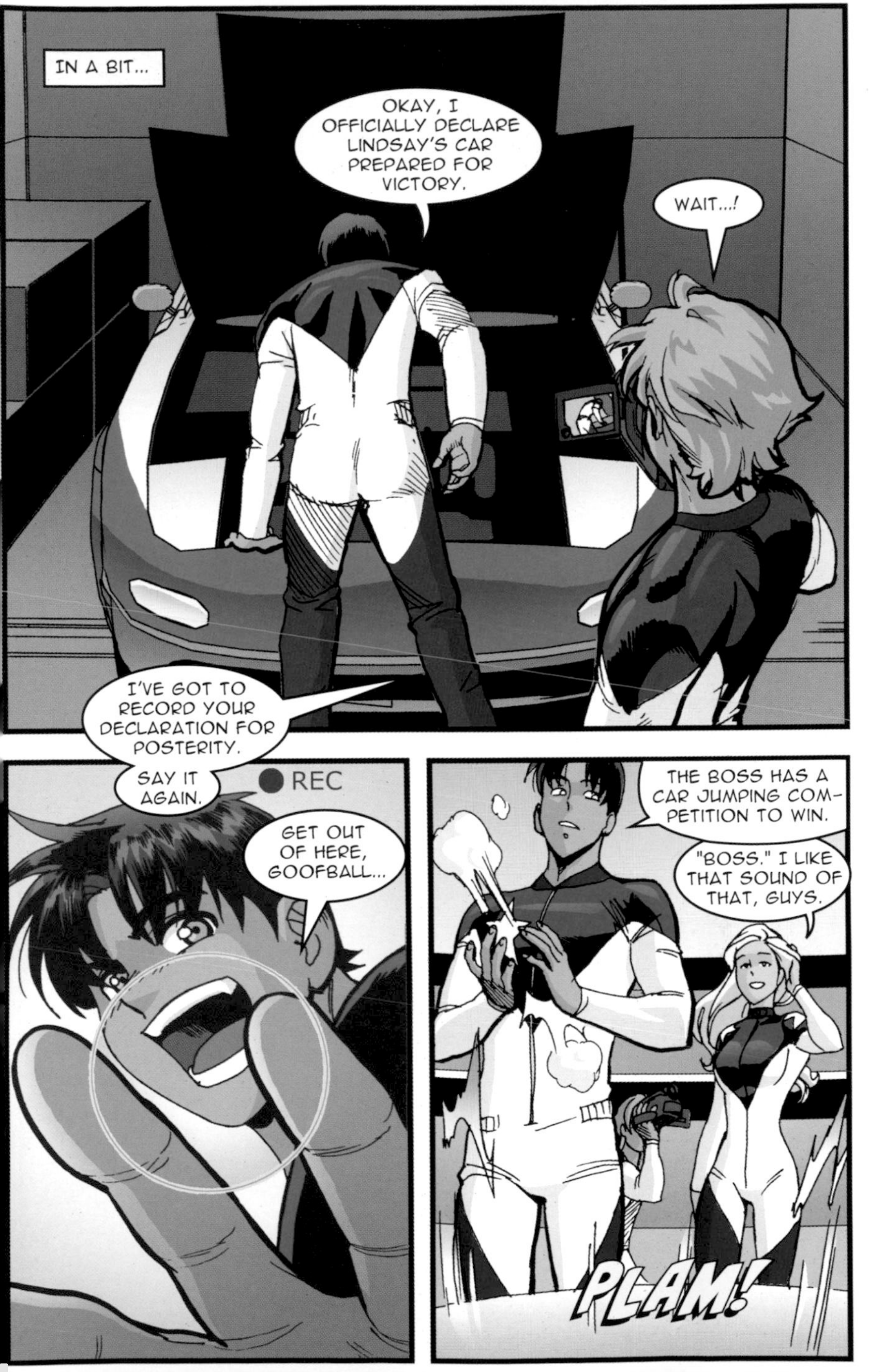
IN A BIT...
OKAY, I OFFICIALLY DECLARE LINDSAY'S CAR PREPARED FOR VICTORY.
WAIT...!
I'VE GOT TO RECORD YOUR DECLARATION FOR POSTERITY.
SAY IT AGAIN.
REC
GET OUT OF HERE, GOOFBALL...
THE BOSS HAS A CAR JUMPING COMPETITION TO WIN.
"BOSS." I LIKE THAT SOUND OF THAT, GUYS.
PLAM!

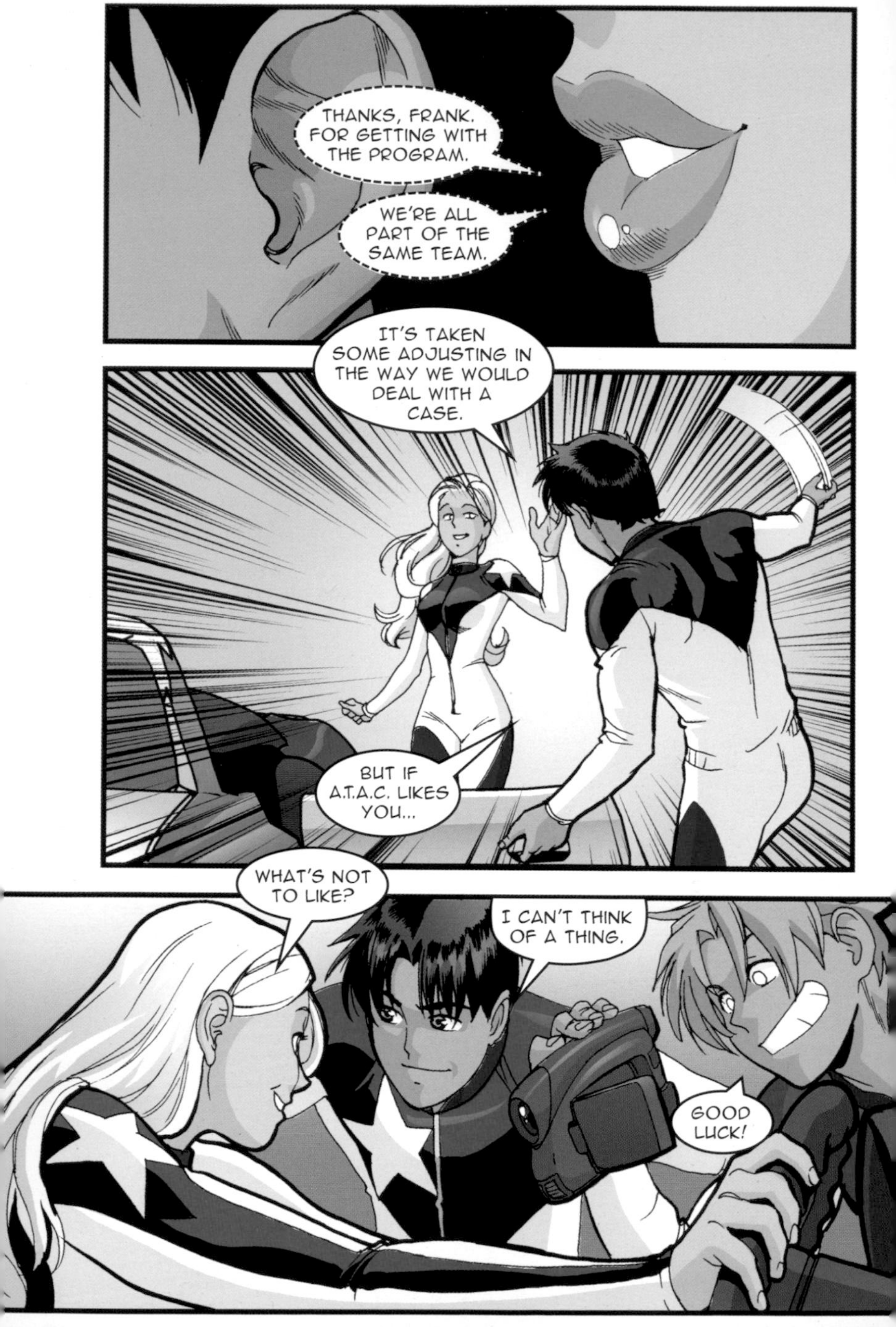
THANKS, FRANK. FOR GETTING WITH THE PROGRAM.
WE'RE ALL PART OF THE SAME TEAM.
IT'S TAKEN SOME ADJUSTING IN THE WAY WE WOULD DEAL WITH A CASE.
BUT IF A.T.A.C. LIKES YOU...
WHAT'S NOT TO LIKE?
I CAN'T THINK OF A THING.
GOOD LUCK!

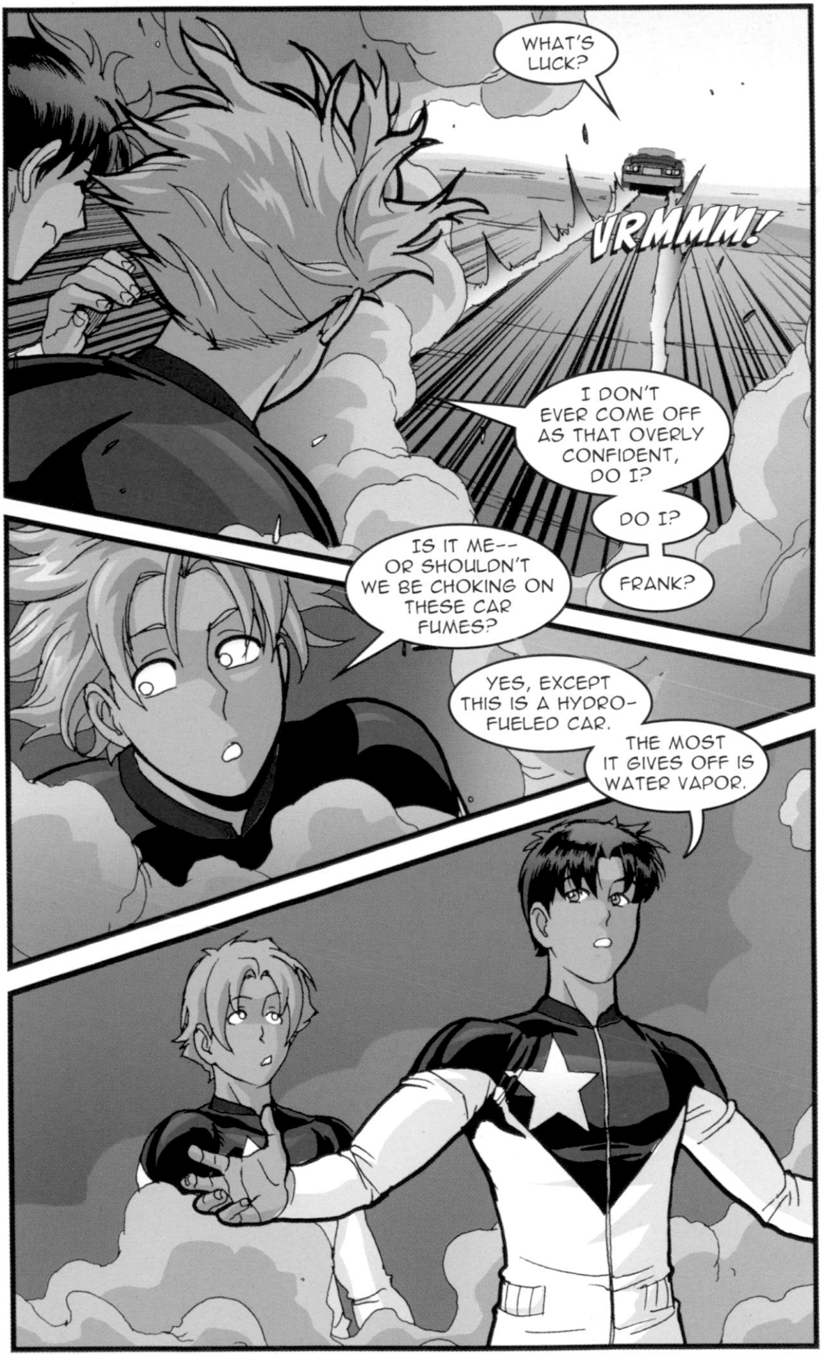
WHAT'S LUCK?
VRMMM!
I DON'T EVER COME OFF AS THAT OVERLY CONFIDENT, DO I?
DO I?
FRANK?
IS IT ME-- OR SHOULDN'T WE BE CHOKING ON THESE CAR FUMES?
YES, EXCEPT THIS IS A HYDRO-FUELED CAR.
THE MOST IT GIVES OFF IS WATER VAPOR.

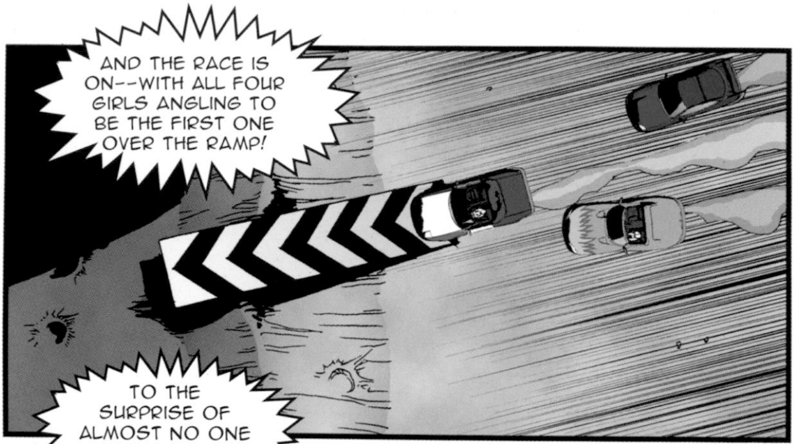
AND THE RACE IS ON--WITH ALL FOUR GIRLS ANGLING TO BE THE FIRST ONE OVER THE RAMP!
TO THE SURPRISE OF ALMOST NO ONE AT ALL --

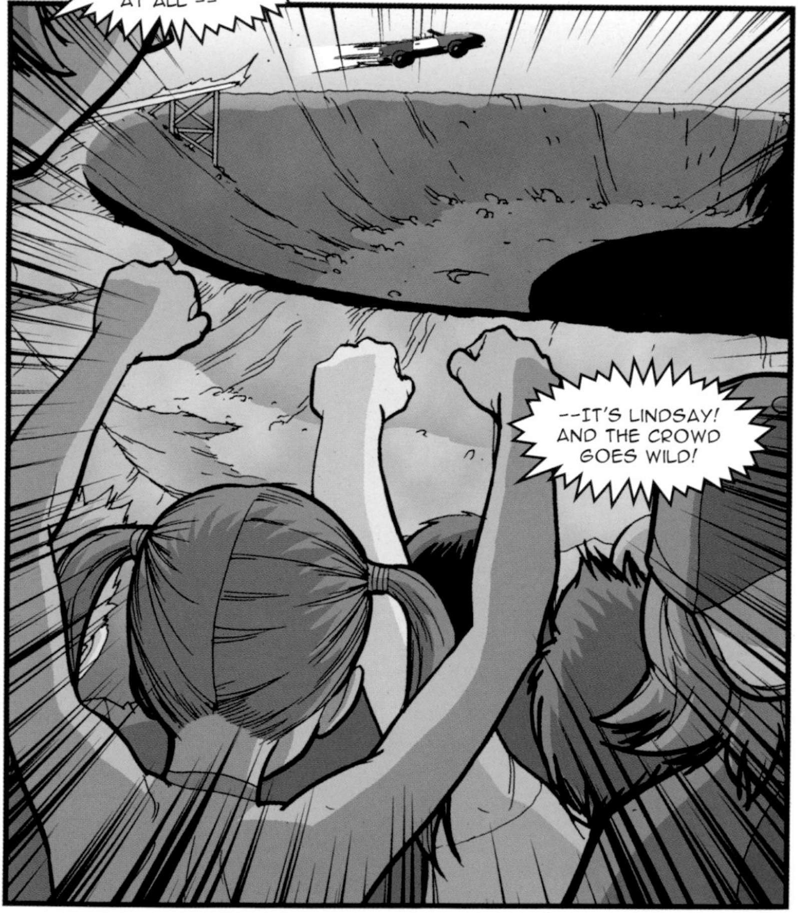
--IT'S LINDSAY! AND THE CROWD GOES WILD!

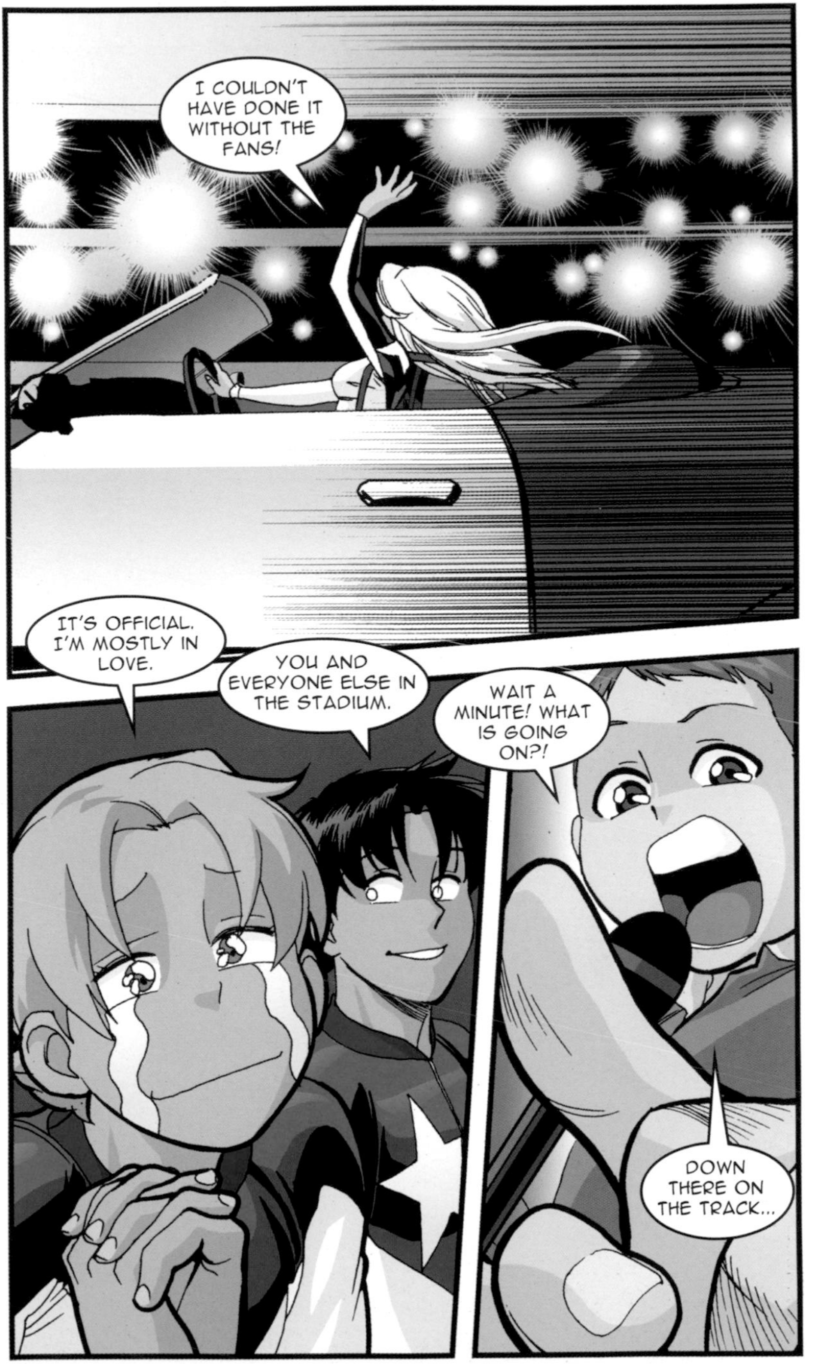
I COULDN'T HAVE DONE IT WITHOUT THE FANS!
IT'S OFFICIAL. I'M MOSTLY IN LOVE.
YOU AND EVERYONE ELSE IN THE STADIUM.
WAIT A MINUTE! WHAT IS GOING ON?!
DOWN THERE ON THE TRACK...

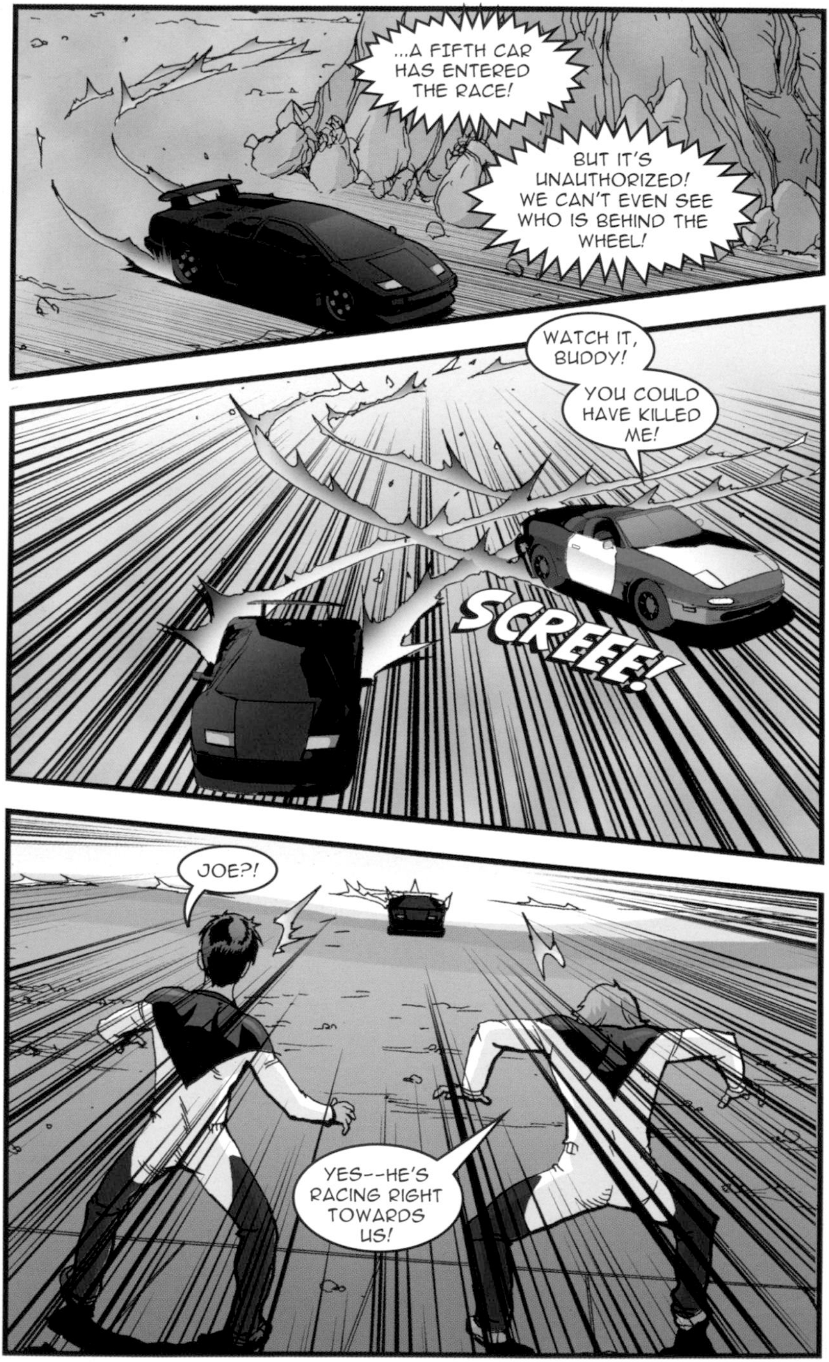
...A FIFTH CAR HAS ENTERED THE RACE!
BUT IT'S UNAUTHORIZED! WE CAN'T EVEN SEE WHO IS BEHIND THE WHEEL!
WATCH IT, BUDDY!
YOU COULD HAVE KILLED ME!
SCREEE!
JOE?!
YES--HE'S RACING RIGHT TOWARDS US!

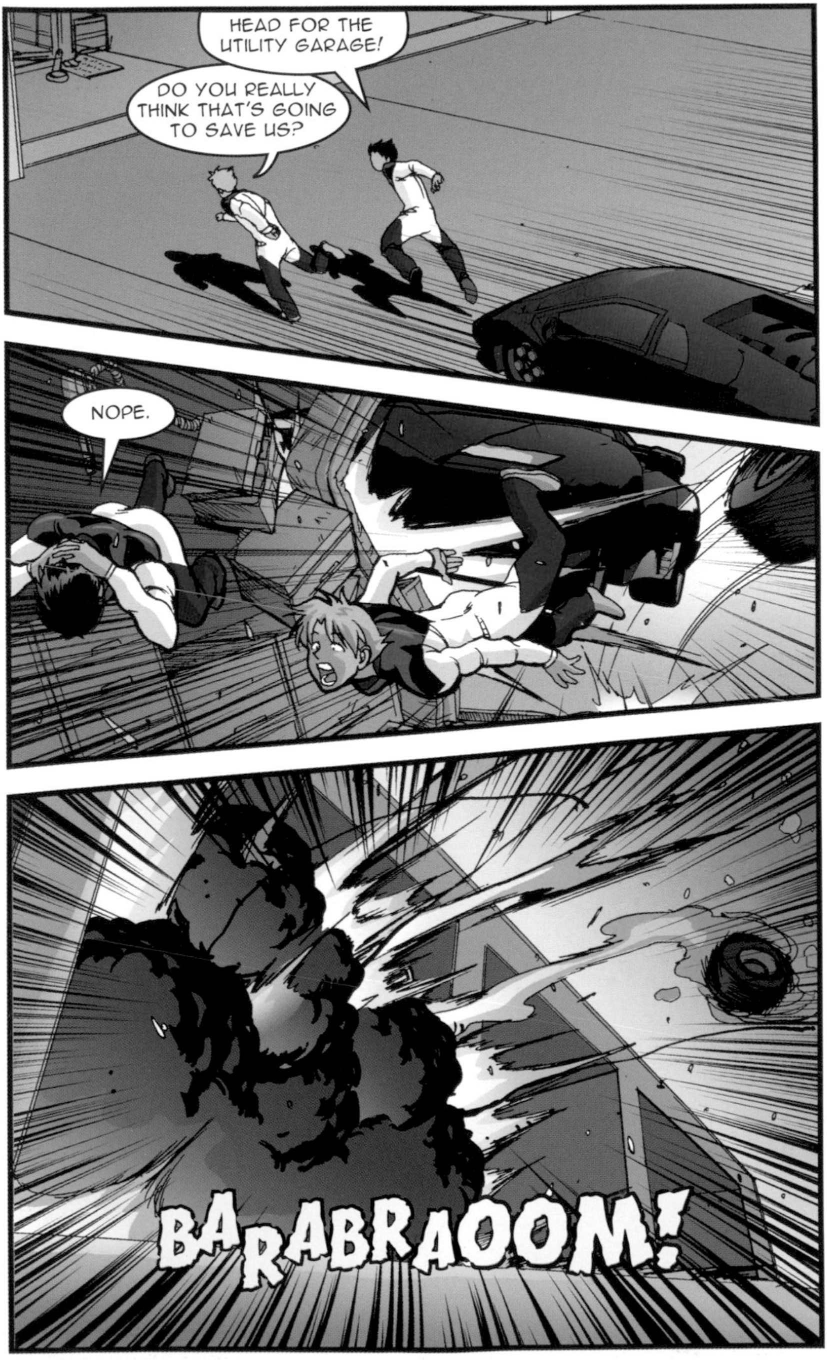
HEAD FOR THE UTILITY GARAGE!
DO YOU REALLY THINK THAT'S GOING TO SAVE US?
NOPE.
BARABRAOOM!

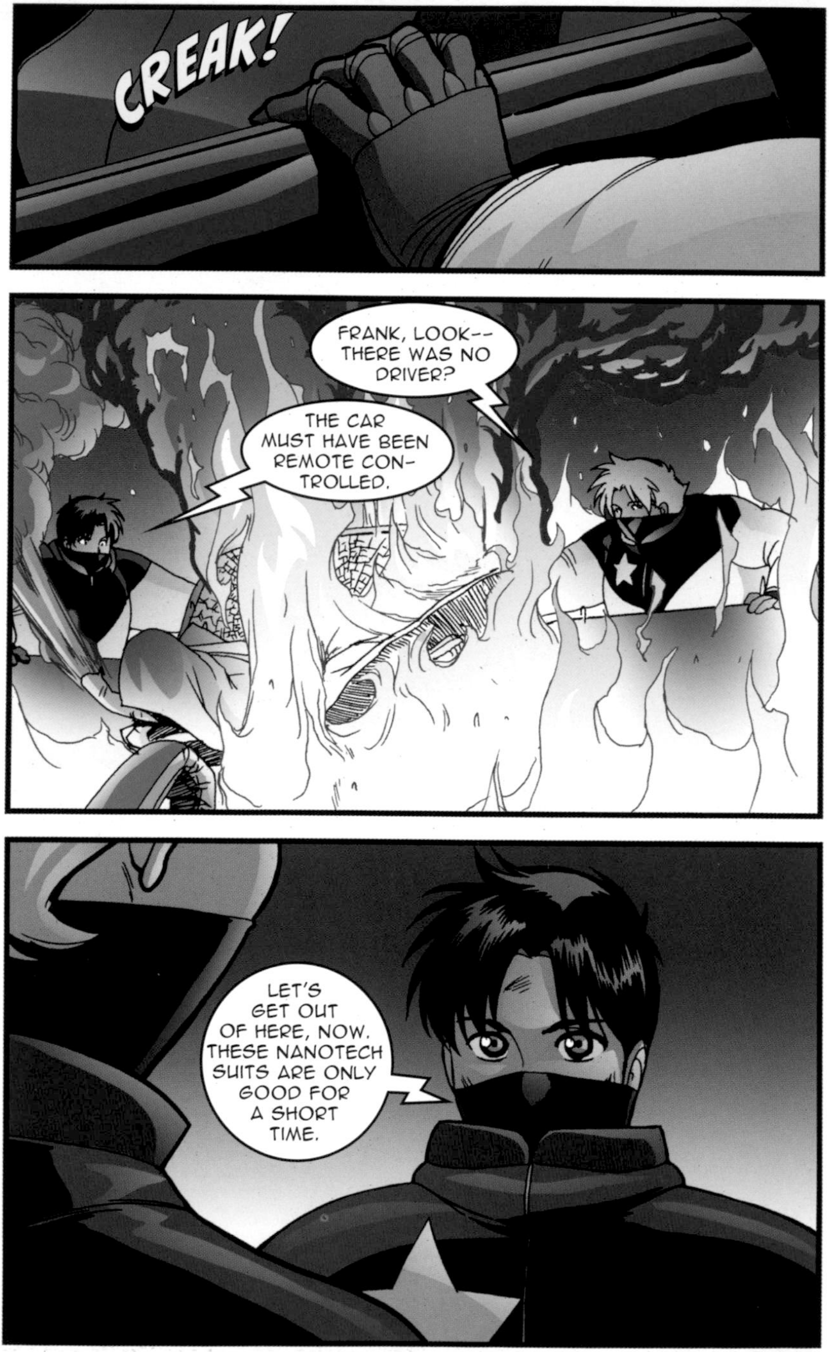
CREAK!
FRANK, LOOK-- THERE WAS NO DRIVER?
THE CAR MUST HAVE BEEN REMOTE CON-TROLLED.
LET'S GET OUT OF HERE, NOW. THESE NANOTECH SUITS ARE ONLY GOOD FOR A SHORT TIME.

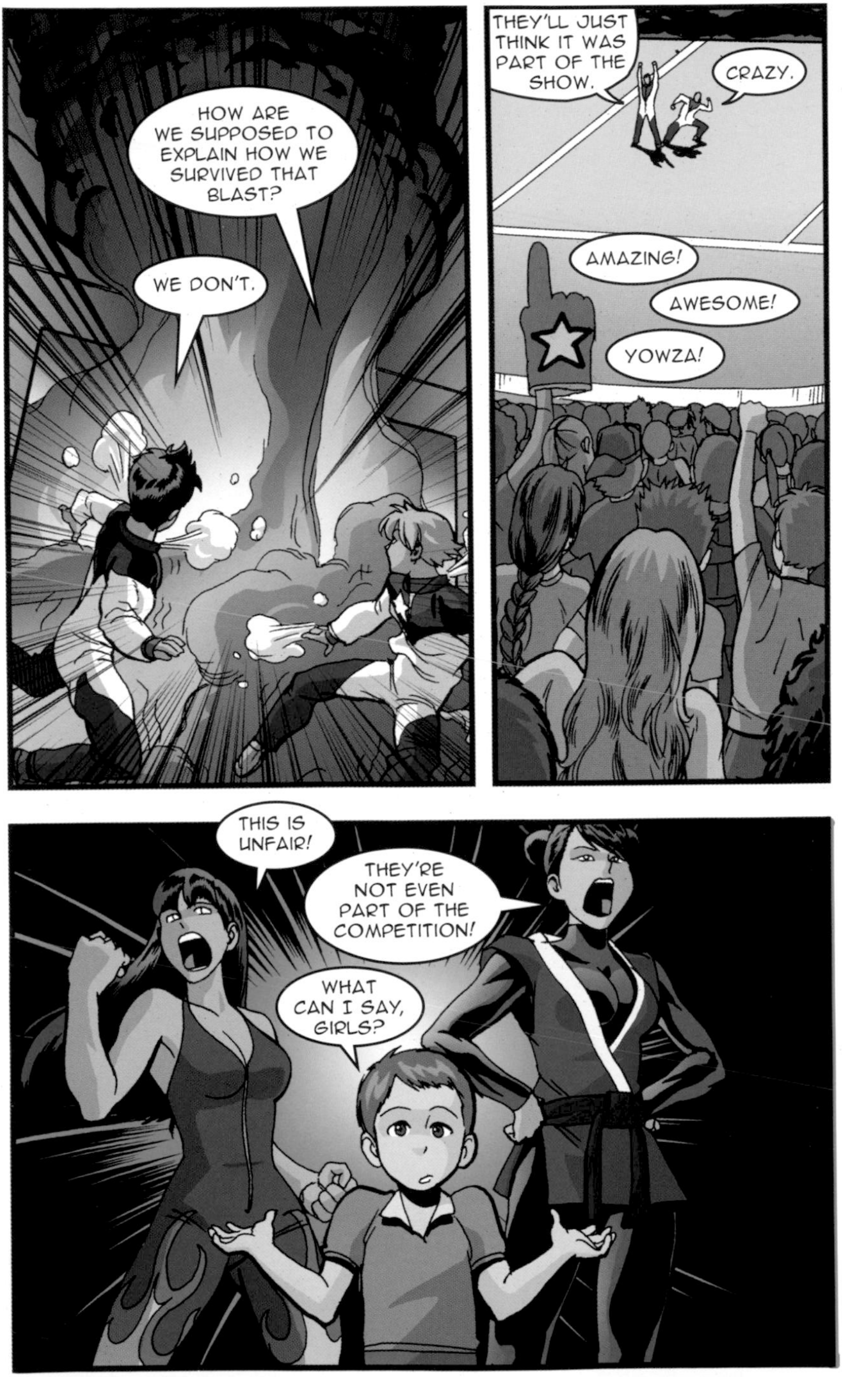
HOW ARE WE SUPPOSED TO EXPLAIN HOW WE SURVIVED THAT BLAST?
WE DON'T.
THEY'LL JUST THINK IT WAS PART OF THE SHOW.
CRAZY.
AMAZING!
AWESOME!
YOWZA!
THIS IS UNFAIR!
THEY'RE NOT EVEN PART OF THE COMPETITION!
WHAT CAN I SAY, GIRLS?

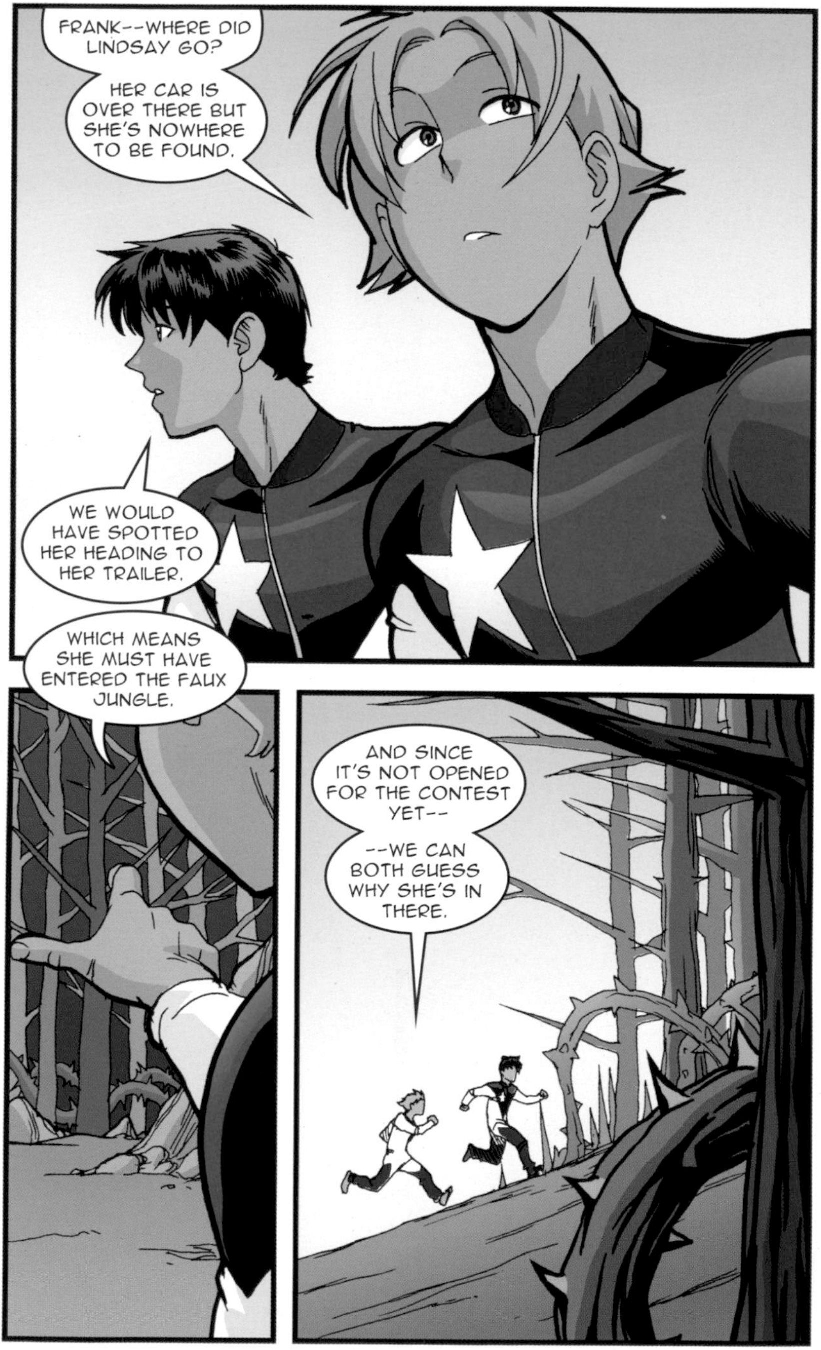
FRANK--WHERE DID LINDSAY GO?
HER CAR IS OVER THERE BUT SHE'S NOWHERE TO BE FOUND.
WE WOULD HAVE SPOTTED HER HEADING TO HER TRAILER.
WHICH MEANS SHE MUST HAVE ENTERED THE FAUX JUNGLE.
AND SINCE IT'S NOT OPENED FOR THE CONTEST YET--
--WE CAN BOTH GUESS WHY SHE'S IN THERE.

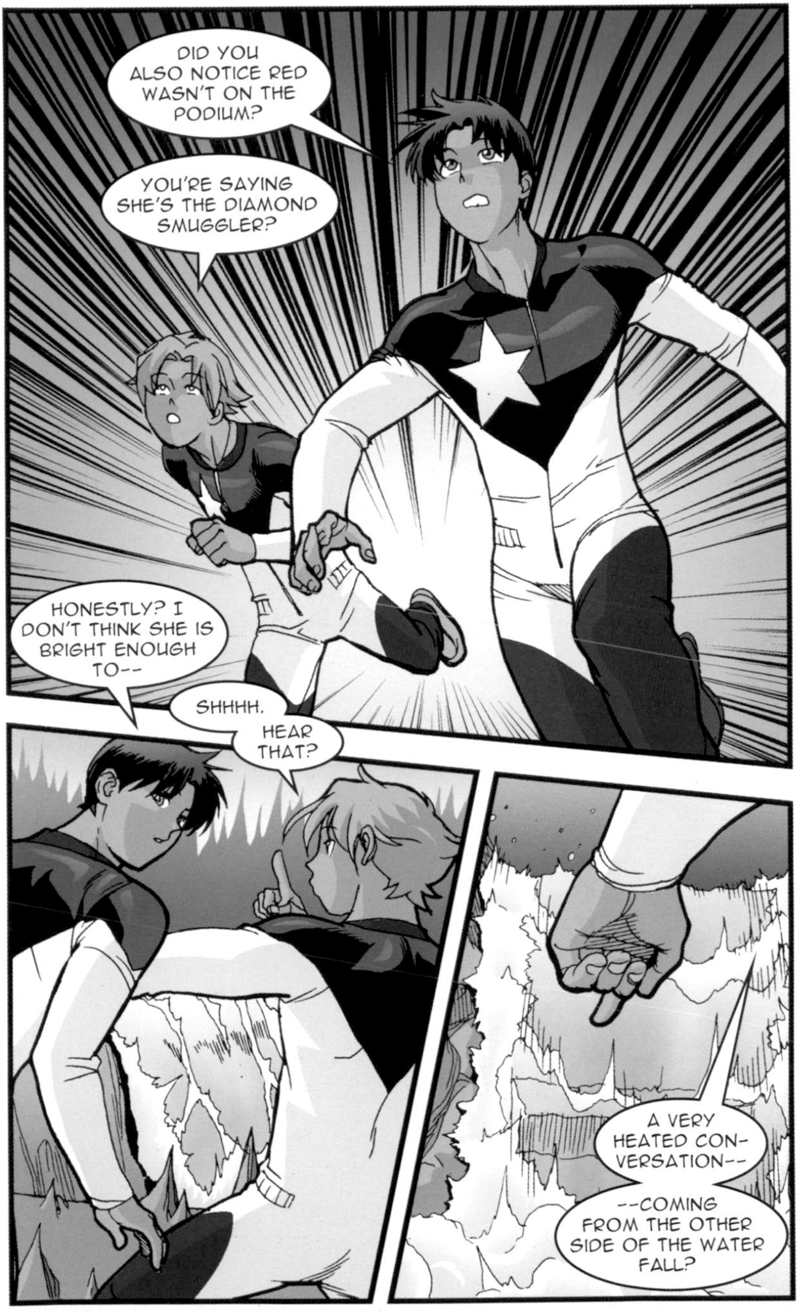
DID YOU ALSO NOTICE RED WASN'T ON THE PODIUM?
YOU'RE SAYING SHE'S THE DIAMOND SMUGGLER?
HONESTLY? I DON'T THINK SHE IS BRIGHT ENOUGH TO--
SHHHH.
HEAR THAT?
A VERY HEATED CON-VERSATION--
--COMING FROM THE OTHER SIDE OF THE WATER FALL?

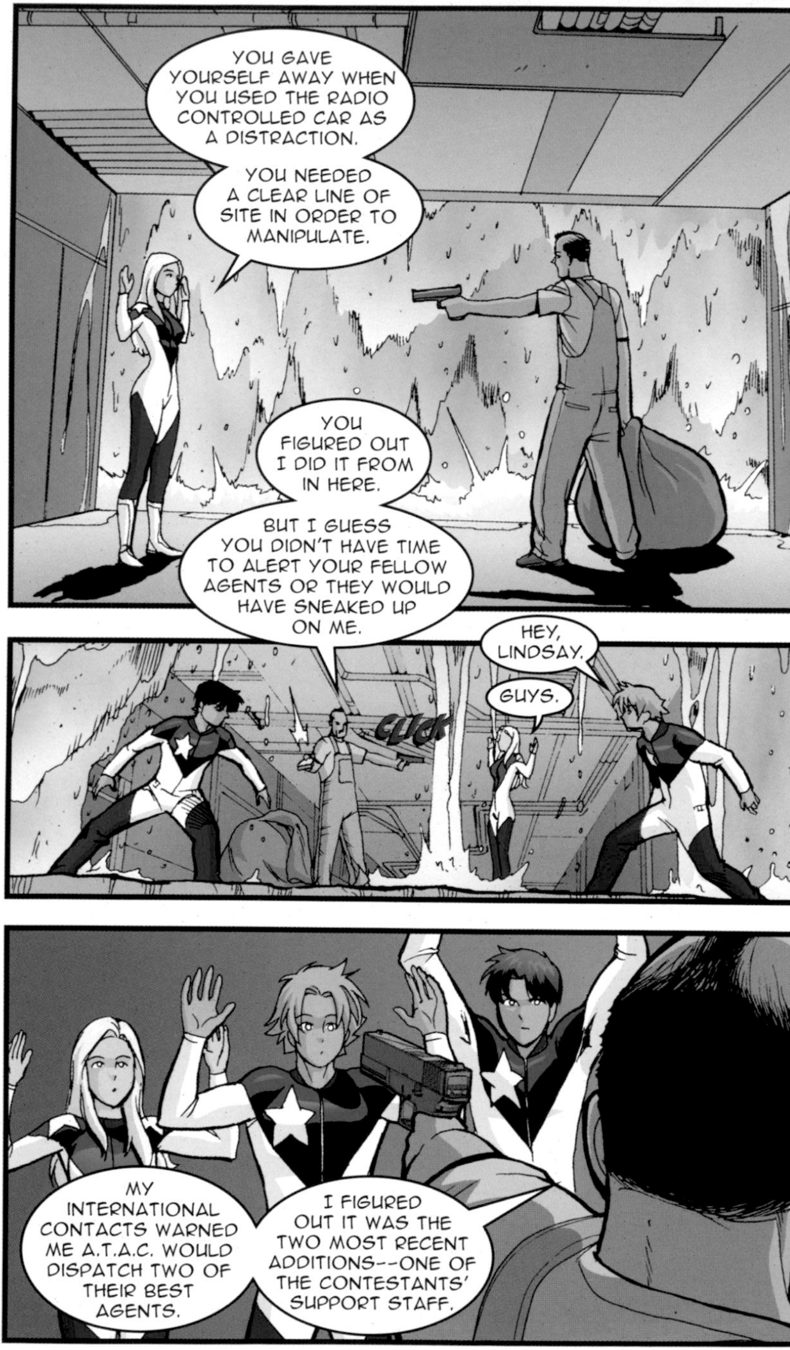
YOU GAVE YOURSELF AWAY WHEN YOU USED THE RADIO CONTROLLED CAR AS A DISTRACTION.
YOU NEEDED A CLEAR LINE OF SITE IN ORDER TO MANIPULATE.
YOU FIGURED OUT I DID IT FROM IN HERE.
BUT I GUESS YOU DIDN'T HAVE TIME TO ALERT YOUR FELLOW AGENTS OR THEY WOULD HAVE SNEAKED UP ON ME.
HEY, LINDSAY.
GUYS.
CLICK
MY INTERNATIONAL CONTACTS WARNED ME A.T.A.C. WOULD DISPATCH TWO OF THEIR BEST AGENTS.
I FIGURED OUT IT WAS THE TWO MOST RECENT ADDITIONS--ONE OF THE CONTESTANTS' SUPPORT STAFF.

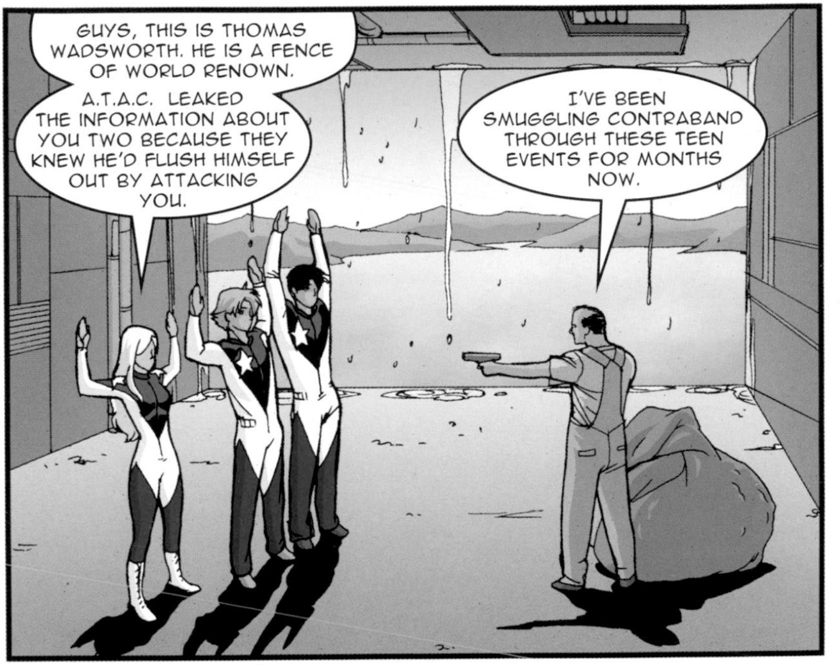
GUYS, THIS IS THOMAS WADSWORTH. HE IS A FENCE OF WORLD RENOWN.
A.T.A.C. LEAKED THE INFORMATION ABOUT YOU TWO BECAUSE THEY KNEW HE'D FLUSH HIMSELF OUT BY ATTACKING YOU.
I'VE BEEN SMUGGLING CONTRABAND THROUGH THESE TEEN EVENTS FOR MONTHS NOW.

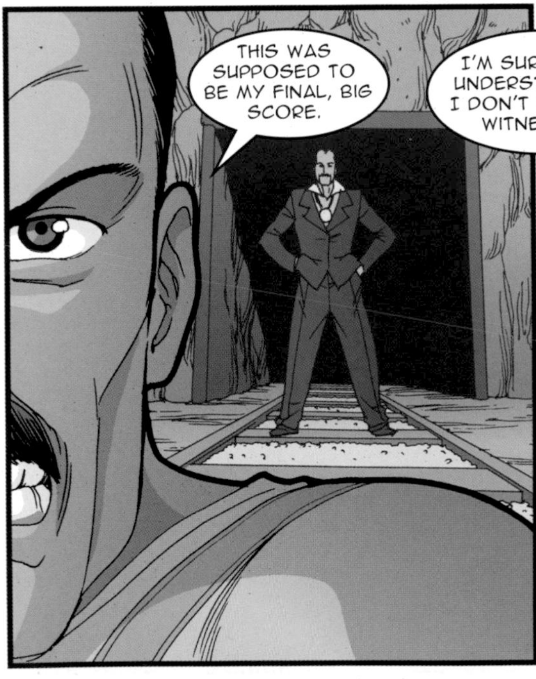
THIS WAS SUPPOSED TO BE MY FINAL, BIG SCORE.

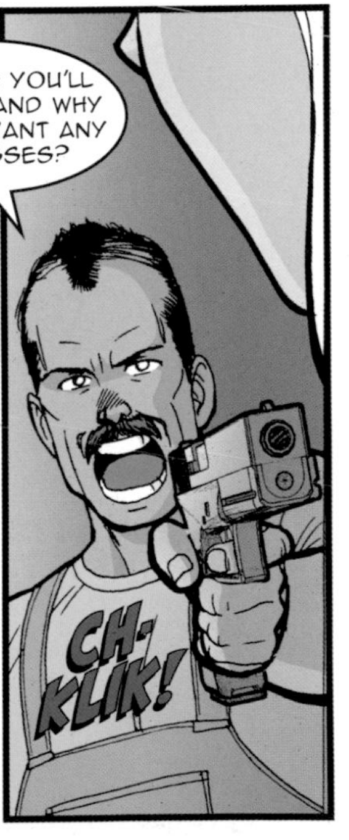
I'M SURE YOU'LL UNDERSTAND WHY I DON'T WANT ANY WITNESSES?
CH-KLIK!

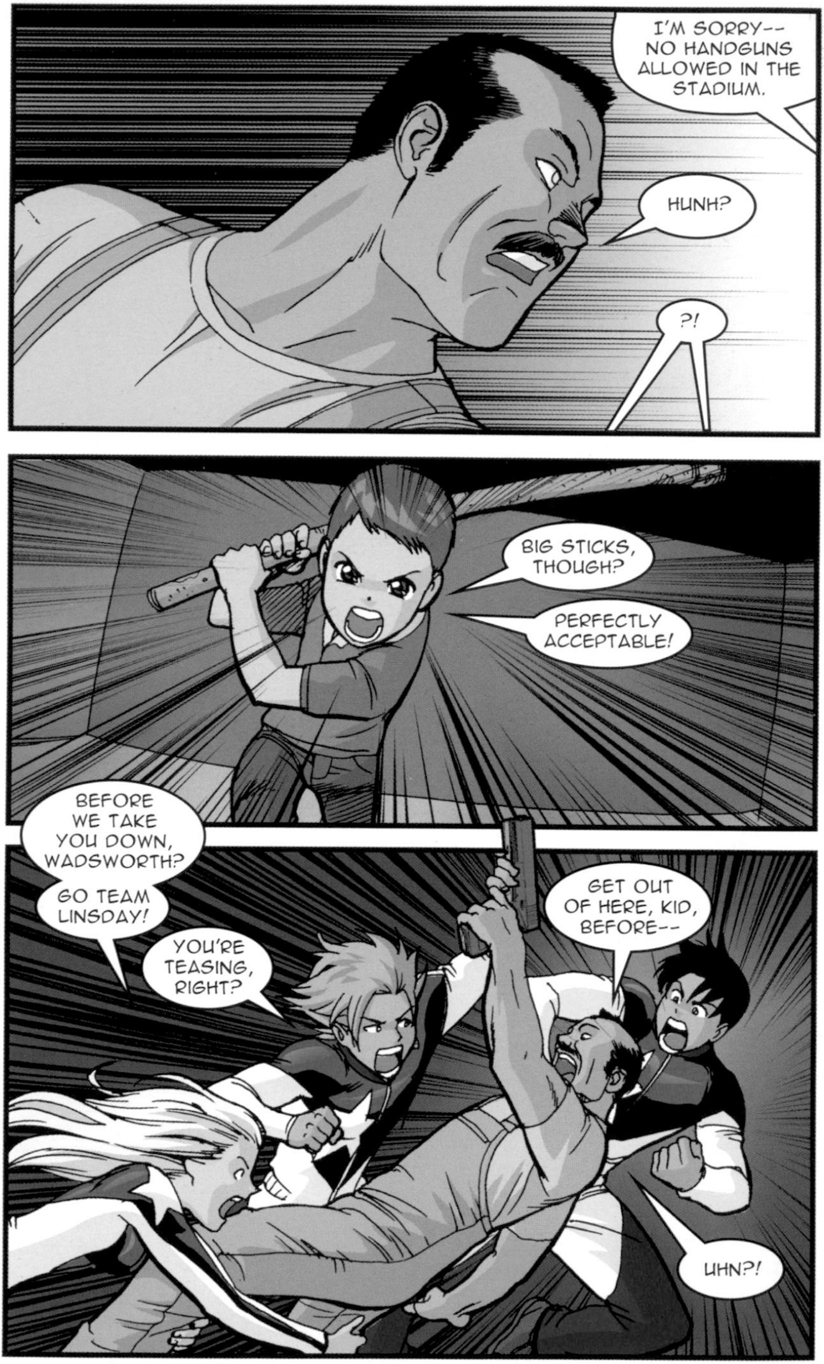
I'M SORRY--
NO HANDGUNS
ALLOWED IN THE
STADIUM.
HUNH?
?!
BIG STICKS,
THOUGH?
PERFECTLY
ACCEPTABLE!
BEFORE
WE TAKE
YOU DOWN,
WADSWORTH?
GO TEAM
LINSDAY!
YOU'RE
TEASING,
RIGHT?
GET OUT
OF HERE, KID,
BEFORE--
UHN?!

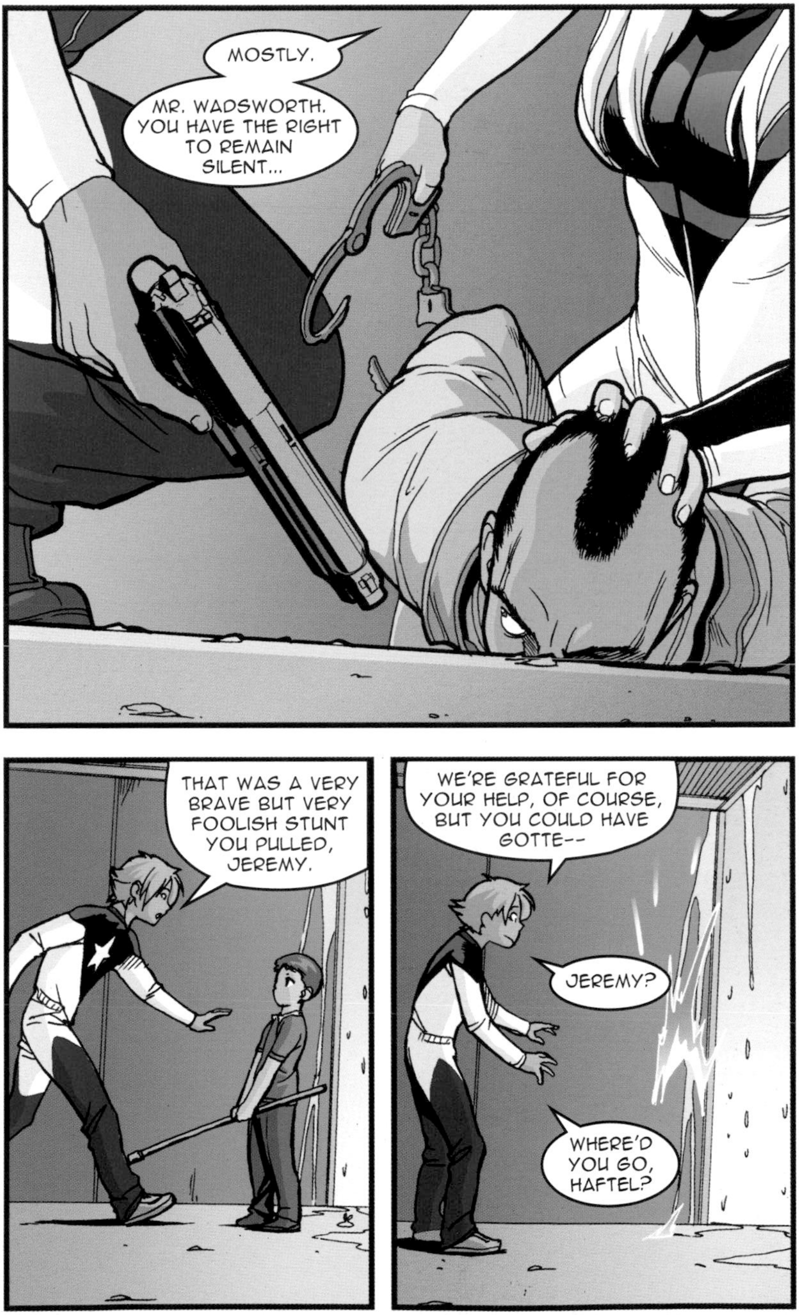
MOSTLY.
MR. WADSWORTH. YOU HAVE THE RIGHT TO REMAIN SILENT...
THAT WAS A VERY BRAVE BUT VERY FOOLISH STUNT YOU PULLED, JEREMY.
WE'RE GRATEFUL FOR YOUR HELP, OF COURSE, BUT YOU COULD HAVE GOTTE--
JEREMY?
WHERE'D YOU GO, HAFTEL?

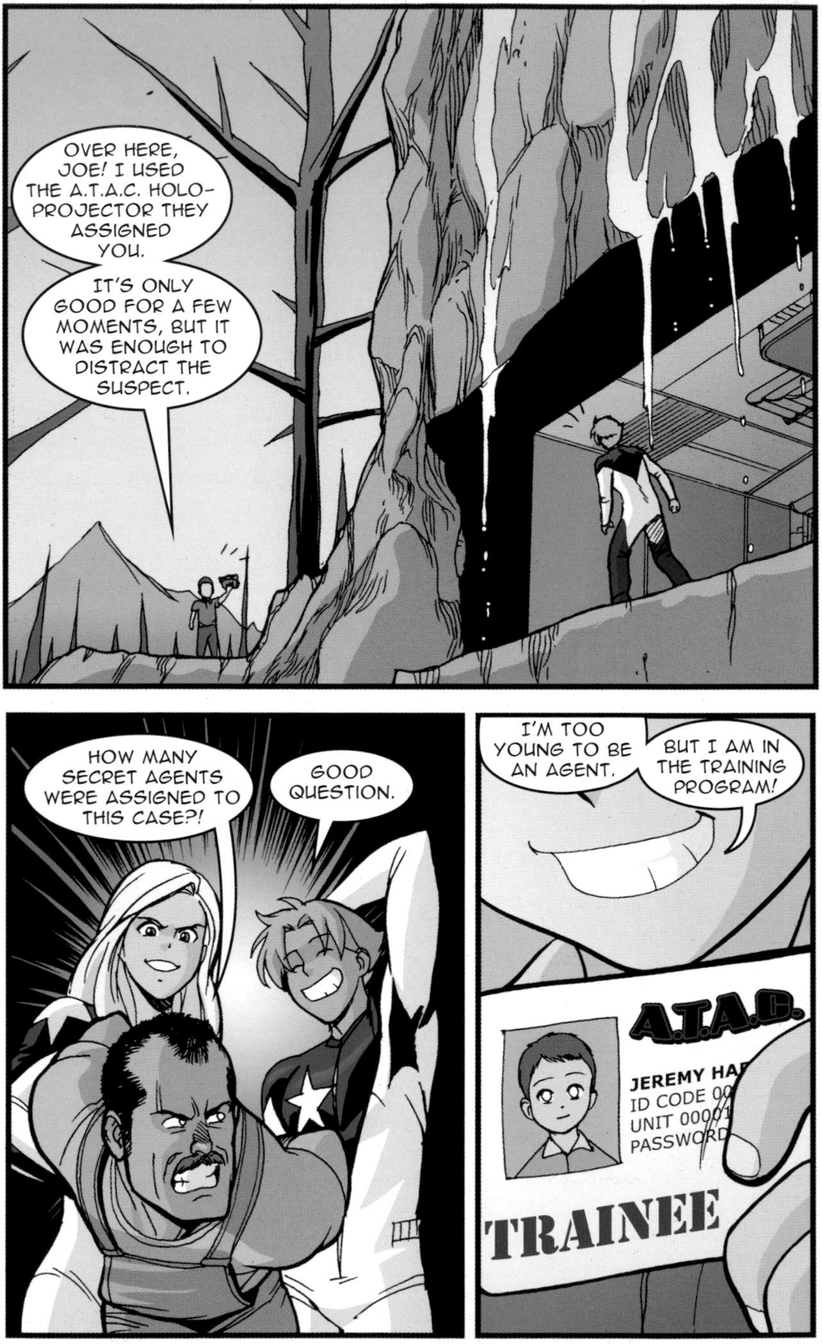
OVER HERE, JOE! I USED THE A.T.A.C. HOLO-PROJECTOR THEY ASSIGNED YOU.
IT'S ONLY GOOD FOR A FEW MOMENTS, BUT IT WAS ENOUGH TO DISTRACT THE SUSPECT.
HOW MANY SECRET AGENTS WERE ASSIGNED TO THIS CASE?!
GOOD QUESTION.
I'M TOO YOUNG TO BE AN AGENT.
BUT I AM IN THE TRAINING PROGRAM!
A.T.A.C.
TRAINEE

AS THE COMPETITION CONTINUES INSIDE THE STADIUM, THE AUTHORITIES HAVE COME TO TAKE THE CRIMINAL AWAY...

WHY DIDN'T ANYONE TELL US ALL THE DETAILS OF THIS CASE BEFORE HAND, DAD?

POLICE

ICE

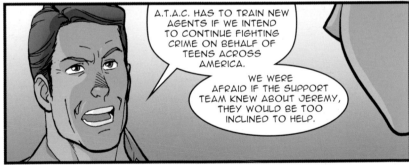

A.T.A.C. HAS TO TRAIN NEW AGENTS IF WE INTEND TO CONTINUE FIGHTING CRIME ON BEHALF OF TEENS ACROSS AMERICA.

WE WERE AFRAID IF THE SUPPORT TEAM KNEW ABOUT JEREMY, THEY WOULD BE TOO INCLINED TO HELP.

AND POSSIBLY UNDERMINE THE WHOLE EXERCISE.

I WAS WONDERING WHY NONE OF THE EVIDENCE POINTED TO THE THREE "SUSPECTS."

YOU WERE KEEPING US *INVOLVED* IN CASE LINDSAY AND JEREMY NEEDED HELP...

...BUT NOT CLOSE ENOUGH TO STEP ON THEIR TOES.

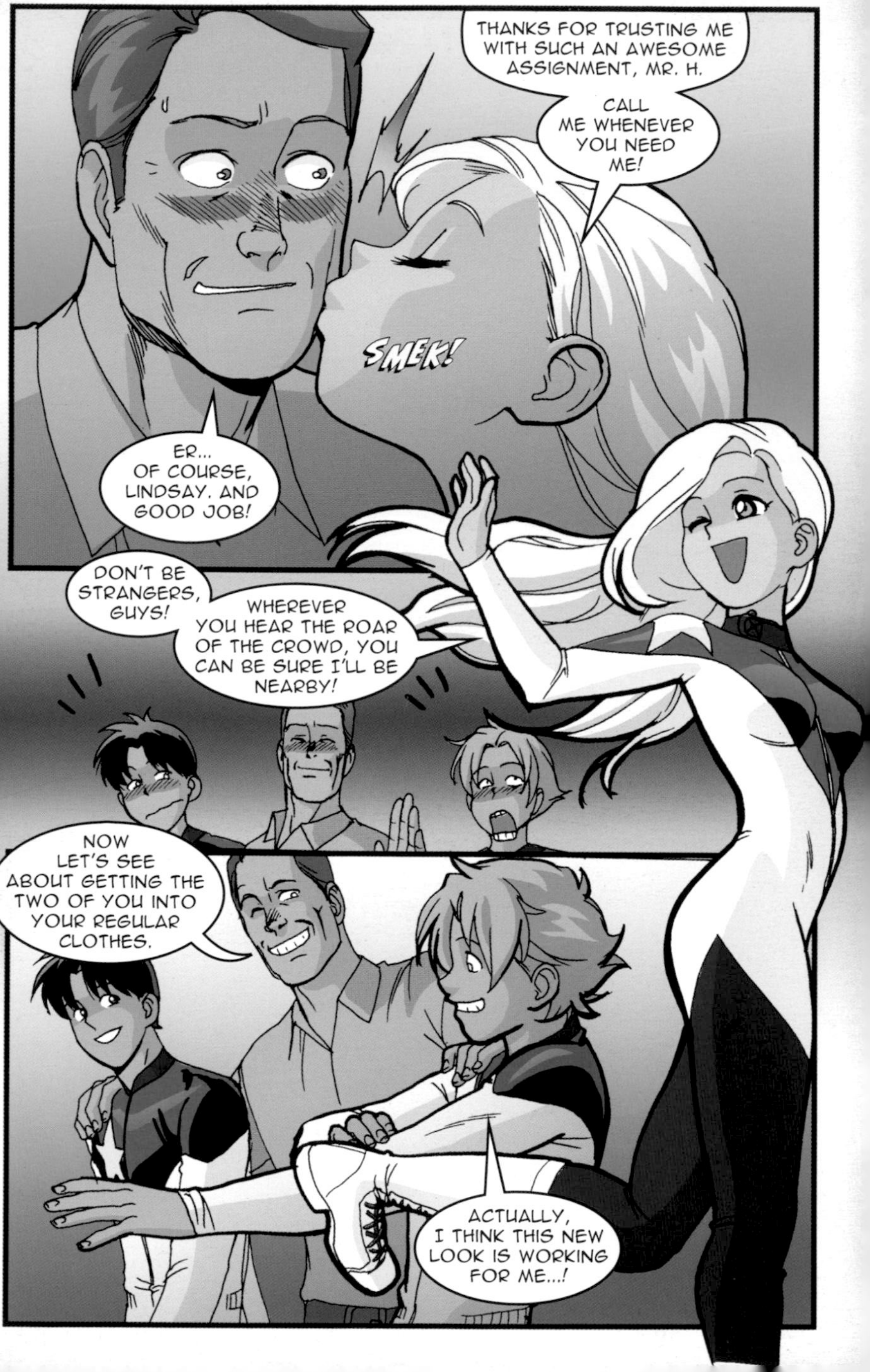
THANKS FOR TRUSTING ME WITH SUCH AN AWESOME ASSIGNMENT, MR. H.
CALL ME WHENEVER YOU NEED ME!
SMEK!
ER... OF COURSE, LINDSAY. AND GOOD JOB!
DON'T BE STRANGERS, GUYS!
WHEREVER YOU HEAR THE ROAR OF THE CROWD, YOU CAN BE SURE I'LL BE NEARBY!
NOW LET'S SEE ABOUT GETTING THE TWO OF YOU INTO YOUR REGULAR CLOTHES.
ACTUALLY, I THINK THIS NEW LOOK IS WORKING FOR ME...!

EPILOGUE: "HERE'S TO USING YOUR HEAD..."

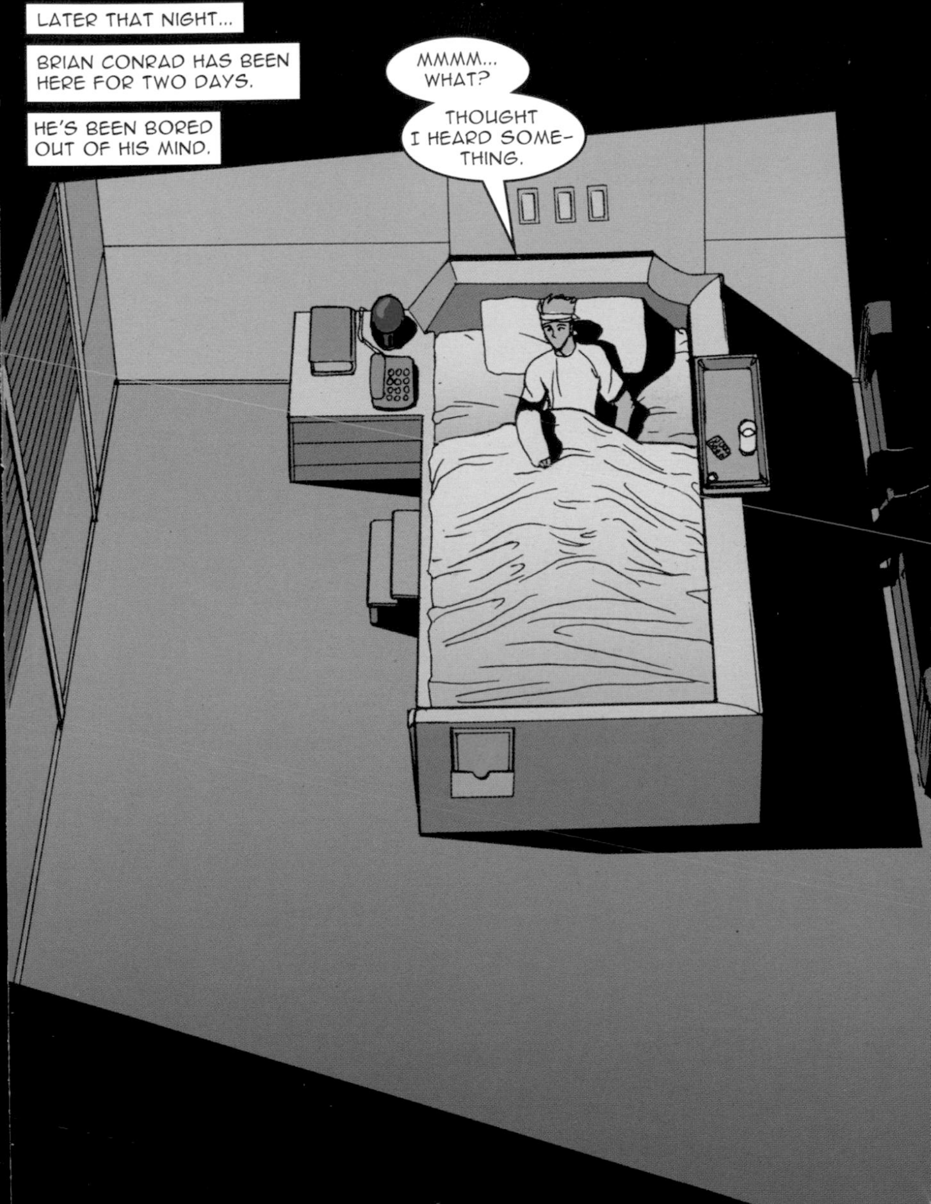
LATER THAT NIGHT...
BRIAN CONRAD HAS BEEN HERE FOR TWO DAYS.
HE'S BEEN BORED OUT OF HIS MIND.
MMMM... WHAT?
THOUGHT I HEARD SOME-THING.

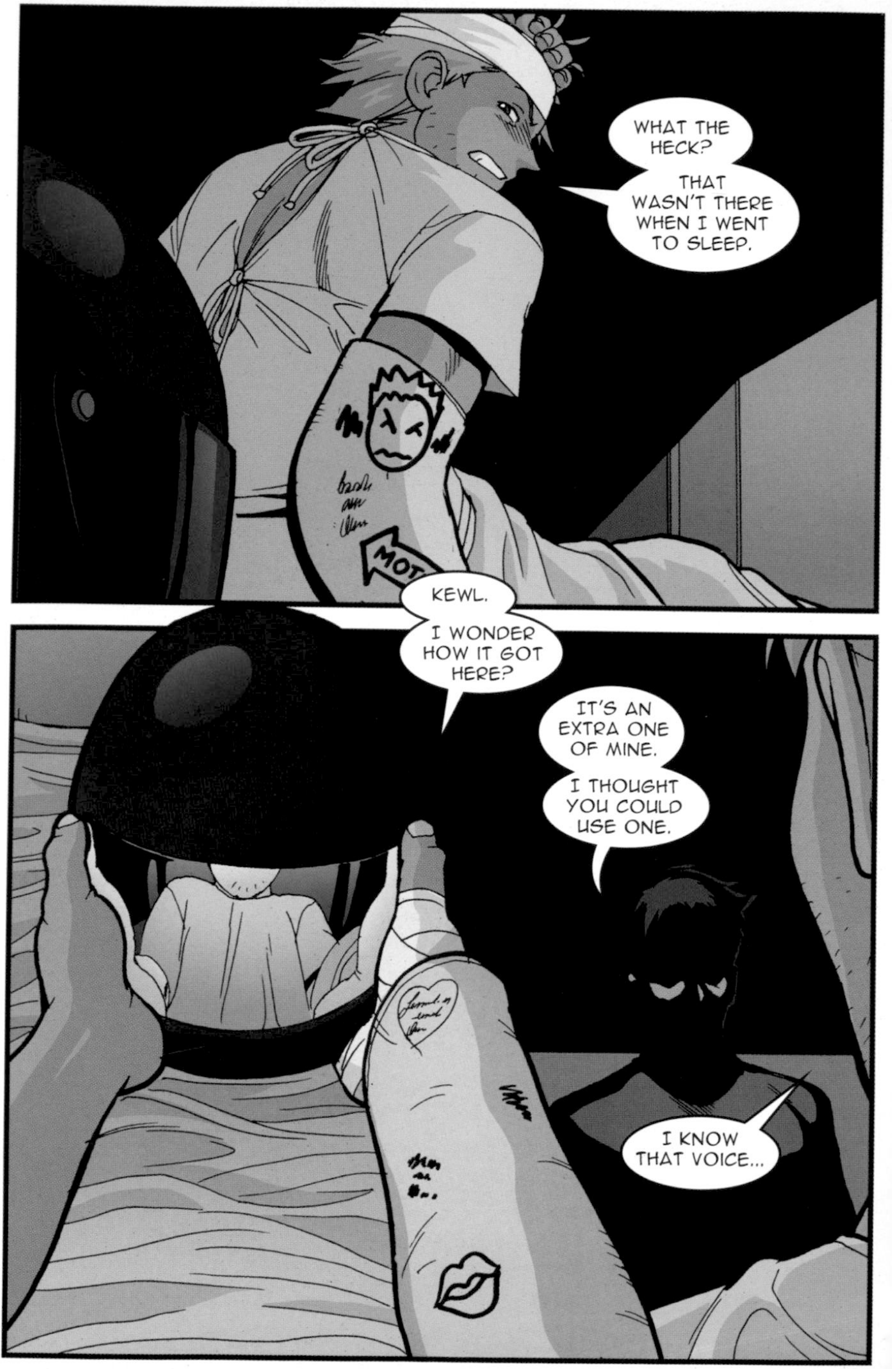
WHAT THE HECK?
THAT WASN'T THERE WHEN I WENT TO SLEEP.
MOT
KEWL.
I WONDER HOW IT GOT HERE?
IT'S AN EXTRA ONE OF MINE.
I THOUGHT YOU COULD USE ONE.
I KNOW THAT VOICE...

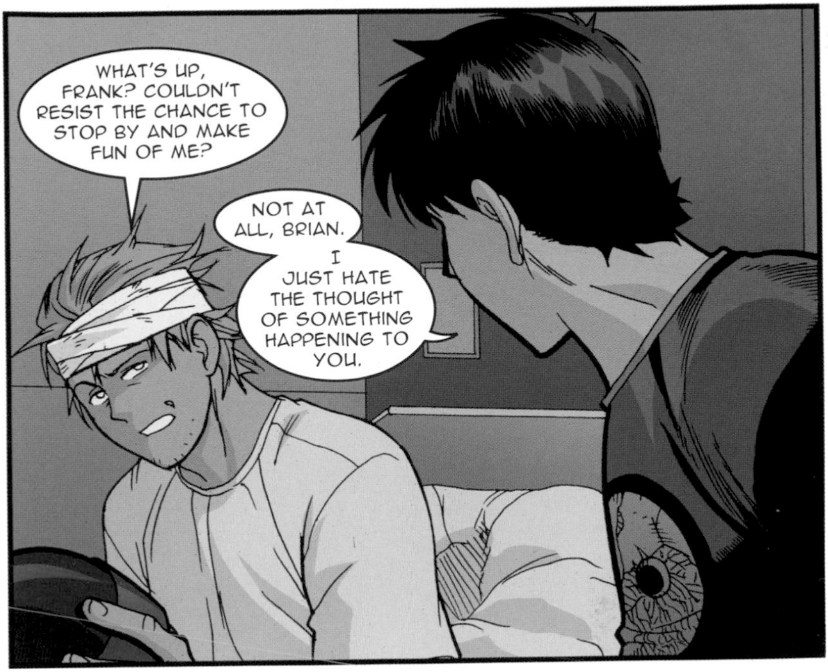
WHAT'S UP, FRANK? COULDN'T RESIST THE CHANCE TO STOP BY AND MAKE FUN OF ME?
NOT AT ALL, BRIAN.
I JUST HATE THE THOUGHT OF SOMETHING HAPPENING TO YOU.

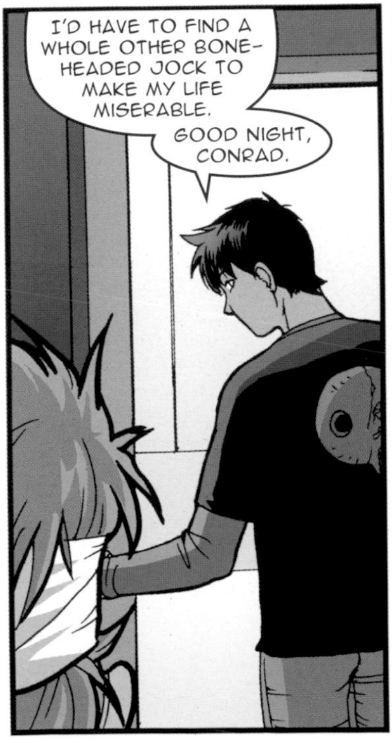
I'D HAVE TO FIND A WHOLE OTHER BONE-HEADED JOCK TO MAKE MY LIFE MISERABLE.
GOOD NIGHT, CONRAD.

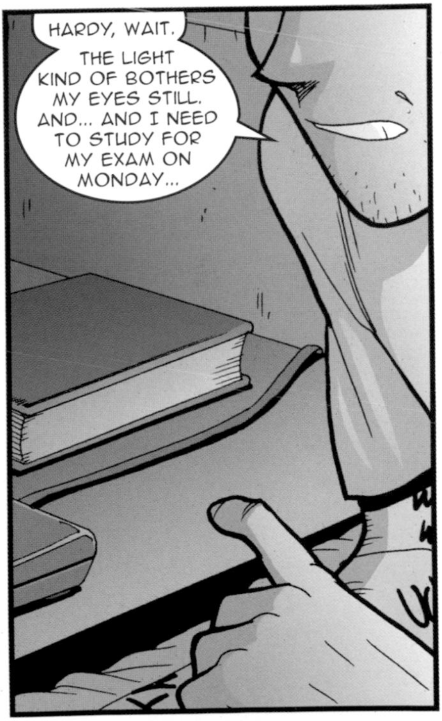
HARDY, WAIT.
THE LIGHT KIND OF BOTHERS MY EYES STILL. AND... AND I NEED TO STUDY FOR MY EXAM ON MONDAY...

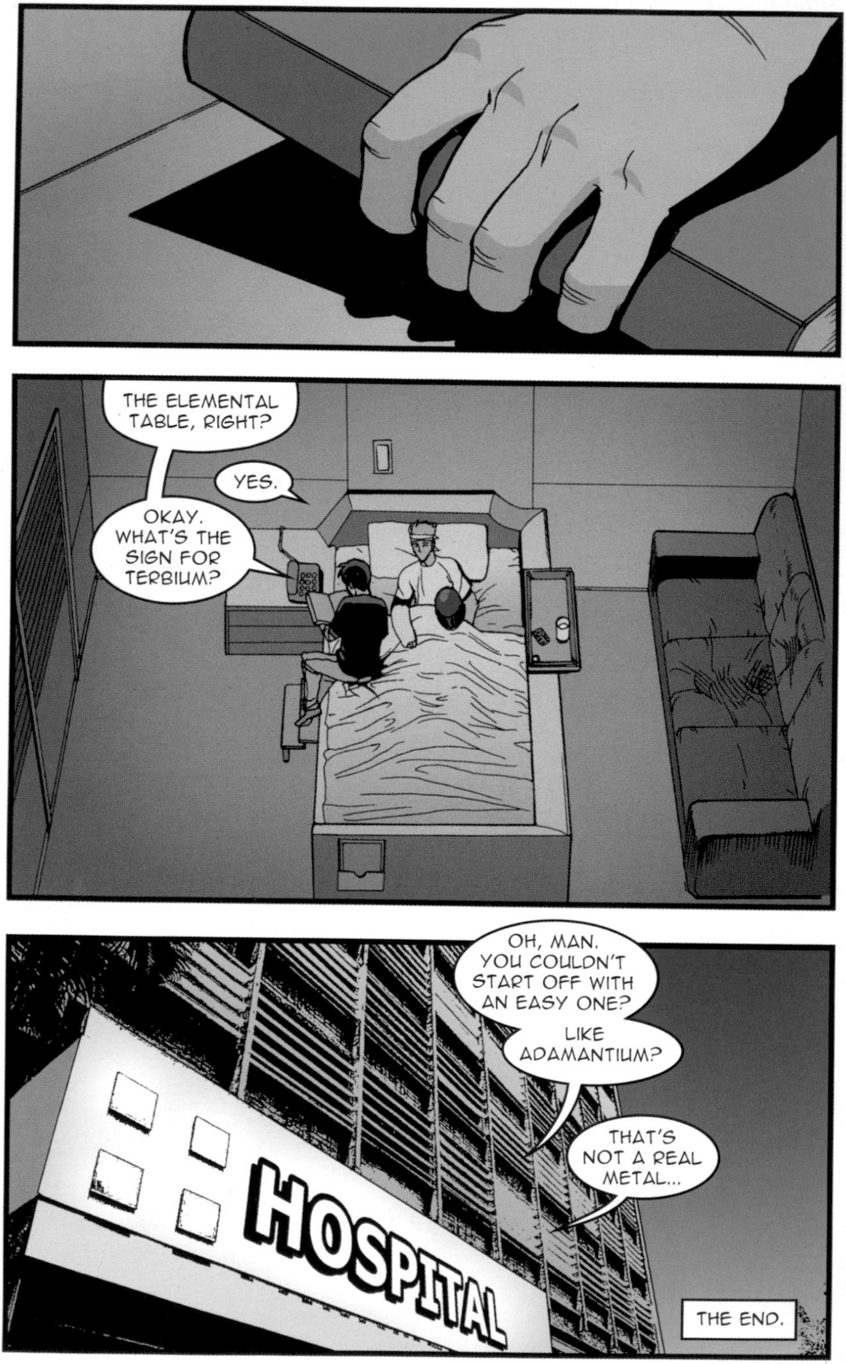
THE ELEMENTAL TABLE, RIGHT?
YES.
OKAY. WHAT'S THE SIGN FOR TERBIUM?
OH, MAN. YOU COULDN'T START OFF WITH AN EASY ONE?
LIKE ADAMANTIUM?
THAT'S NOT A REAL METAL...
HOSPITAL
THE END.

"Special Preview of THE HARDY BOYS #14 "Haley Danelle's Best Eight"

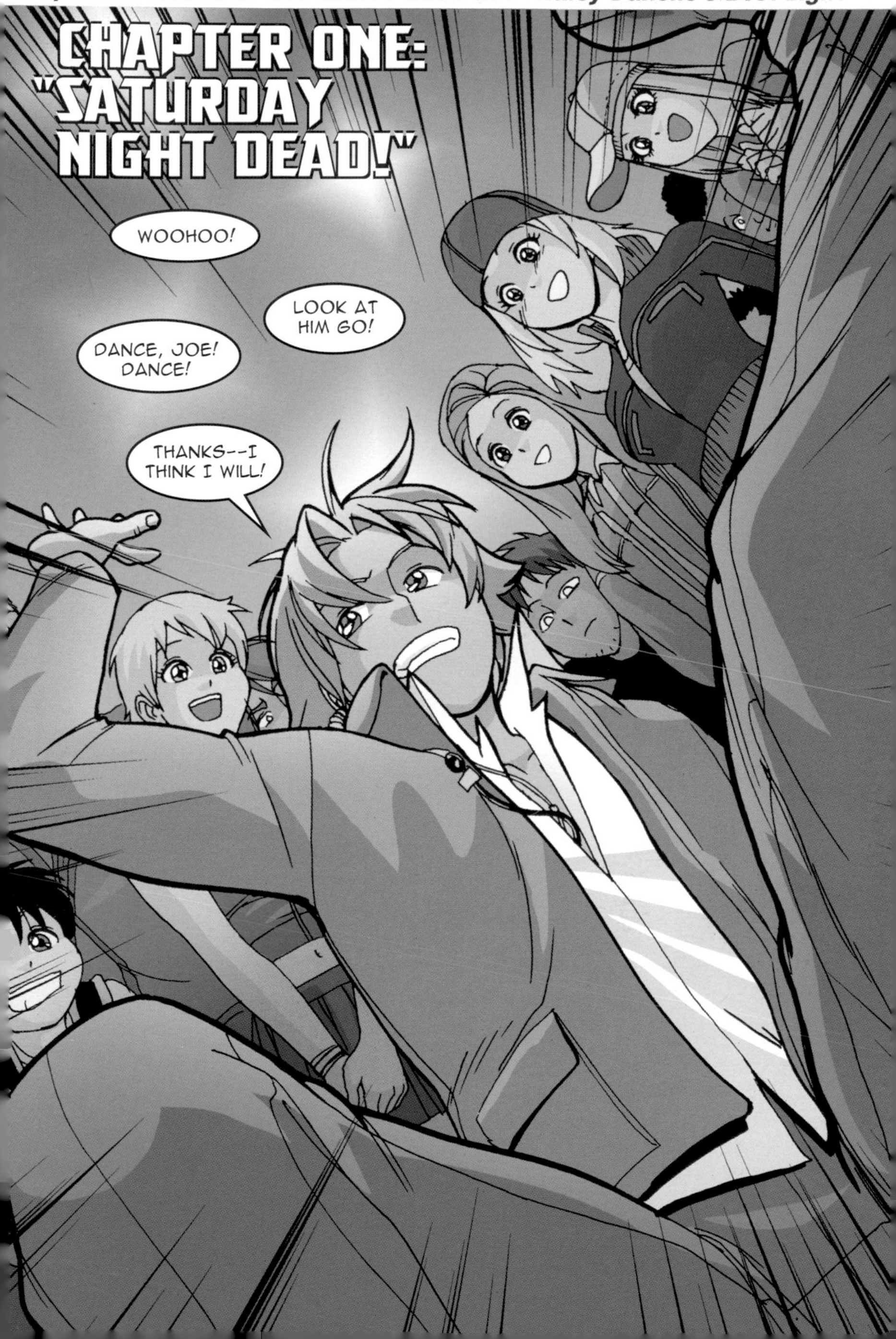
CHAPTER ONE:
"SATURDAY NIGHT DEAD!"
WOOHOO!
LOOK AT HIM GO!
DANCE, JOE! DANCE!
THANKS--I THINK I WILL!

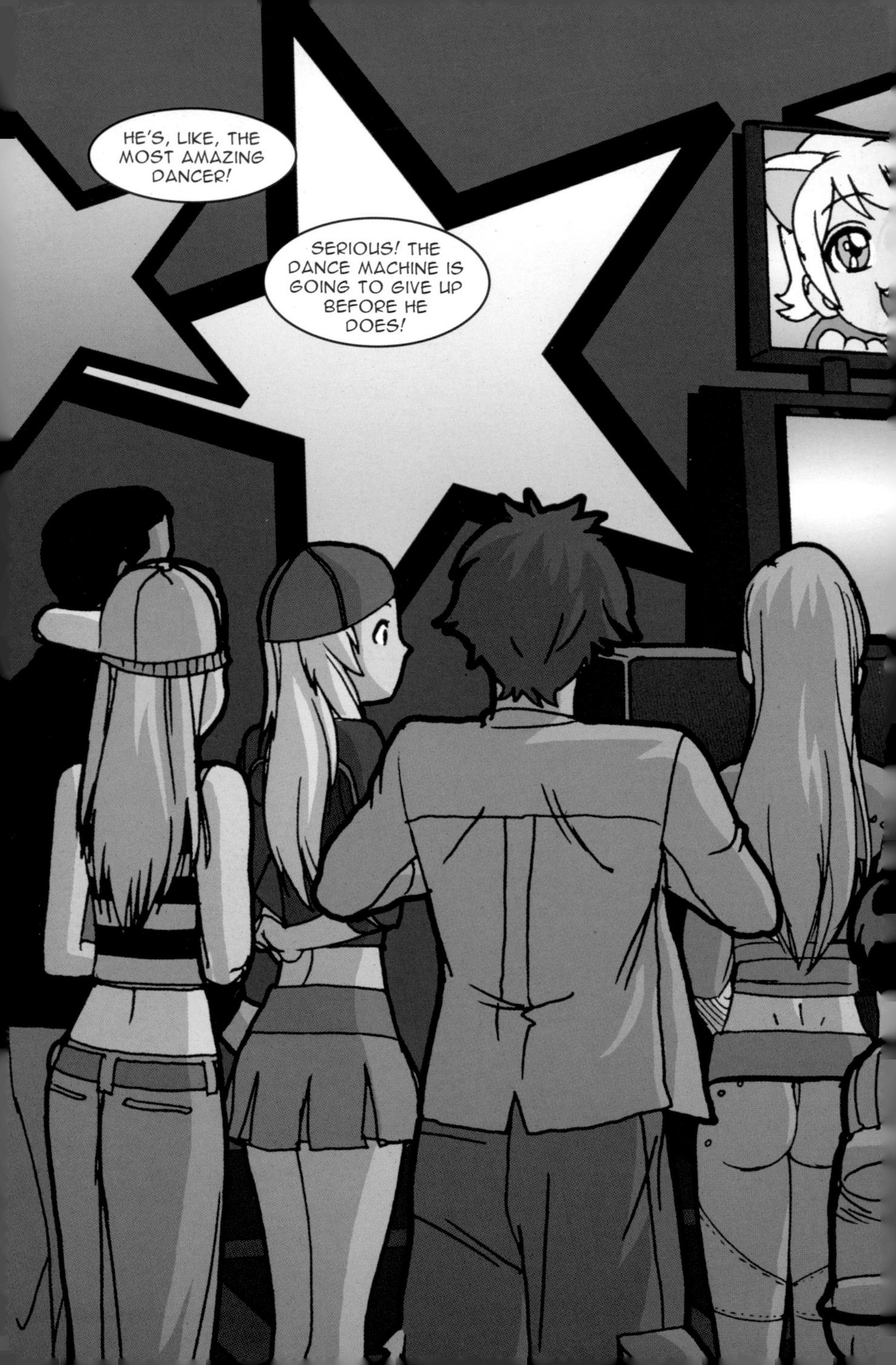
HE'S, LIKE, THE MOST AMAZING DANCER!
SERIOUS! THE DANCE MACHINE IS GOING TO GIVE UP BEFORE HE DOES!

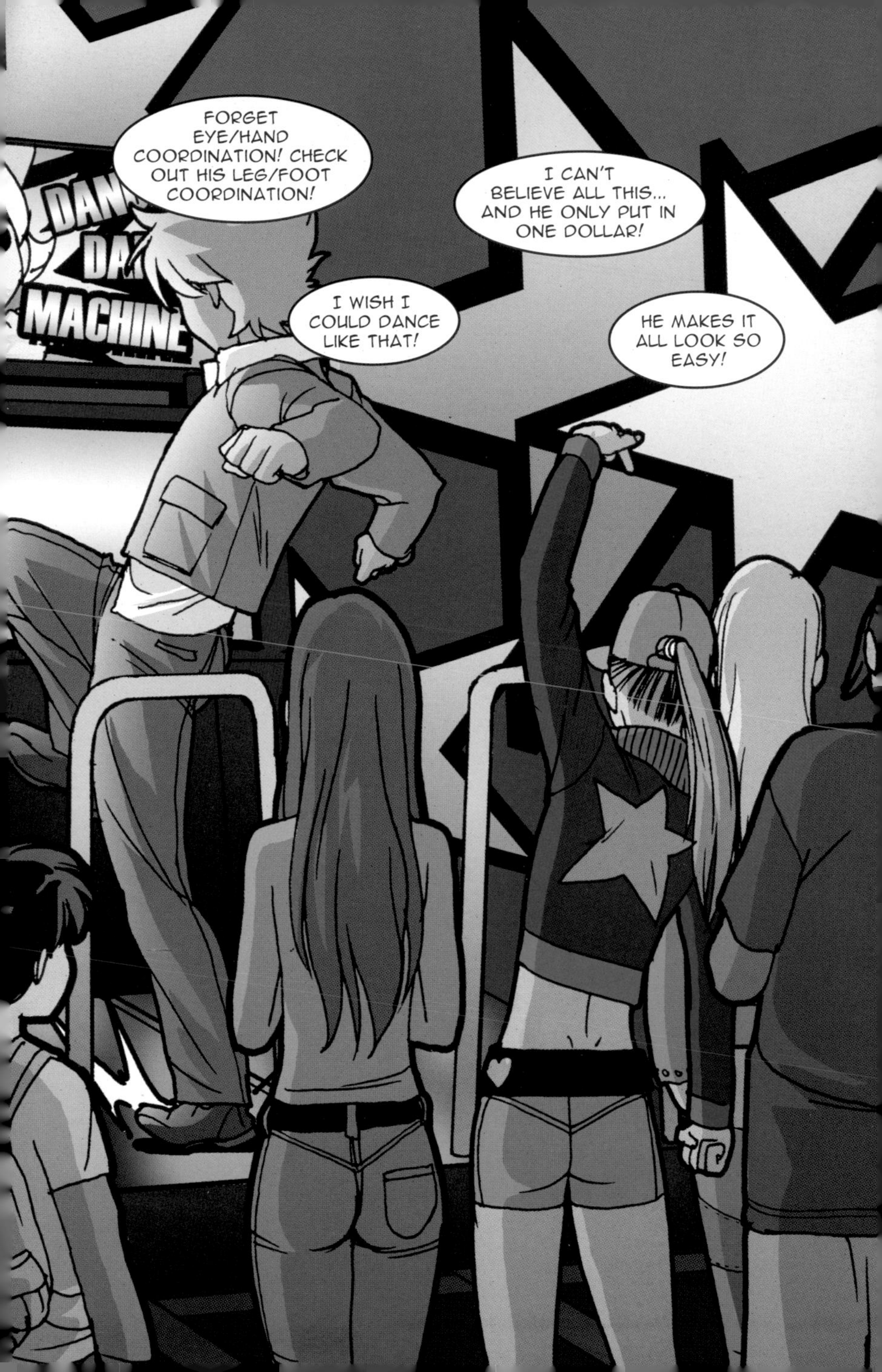
DANCE DANCE MACHINE
FORGET EYE/HAND COORDINATION! CHECK OUT HIS LEG/FOOT COORDINATION!
I WISH I COULD DANCE LIKE THAT!
I CAN'T BELIEVE ALL THIS... AND HE ONLY PUT IN ONE DOLLAR!
HE MAKES IT ALL LOOK SO EASY!

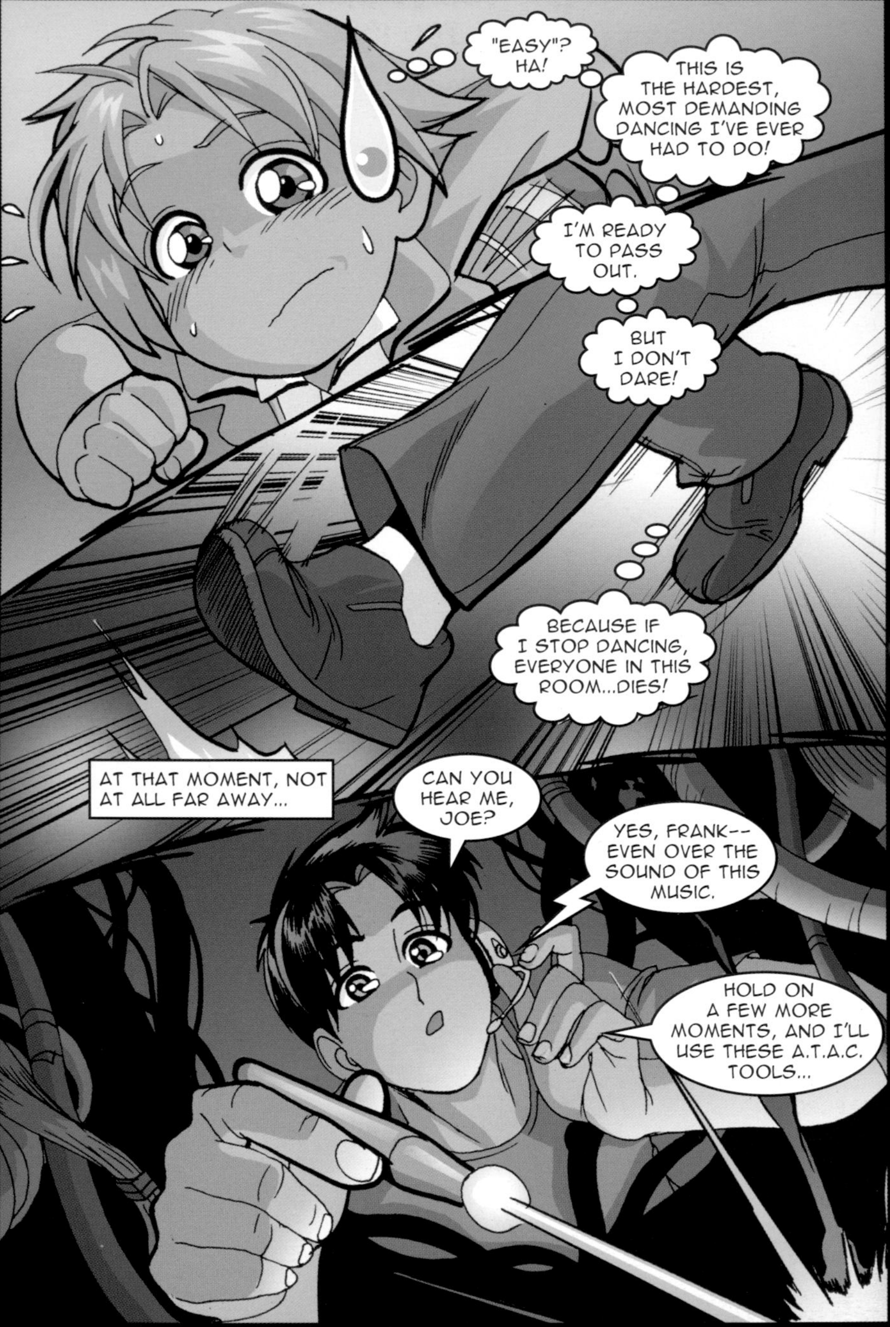

"EASY"? HA!
THIS IS THE HARDEST, MOST DEMANDING DANCING I'VE EVER HAD TO DO!
I'M READY TO PASS OUT.
BUT I DON'T DARE!
BECAUSE IF I STOP DANCING, EVERYONE IN THIS ROOM...DIES!
AT THAT MOMENT, NOT AT ALL FAR AWAY...
CAN YOU HEAR ME, JOE?
YES, FRANK-- EVEN OVER THE SOUND OF THIS MUSIC.
HOLD ON A FEW MORE MOMENTS, AND I'LL USE THESE A.T.A.C. TOOLS...

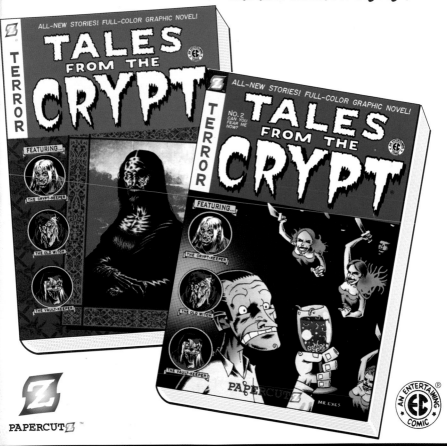

NANCY DREW

A NEW GRAPHIC NOVEL EVERY 3 MONTHS!

NEW STORY! FULL-COLOR GRAPHIC NOVEL
NANCY DREW
girl detective
#12
DRESS REVERSAL
BASED ON THE SERIES BY CAROLYN KEENE
PETRUCHA & KINNEY
MURASE & GUZMAN
ON SALE NOW!

#1 "The Demon of River Heights"
ISBN 1-59707-000-9 pb.
#2 "Writ In Stone" ISBN 1-59707-002-5 pb.
#3 "The Haunted Dollhouse"
ISBN 1-59707-008-4 pb.
#4 "The Girl Who Wasn't There"
ISBN 1-59707-012-2 pb.
#5 "The Fake Heir" ISBN 1-59707-024-6 pb.
#6 "Mr. Cheeters Is Missing"
ISBN 1-59707-030-0 pb.
#7 "The Charmed Bracelet"
ISBN 1-59707-036-X pb.
#8 "Global Warning" ISBN 1-59707-051-3 pb.
#9 "Ghost in the Machinery"
ISBN 1-59707-058-0 pb.
#10 "The Disoriented Express"
ISBN 1-59707-066-1 pb.
#11 "Monkey Wrench Blues"
ISBN 1-59707-076-9 pb.
NEW #12 "Dress Reversal"
ISBN 1-59707-086-6 pb.

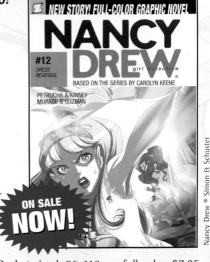

All: Pocket sized, 96-112pp., full color, $7.95
Also available in hardcover! $12.95 each.

Nancy Drew
Boxed Set #1-4
384 pages of color comics!
ISBN 1-59707-038-6

Nancy Drew
Boxed Set #5-8
432 pages of color comics!
$29.95 ISBN 1-59707-074-4

NEW STORIES! FULL-COLOR GRAPHIC NOVELS
NANCY DREW
girl detective
BASED ON THE SERIES BY CAROLYN KEENE
SPECIALLY PRICED BOX SET OF #1-4!
PAPERCUTZ

ALL-NEW, FULL-COLOR GRAPHIC NOVEL
ZORRO
#1
SCARS!
DON McGREGOR • SIDNEY LIMA
SEE THE NEW MAJOR MOTION PICTURE "THE LEGEND OF ZORRO"
PAPERCUTZ

ZORRO

#1 "Scars!" ISBN 1-59707-016-5
#2 "Drownings!" ISBN 1-59707-018-1
#3 "Vultures!" ISBN 1-59707-020-3
#4 "Spies in Space" ISBN 1-59707-055-6
Each: 5x7 1/2, 96pp., full color paperback: $7.95
Also available in hardcover! $12.95 each.

At your store or order at Papercutz, 40 Exchange Place, Ste. 1308,
New York NY 10005, 1-800-886-1223

PAPERCUTZ

THE HARDY BOYS

UNDERCOVER BROTHERS™

ATAC BRIEFING FOR AGENTS FRANK AND JOE HARDY

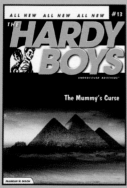

#13: THE MUMMY'S CURSE
Available December 2006

MISSION:

A man has been murdered, possibly over a map to a precious golden mummy. Are there other treasure-hunters trying to find the location of the tomb? Could there be a curse surrounding the ancient mummy and his treasure?

LOCATION:

Cairo, Egypt, and the surrounding area.

SUSPECTS:

Several people on an expedition are suspects. you have to find them before they find the mummy . . . and his treasure!

THIS MISSION REQUIRES YOUR IMMEDIATE ATTENTION. PICK UP A COPY OF *THE MUMMY'S CURSE* AND GET ON THE CASE!

WATCH OUT FOR PAPERCUTZ™

If this is your very first Papercutz graphic novel, then allow me, Jim Salicrup, your humble and lovable Editor-in-Chief, to welcome you to the Papercutz Backpages where we check out what's happening in the ever-expanding Papercutz Universe! If you're a long-time Papercutz fan, then welcome back, friend!

Things really have been popping at Papercutz! In the last few editions of the Backpages we've announced new titles such as TALES FROM THE CRYPT, CLASSICS ILLUSTRATED, and CLASSICS ILLUSTRATED DELUXE. Well, guess what? The tradition continues, and we're announcing yet another addition to our line-up of blockbuster titles. So, what is our latest and greatest title? We'll give you just one hint -- the stars of the next Papercutz graphic novel series just happen to be the biggest, most exciting line of constructible action figures ever created! That's right -- BIONICLE is coming! Check out the power-packed preview pages ahead!

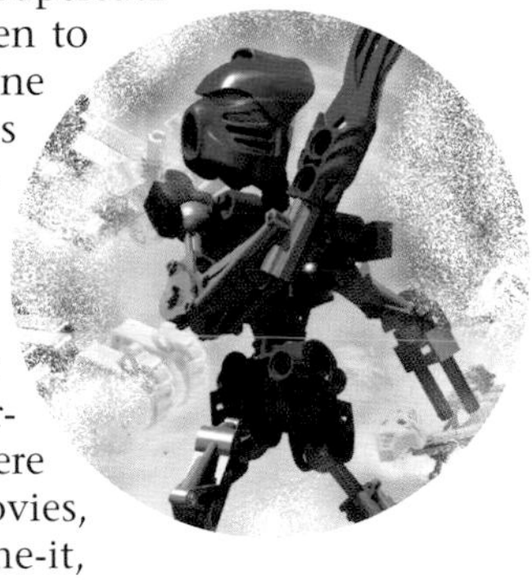

Before I run out of room, let me say that we're always interested in what you think! Are there characters, TV shows, movies, books, videogames, you-name-it, that you'd like to see Papercutz turn into graphic novels? Don't be shy, let's us know! You can contact me at salicrup@papercutz.com or Jim Salicrup, PAPERCUTZ, 40 Exchange Place, Ste. 1308, New York, NY 10005 and let us know how we're doing. After all, we want you to be as excited about Papercutz as we are!

Thanks,

Jim

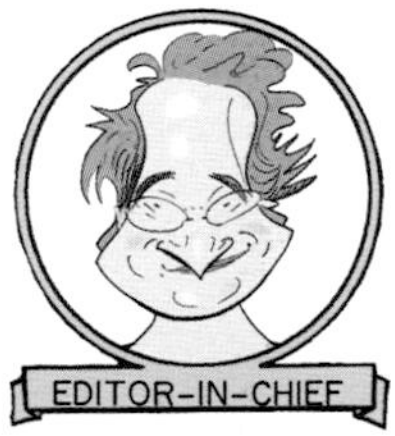
EDITOR-IN-CHIEF

Caricature drawn by Steve Brodner at the MoCCA Art Fest.

TWO DOZEN TEEN DETECTIVE GRAPHIC NOVELS NOW IN PRINT!

NEW STORY! FULL-COLOR GRAPHIC NOVEL
NANCY DREW
girl detective
#12
DRESS REVERSAL
BASED ON THE SERIES BY CAROLYN KEENE
PETRUCHA & KINNEY
MURASE & GUZMAN
PAPERCUTZ

You know, while it's exciting to be adding so many new titles, we don't want anyone to think we've forgotten any of our previous Papercutz publications! For example, can you believe there are now two dozen all-new, full-color graphic novels starring America's favorite teen sleuths?! Let's check out what's happening in the 12th volume of NANCY DREW...

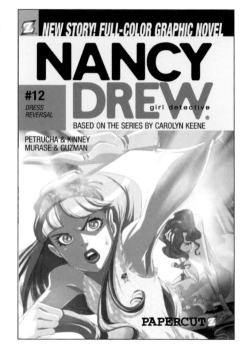

Writers Stefan Petrucha and Sarah Kinney and artists Sho Murase and Carlos Jose Guzman present Nancy's latest case, "Dress Reversal." After showing up at River Height's social event of the year, in the identical dress as the party's hostess, Deirdre Shannon, things get worse for Nancy when she's suddenly kidnapped! That leaves Bess, George, and Ned to solve the mystery of the missing Girl Detective.

That's all in NANCY DREW #12 "Dress Reversal," on sale sale at bookstores everywhere and online booksellers.

Behold. . .

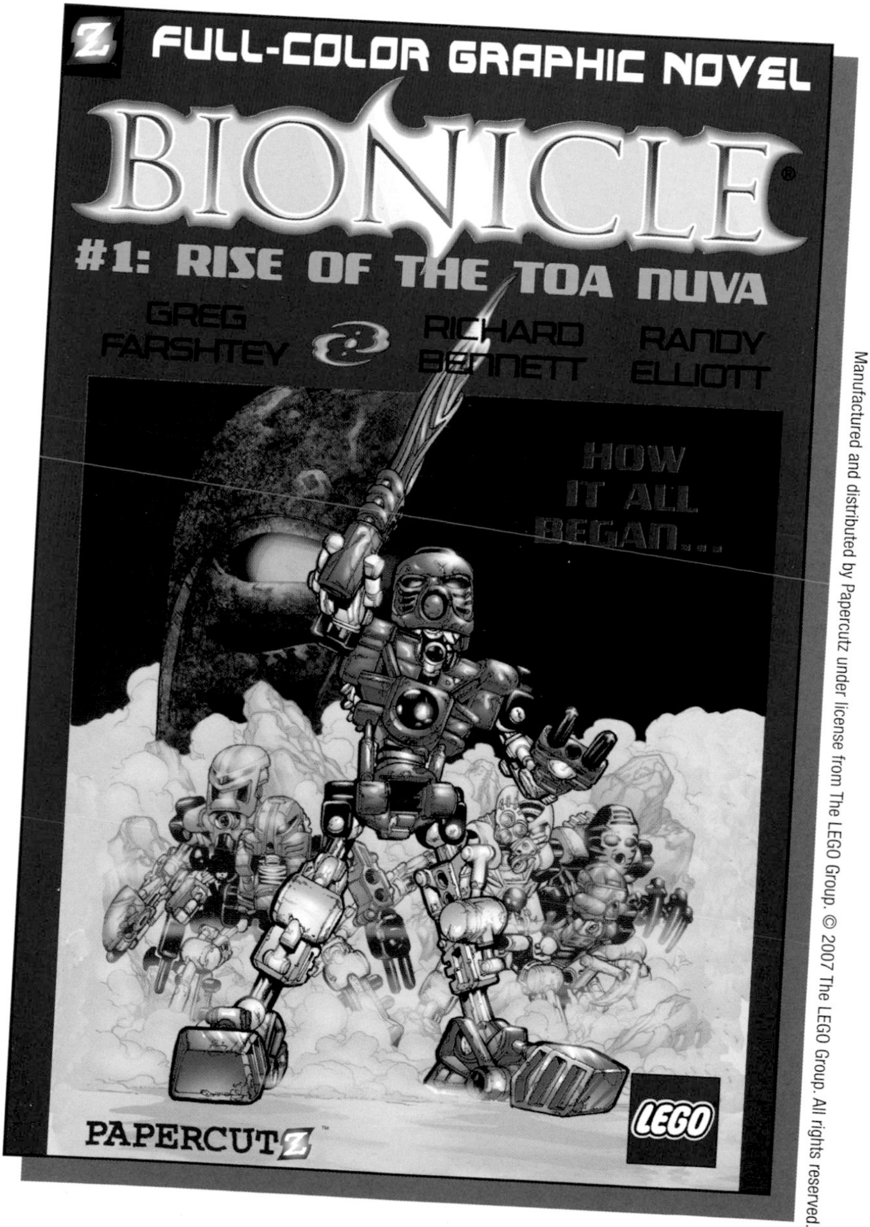
FULL-COLOR GRAPHIC NOVEL
BIONICLE®
#1: RISE OF THE TOA NUVA
GREG FARSHTEY
RICHARD BENNETT
RANDY ELLIOTT
HOW IT ALL BEGAN...
PAPERCUTZ™
LEGO

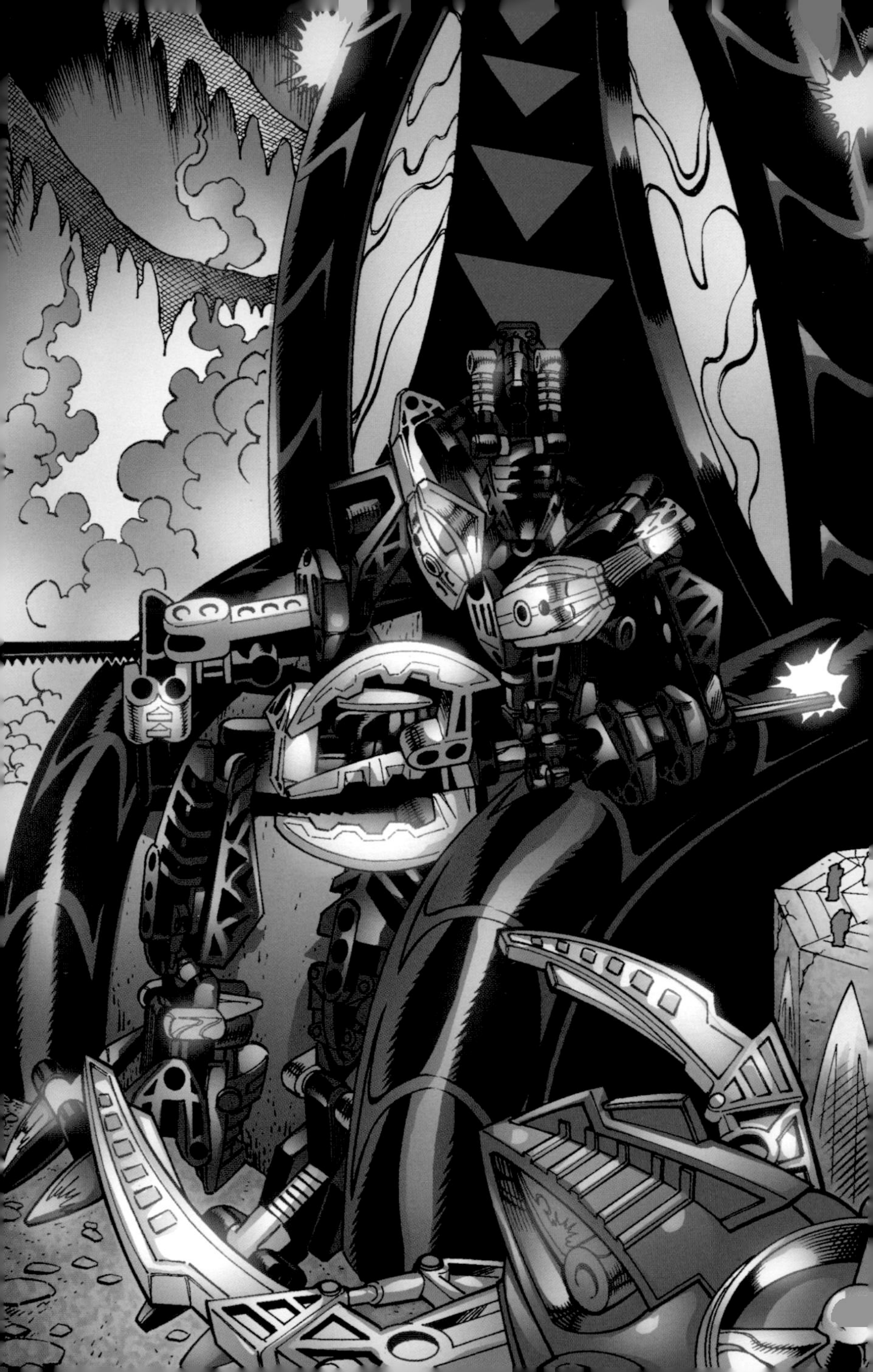

At the start of the new millennium, a new line of toys from LEGO made their dramatic debut. Originally released in six color-coded canisters, each containing a constructible, fully-poseable, articulated character, BIONICLE was an instant hit!

The BIONICLE figures were incredibly intriguing. With their exotic names hinting at a complex history, fans were curious to discover more about these captivating characters. Even now, over six years later, there are still many unanswered questions surrounding every facet of the ever-expanding BIONICLE universe.

A comicbook, written by leading BIONICLE expert and author of most of the BIONICLE novels Greg Farshtey, was created by DC Comics and given away to members of the BIONICLE fan club. The action-packed comics revealed much about these mysterious biomechanical (part biological, part mechanical) beings and the world they inhabited. A world filled with many races, most prominent being the Matoran. A world once protected millennia ago by a Great Spirit known as Mata Nui, who has fallen asleep. A world that has begun to decay as its inhabitants must defend themselves from the evil forces of Makuta.

The first story arc of the comics called "The BIONICLE Chronicles," begins when six heroic beings known as Toa arrive on a tropical-like island which is also named Mata Nui. The Toa may just be the saviors the people of Mata Nui need, if they can avoid fighting with themselves, not to mention the Bohrok and the Rahkshise early comics are incredibly hard-to-find, and many new BIONICLE fans have never seen these all-important early chapters in this epic science fantasy. But soon, those comics will be collected as the first two volumes in the Papercutz series of BIONICLE graphic novels.

These early comics are incredibly hard-to-find, and many new BIONICLE fans have never seen these all-important early chapters in this epic science fantasy. But soon, those comics will be collected as the first two volumes in the Papercutz series of BIONICLE graphic novels.

In the following pages, enjoy a special preview of BIONICLE graphic novel #1...

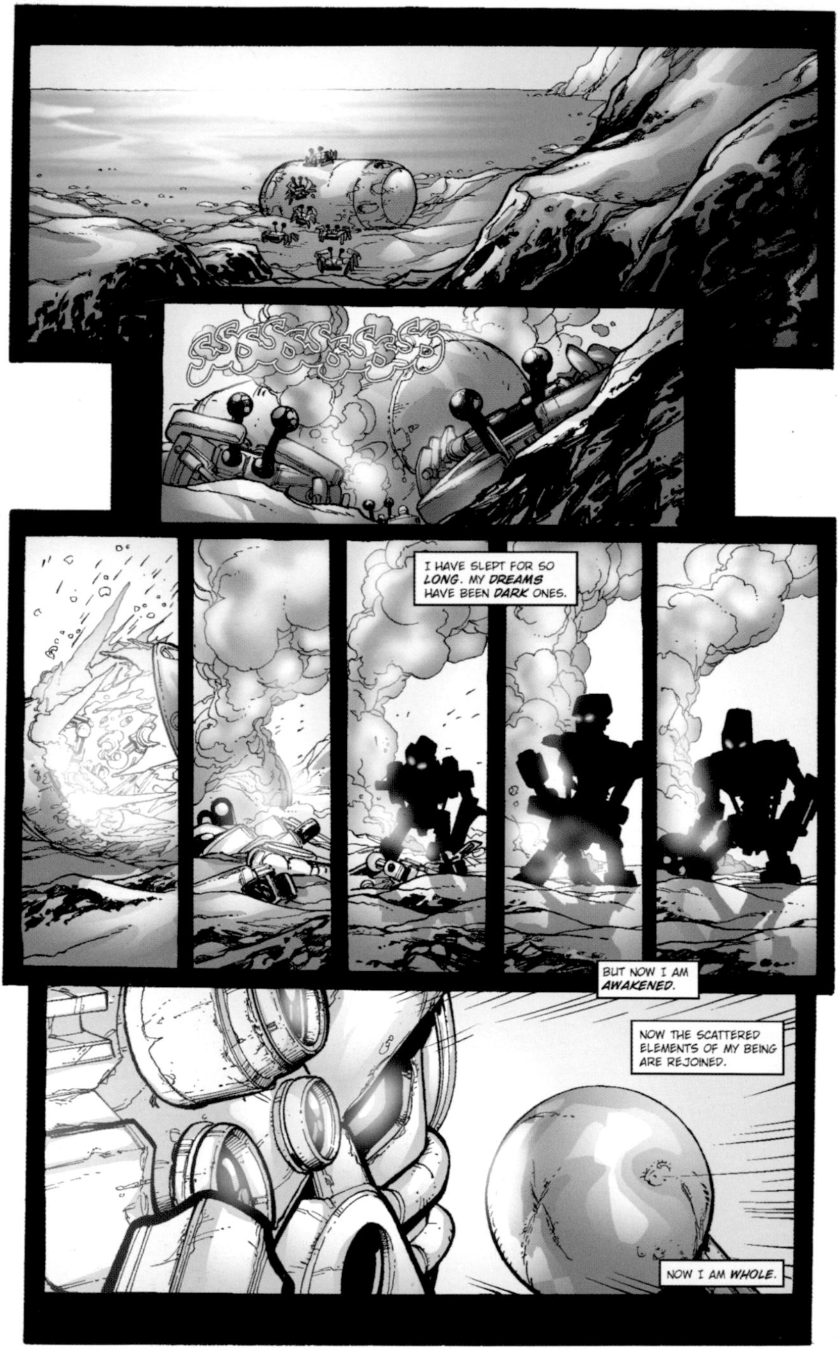
SSSSSSSSSS
I HAVE SLEPT FOR SO LONG. MY DREAMS HAVE BEEN DARK ONES.
BUT NOW I AM AWAKENED.
NOW THE SCATTERED ELEMENTS OF MY BEING ARE REJOINED.
NOW I AM WHOLE.

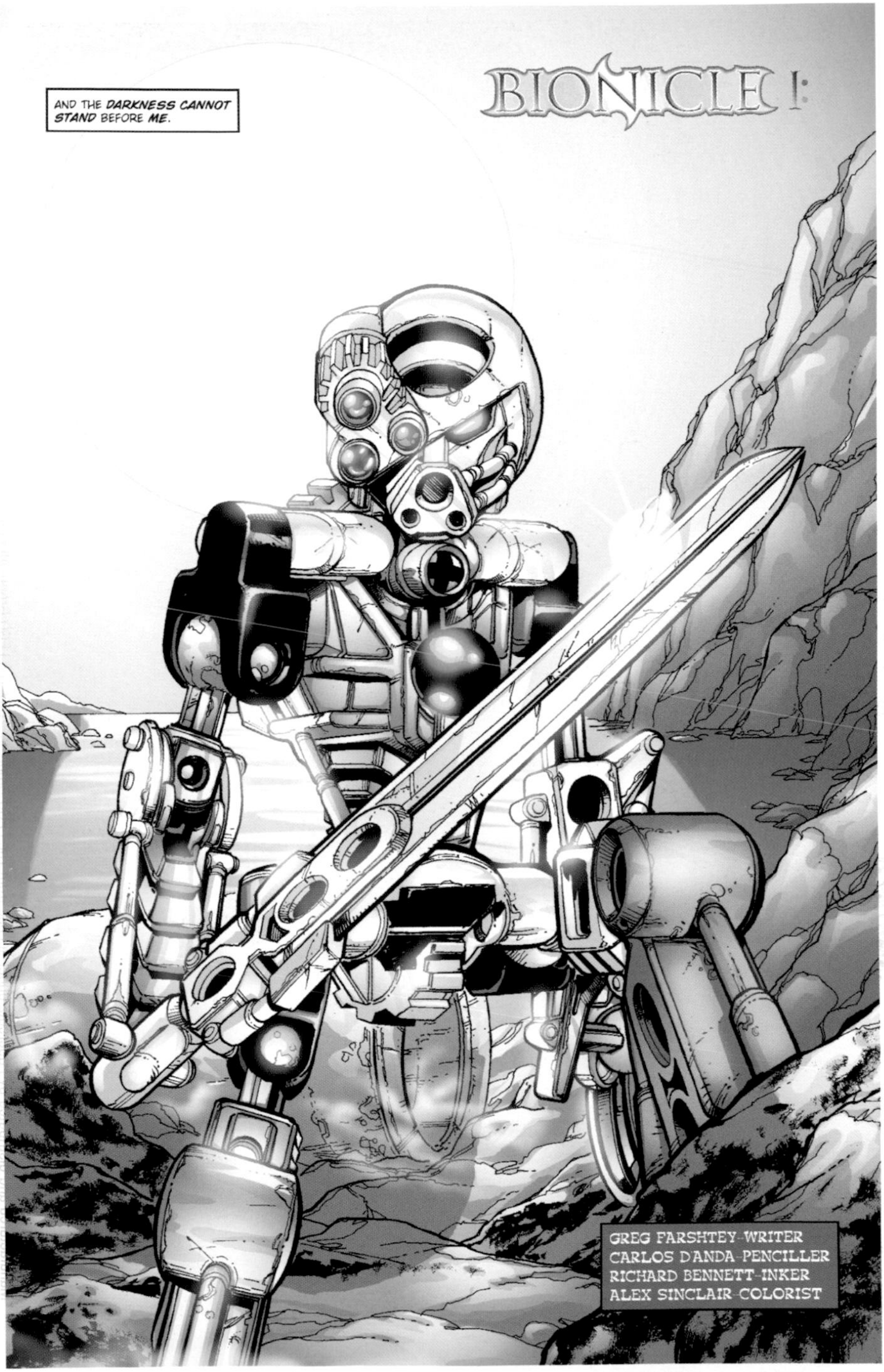
AND THE DARKNESS CANNOT STAND BEFORE ME.
BIONICLE I:
GREG FARSHTEY–WRITER
CARLOS D'ANDA–PENCILLER
RICHARD BENNETT–INKER
ALEX SINCLAIR–COLORIST

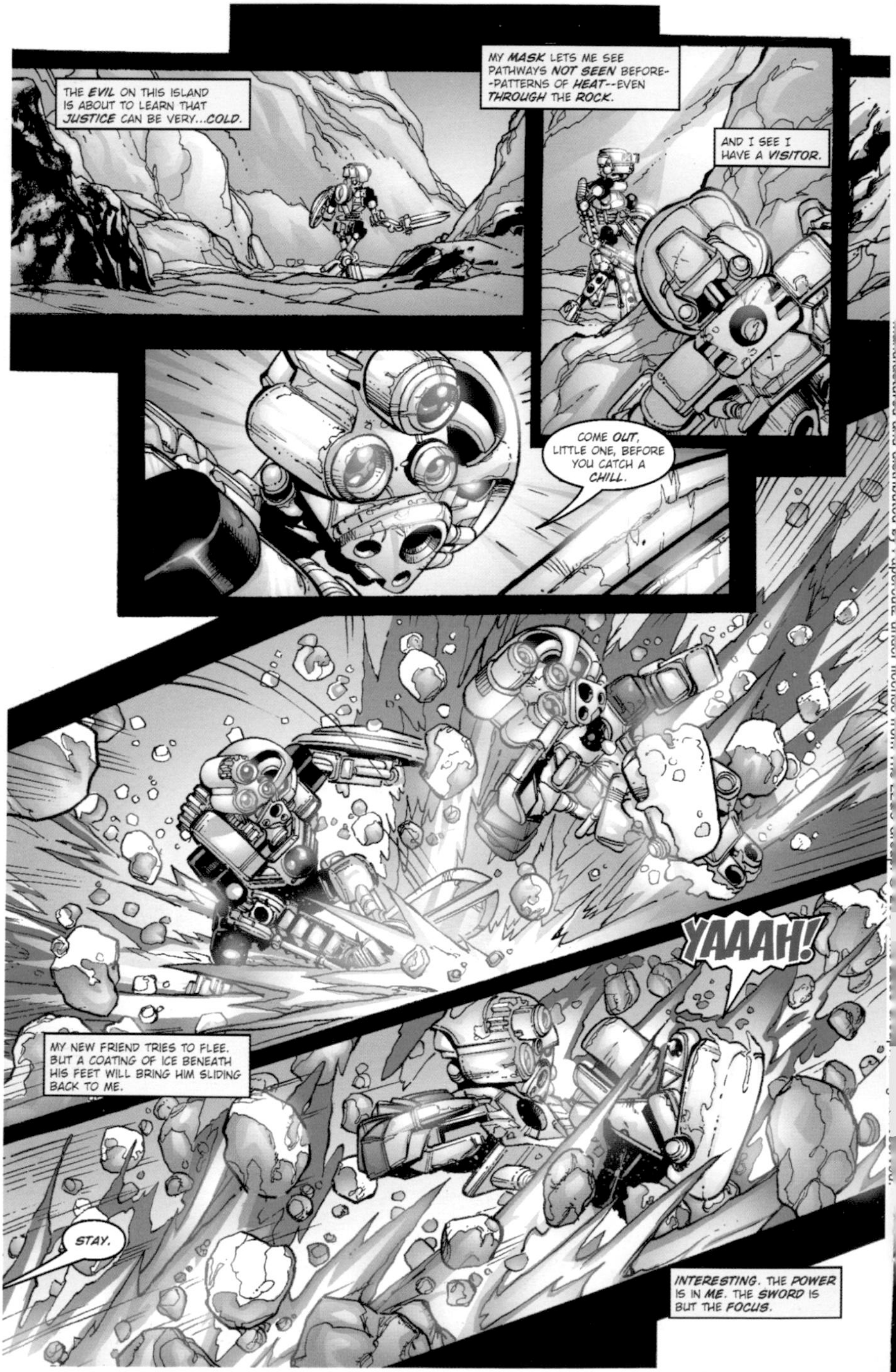

THE EVIL ON THIS ISLAND IS ABOUT TO LEARN THAT JUSTICE CAN BE VERY...COLD.
MY MASK LETS ME SEE PATHWAYS NOT SEEN BEFORE--PATTERNS OF HEAT--EVEN THROUGH THE ROCK.
AND I SEE I HAVE A VISITOR.
COME OUT, LITTLE ONE, BEFORE YOU CATCH A CHILL.
YAAAH!
MY NEW FRIEND TRIES TO FLEE. BUT A COATING OF ICE BENEATH HIS FEET WILL BRING HIM SLIDING BACK TO ME.
STAY.
INTERESTING. THE POWER IS IN ME. THE SWORD IS BUT THE FOCUS.

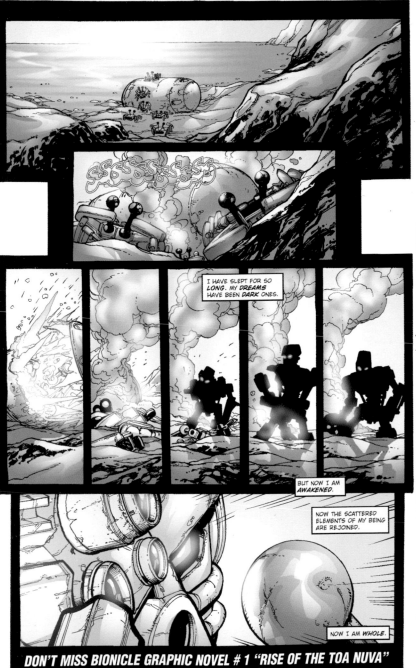

DON'T MISS BIONICLE GRAPHIC NOVEL # 1 "RISE OF THE TOA NUVA"

CLASSICS
Illustrated

Featuring Stories by the World's Greatest Authors

Returns in two new series from Papercutz!

The original, best-selling series of comics adaptations of the world's greatest literature, CLASSICS ILLUSTRATED, returns in two new formats--the original, featuring abridged adaptations of classic novels, and CLASSICS ILLUSTRATED DELUXE, featuring longer, more expansive adaptations-from graphic novel publisher Papercutz. "We're very proud to say that Papercutz has received such an enthusiastic reception from librarians and school teachers for its NANCY DREW and HARDY BOYS graphic novels as well as THE LIFE OF POPE JOHN PAUL II...*IN COMICS!*, that it only seemed logical for us to bring back the original CLASSICS ILLUSTRATED comicbook series beloved by parents, educators, and librarians," explained Papercutz Publisher, Terry Nantier. "We can't thank the enlightened librarians and teachers who have supported Papercutz enough. And we're thrilled that they're so excited about CLASSICS ILLUSTRATED."

Upcoming titles include The Invisible Man, Tales from the Brothers Grimm, and Robinson Crusoe.

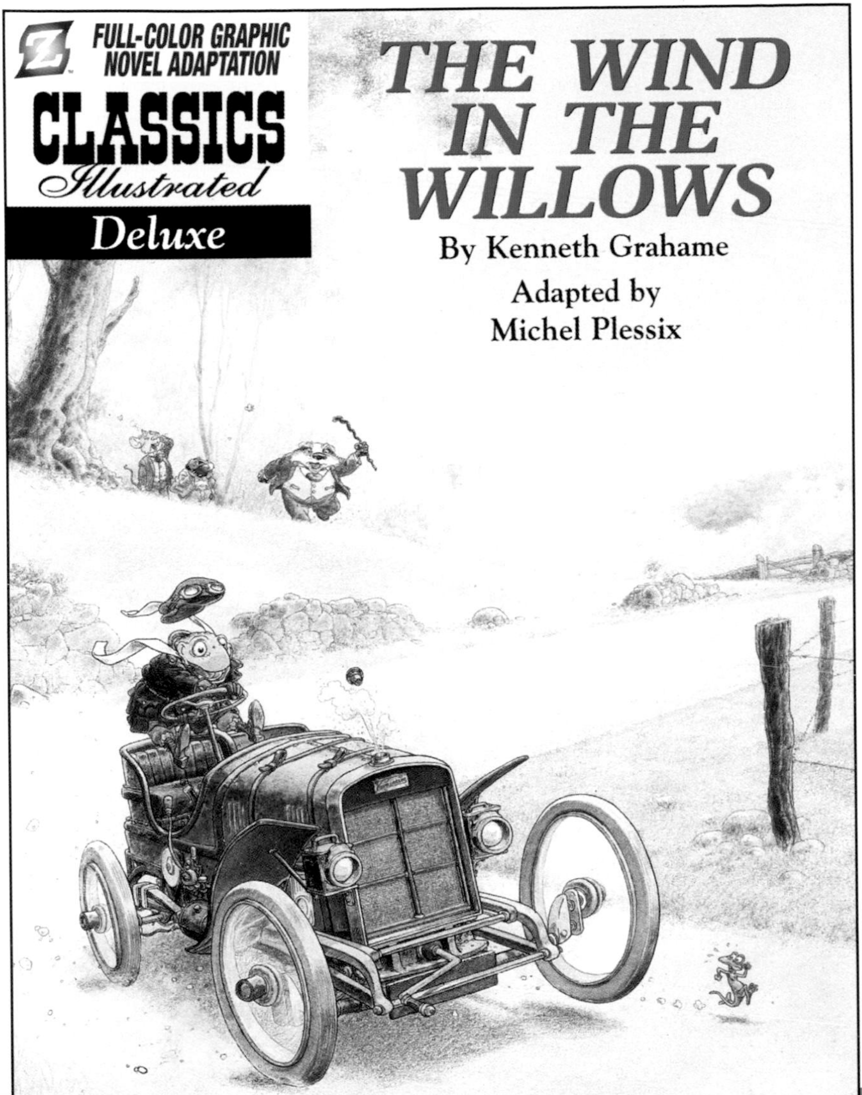
FULL-COLOR GRAPHIC NOVEL ADAPTATION
CLASSICS Illustrated
Deluxe
THE WIND IN THE WILLOWS
By Kenneth Grahame
Adapted by
Michel Plessix
PAPERCUTZ

CLASSICS Illustrated
THE THREE MUSKETEERS

CLASSICS Illustrated
Ivanhoe

CLASSICS Illustrated
THE LAST OF THE MOHICANS

CLASSICS Illustrated
Robin Hood

CLASSICS Illustrated
ARABIAN NIGHTS

CLASSICS Illustrated
LES MISERABL

CLASSICS Illustrated
THE HOUSE OF THE SEVEN GABLES

A Short History of CLASSICS ILLUSTRATED...

CLASSICS Illustrated
THE MAN IN THE IRON MASK

William B. Jones Jr. is the author of Classics Illustrated: A Cultural History, which offers a comprehensive overview of the original comic-book series and the writers, artists, editors, and publishers behind-the-scenes. With Mr. Jones Jr.'s kind permission, here's a very short overview of the history of CLASSICS ILLUSTRATED adapted from his 2005 essay on Albert Kanter.

CLASSICS Illustrated
THE TOILERS OF THE SEA

CLASSICS ILLUSTRATED was the creation of Albert Lewis Kanter, a visionary publisher, who from 1941 to 1971, introduced young readers worldwide to the realms of literature, history, folklore, mythology, and science in over 200 titles in such comicbook series as CLASSICS ILLUSTRATED and CLASSICS ILLUSTRATED JUNIOR. Kanter, inspired by the success of the first comicbooks published in the early 30s and late 40s, believed he

CLASSICS Illustrated
The Song of Hiawatha

CLASSICS Illustrated
Two Years before The Mast

CLASSICS Illustrated
FRANKENSTEIN

CLASSICS Illustrated
The PRINCE and the PAUPER

CLASSICS Illustrated

CLASSICS Illustrated
THE BLACK ARROW

CLASSICS Illustrated
TYPEE

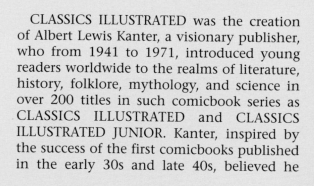

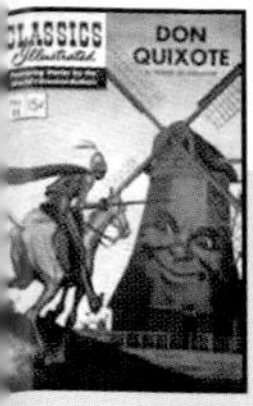
CLASSICS Illustrated
DON QUIXOTE
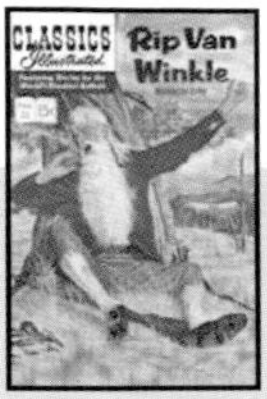
CLASSICS Illustrated
Rip Van Winkle
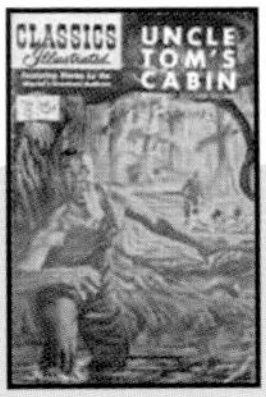
CLASSICS Illustrated
UNCLE TOM'S CABIN
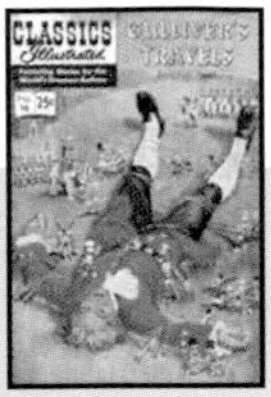
CLASSICS Illustrated
GULLIVER'S TRAVELS
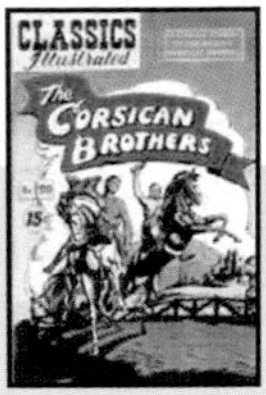
CLASSICS Illustrated
The CORSICAN BROTHERS
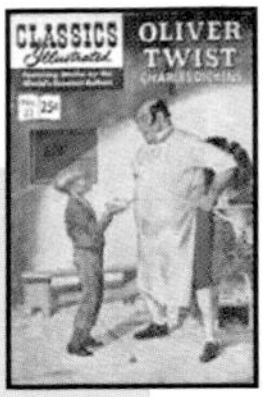
CLASSICS Illustrated
OLIVER TWIST
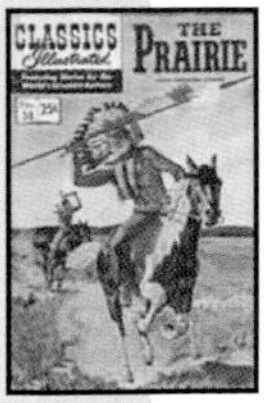
CLASSICS Illustrated
THE PRAIRIE
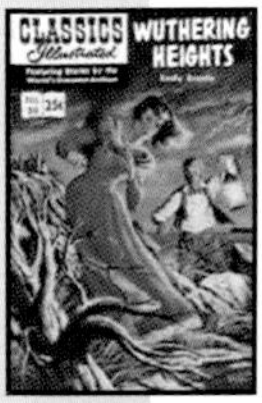
CLASSICS Illustrated
WUTHERING HEIGHTS
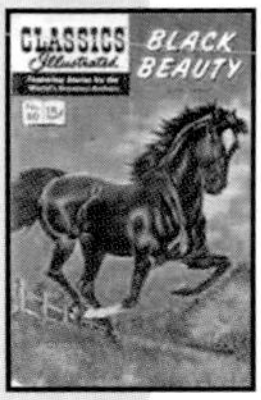
CLASSICS Illustrated
BLACK BEAUTY
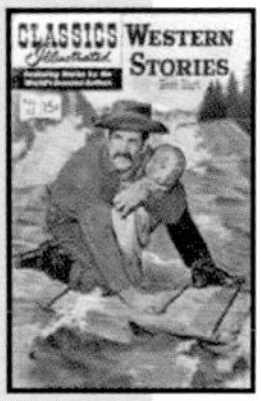
CLASSICS Illustrated
WESTERN STORIES

could use the same medium to introduce young readers to the world of great literature. CLASSIC COMICS (later changed to CLASSICS ILLUSTRATED in 1947) was launched in 1941, and soon the comicbook adaptations of Shakespeare, Stevenson, Twain, Verne, and other authors, were being used in schools and endorsed by educators.

CLASSICS ILLUSTRATED was translated and distributed in countries such as Canada, Great Britain, the Netherlands, Greece, Brazil, Mexico, and Australia. The genial publisher was hailed abroad as "Papa Kassiker." By the beginning of the 1960s, CLASSICS ILLUSTRATED was the largest childrens publication in the world. The original CLASSICS ILLUSTRATED series adapted into comics 169 titles; among these were Frankenstein, 20,000 Leagues Under the Sea, Treasure Island, Julius Caesar, and Faust.

Albert L. Kanter died, March 17, 1973, leaving behind a rich legacy for the millions of readers whose imaginations were awakened by CLASSICS ILLUSTRATED.

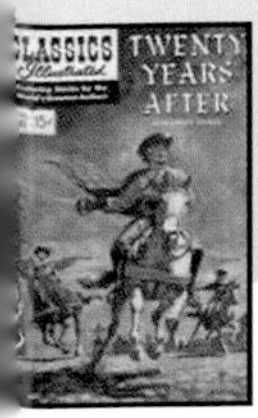
CLASSICS Illustrated
TWENTY YEARS AFTER
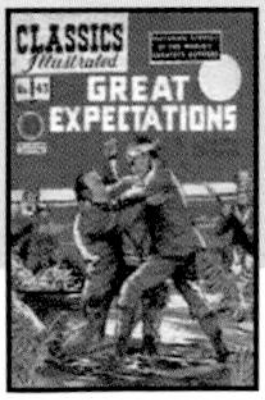
CLASSICS Illustrated
GREAT EXPECTATIONS
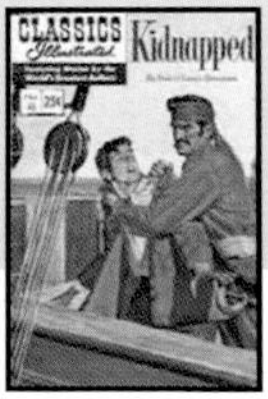
CLASSICS Illustrated
Kidnapped
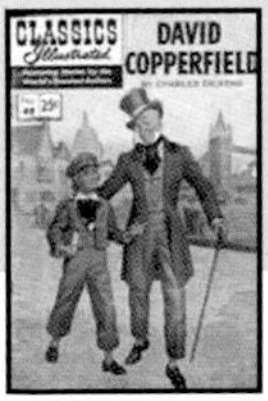
CLASSICS Illustrated
DAVID COPPERFIELD
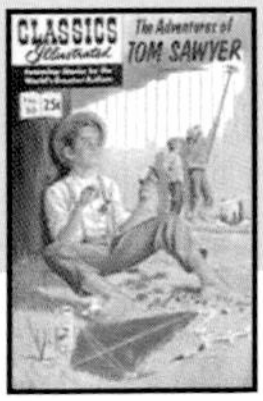
CLASSICS Illustrated
The Adventures of TOM SAWYER
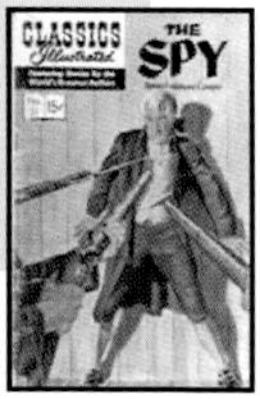
CLASSICS Illustrated
THE SPY

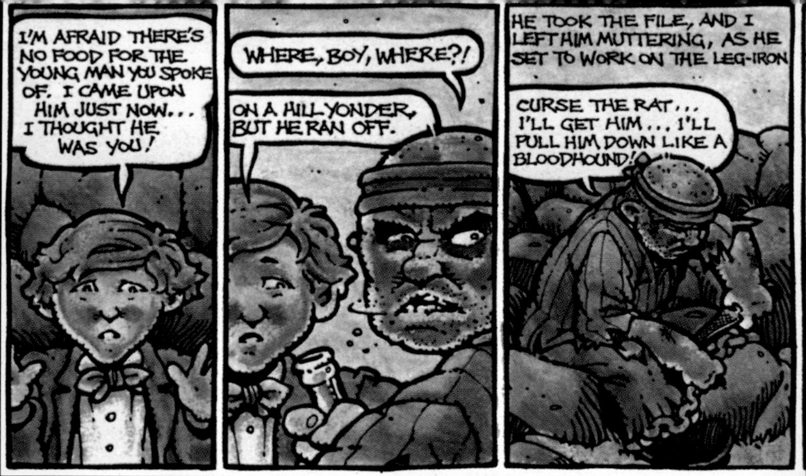
I'M AFRAID THERE'S NO FOOD FOR THE YOUNG MAN YOU SPOKE OF. I CAME UPON HIM JUST NOW... I THOUGHT HE WAS YOU!
WHERE, BOY, WHERE?!
ON A HILL YONDER, BUT HE RAN OFF.
HE TOOK THE FILE, AND I LEFT HIM MUTTERING, AS HE SET TO WORK ON THE LEG-IRON
CURSE THE RAT... I'LL GET HIM... I'LL PULL HIM DOWN LIKE A BLOODHOUND!

CLASSICS ILLUSTRATED was re-launched in 1990 in graphic novel/book form by the Berkley Publishing Group and First Publishing, Inc. featuring all-new adaptations by such top graphic novelists as Rick Geary, Bill Sienkiewicz, Kyle Baker, Gahan Wilson, and others. "First had the right idea, they just came out about 15 years too soon. Now bookstores are ready for graphic novels such as these," Jim explains. Many of these excellent adaptations have been acquired by Papercutz and will make up the new series of CLASSICS ILLUSTRATED titles.

The first volume of the new CLASSICS ILLUSTRATED series presents graphic novelist Rick Geary's adaptation of "Great Expectations" by Charles Dickens, the bittersweet tale of one boy's adolescence, and of the choices he makes to shape his destiny. Into an engrossing mystery, Dickens weaves a heartfelt inquiry into morals and virtues-as the orphan Pip, the convict Magwitch, the beautiful Estella, the bitter Miss Havisham, the goodhearted Biddy, the kind Joe and other memorable characters entwine in a battle of human nature. Rick Geary's delightful illustrations capture the newfound awe and frustrations of young Pip as he comes of age, and begins to understand the opportunities that life presents.

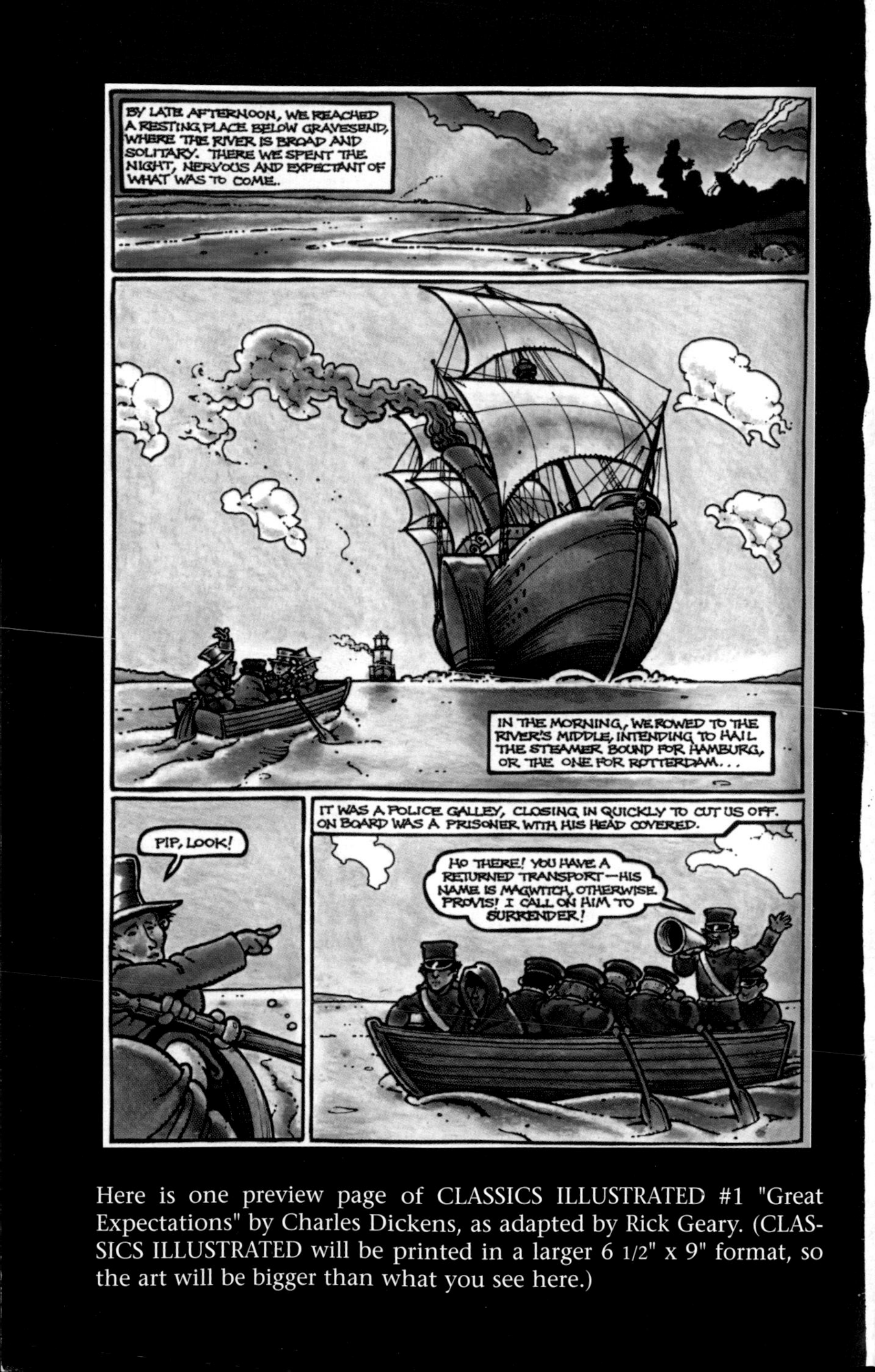
BY LATE AFTERNOON, WE REACHED A RESTING PLACE BELOW GRAVESEND, WHERE THE RIVER IS BROAD AND SOLITARY. THERE WE SPENT THE NIGHT, NERVOUS AND EXPECTANT OF WHAT WAS TO COME.
IN THE MORNING, WE ROWED TO THE RIVER'S MIDDLE, INTENDING TO HAIL THE STEAMER BOUND FOR HAMBURG, OR THE ONE FOR ROTTERDAM...
PIP, LOOK!
IT WAS A POLICE GALLEY, CLOSING IN QUICKLY TO CUT US OFF. ON BOARD WAS A PRISONER WITH HIS HEAD COVERED.
HO THERE! YOU HAVE A RETURNED TRANSPORT—HIS NAME IS MAGWITCH, OTHERWISE PROVIS! I CALL ON HIM TO SURRENDER!

Here is one preview page of CLASSICS ILLUSTRATED #1 "Great Expectations" by Charles Dickens, as adapted by Rick Geary. (CLASSICS ILLUSTRATED will be printed in a larger 6 1/2" x 9" format, so the art will be bigger than what you see here.)

FULL-COLOR GRAPHIC NOVEL ADAPTATION

CLASSICS *Illustrated*®

Featuring Stories by the World's Greatest Authors

GREAT EXPECTATIONS

By Charles Dickens

Adapted by Richard Geary

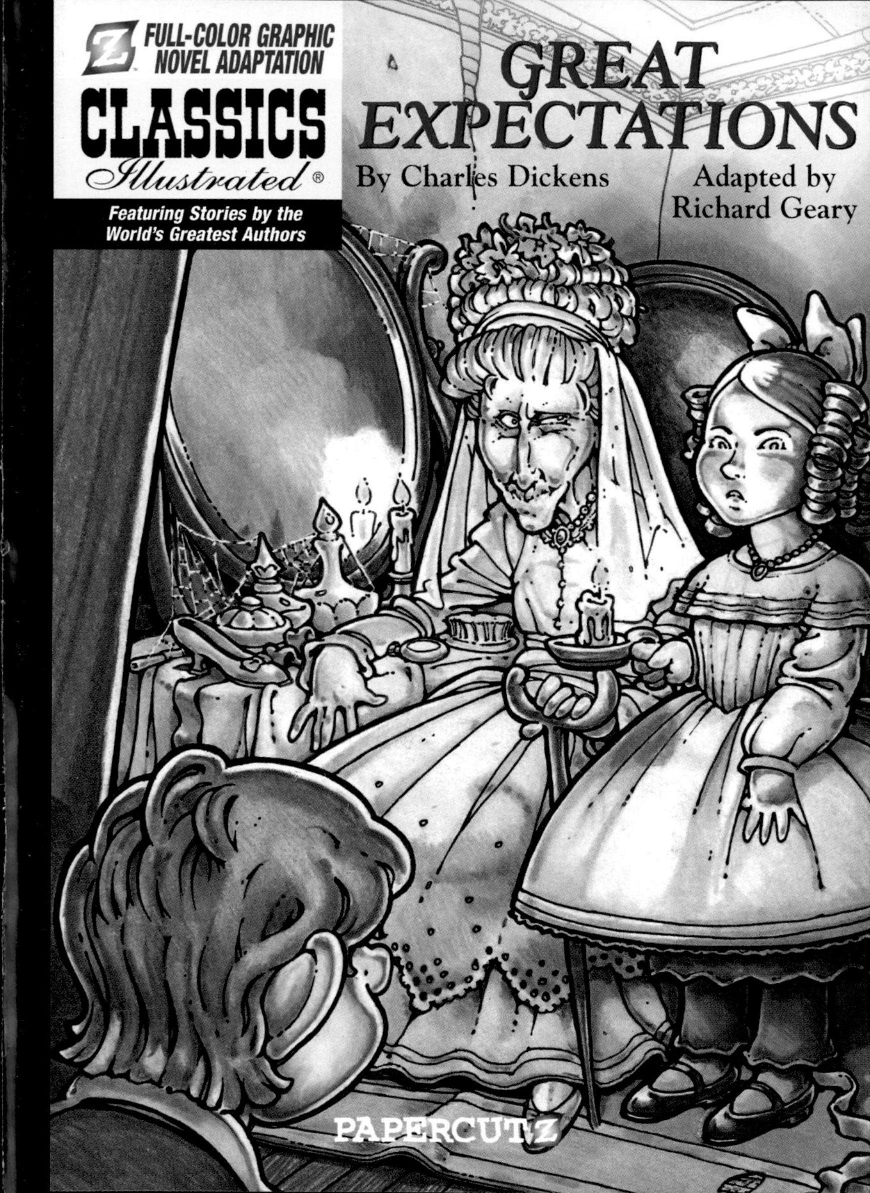

PAPERCUTZ